SAVAGES

THE SAINT-ETIENNE QUARTET, VOLUME 1:

THE WEDDING

THE NERROUCHE FAMILY

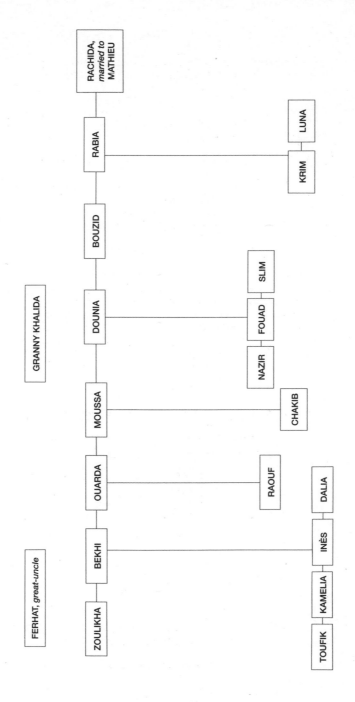

THE WEDDING

Prologue

A Family Reunion

France's 'next president' – one of the eight contenders still in the running – was known to enjoy music, but very few people had anticipated that the Socialist candidate's melomania would fuel such heated debate behind the scenes during the campaign. Every time he caught a word in a conversation that reminded him of a song, Idder Chaouch would start humming it, regardless of his audience – family members or strangers, kissable babies in the crowd, loud-mouthed lawyers in his staff, smug-faced journalists, off-key political opponents, close friends or envious allies awaiting his downfall – no matter who they were, he would hum in front of them; and when he was in a good mood – that is, almost every day – it got worse: he couldn't resist the impulse of singing the lyrics out loud, in his beautiful, unpretentious voice, clear and smooth like the skin on top of his hands.

Before entering the rat race to the highest office, Chaouch had served as the mayor of Grogny. In this once monotonous and sad suburban ethnic neighbourhood, Mayor Chaouch, over the course of his two terms, had planted trees and designed gardens and reduced crime and the public debt. He'd also created music schools that were free for underprivileged kids and built an auditorium that resembled a triumphal arch when seen from the motorway leading to Roissy Airport.

A reporter mentioned this Napoleonic symbolism during a photo-op: was it intentional? Chaouch didn't back away from the question, he didn't confront it either, he just chanted the chorus of the three fairies at the beginning of *The Magic Flute*:

'*Triumph! Triumph! Triumph! Sie ist vollbracht, die Heldentat!*'

How could anyone doubt that Chaouch would make a great president? He knew Mozart's operas by heart! And of course he was not only charming but handsome: you wouldn't have guessed at first glance that he was in his late forties. He had full lips, strong and youthful curly hair, shining brown eyes. His smile spread pleasantly across his oval face, and he was starting to wrinkle at the temples, though even these wrinkles deepened the laughter in his eyes instead of dimming it.

As a young man he had ranked first in the crazily selective Ecole Nationale d'Administration; but he hadn't chosen the boring and prestigious administrative career that lay ahead of him. It was the first time that this had happened since the School had been created two centuries earlier (incidentally, by Napoleon). Young Chaouch had needed to stretch his eager legs beyond the limits of his native hexagon. Instead of pursuing a path paved with gold in the back alleys of the French State, he had taken off to the New World, and for a few years in the nineties he taught economics at the Harvard Kennedy School. He had a wicked sense of humour. Everyone loved him there – students, professors, baristas, piano tuners. He was a man of many gifts, blessed with a brilliant mind, although his most distinctive trait was his generous and spontaneous and egalitarian way of dealing with people – from the uncomplicated likes of Papageno to the Prince Taminos of this world.

His senior advisers, however, as well as his Queen of the Night, regarded all this singing business – a living proof of his joyful nature – as a liability: it made him look eccentric, funny, unpresidential, not to mention dangerously un-Gallic, given that many of the songs in his repertoire happened to be opera tunes in Italian or German, jazz standards and pop hits sung in American English. No one had ever won a French election by showing that they mastered the *langue de Shakespeare*. Quite the contrary; French politicians were fiercely proud of speaking English with a pronounced accent – well aware that ninety per cent of their constituency would mock them lovingly for doing so, and that politics in its age of relative powerlessness also lies in the art of being made fun of in a likeable way.

Chaouch didn't partake in any of this cynical wisdom. Still, he was being ridiculed by his many detractors; and music – of all hazards – was becoming his Achilles heel. Right-wing magazines started to call him the *songster candidate*. They deemed him a fraud, an entertainer, a glittering icon – they even called him a pop star! Somebody had to take action. His spin doctors didn't know how to emphasize how serious this deceptively petty matter was. So Madame Chaouch stepped in. They had a five-minute talk after lunch; Chaouch promised he would curb his lyrical enthusiasm.

But at the end of that same day, he was attending a campaign event in Lyon, meeting with the left-leaning president of the General Council of the region. The public conference was televised. Ten minutes after the beginning of his speech, someone shouted something in the audience. Chaouch loved hecklers and being able to free himself from the dullness of a monologue about fiscal reform; besides, he enjoyed exercising his wit with improvised sparring partners. But this particular partner had attacked him for his Algerian background, and was advising him to run for president of Araby instead. The use of this old-fashioned and improper term was more than enough to trigger the melodic function in the candidate's mischievous brain:

'Well . . . *I am the sheik of Araby . . . your love belongs to me . . .*'

The crowd burst out laughing, they cheered and they applauded, and Chaouch got back to his five-point plan to make the tax system more equitable, and to improve solidarity.

One might say he had his own brand of wisdom. Who knows, this may even have been a strategy from the start – lulling the enemy to sleep; singing his way to the top of the world. For he was definitely getting there. And he knew it better than his advisers, better than the pollsters, better than anyone – well, almost anyone.

At the candidate's request, an American big-data expert had been hired to provide the Paris-based staff with the most recent black magic from the tech industries. She wanted to work from Chicago where she was based, but Chaouch didn't like working with people he couldn't touch. He wanted to see real human beings, to hear actual voices, unmediated by echoey conference lines; he needed hands to high-five, smiles to reward with his own, shoulders to pat enthusiastically.

Sari Essman possessed such shoulders, in abundance, so to speak: she was indeed an accomplished Crossfitter, albeit of the nerdy kind; her rippling upper body contrasted powerfully with her pale, glassy-eyed and thick-spectacled mousy face. Still in her early thirties, she was making a fortune foreseeing and nudging the outcomes of national elections all over the world. Her methods were disquietingly accurate; she had offered her services to the previous US Democratic presidential campaign, and was now determined to help crown the 'French Obama', as the American media had dubbed Chaouch – and she was working pro bono this time, firstly because French campaigns were cash poor compared to American ones, and also because she had heard the left-wing candidate sing her long-forgotten favourite tune in a leaked video on YouTube.

Usually Sari Essman was not prone to sentimentality; in her free time she participated in those heroic Crossfit contests, where she squatted and deadlifted and snatched boulders and sprinted miles while carrying her own body weight and did endless series of muscle-ups – that wicked exercise involving two rings simply floating in the air, a bionic pull-up of sorts. She hadn't managed to make the top rankings yet – most of her competitors were full-time She-Hulks, while she was coding and analysing data and meeting with important people in between her daily workouts.

This unexpected trip to the South of France made her miss a regional event in her beloved blizzard-bound home state. But early spring in Petite Camargue made up for the loss – the place was lovely: vineyards and poppy fields surrounded by majestic lines of cypresses; blooming fruit trees everywhere; and Camargue horses playfully racing alongside the black

SUVs of the motorcade. Chaouch had decided to spend a whole weekend in this poverty-stricken region where the extreme right party registered its highest scores. Many people living in these small towns were seasonal workers – unemployment rates grew faster here than anywhere in France. Sari Essman had studied the numbers on the plane – by now she and her data probably understood the *département* better than its own representatives.

The first time she saw the candidate, he was delivering a speech in the outskirts of a small village, in front of a leery crowd that was ostensibly divided into two groups. Chaouch's campaign manager told her that the locals stood on the left, while on the right she could see the Arabs from nearby housing projects. Could she, really? Sari Essman's ethnic radar was no good at differentiating these olive-skinned, dark-haired, bushy-browed villagers. Like all Americans, she could identify a light-coloured black person in a fraction of a second; but these Mediterranean folks all had the same strong noses, the same eye colour, they all folded their arms in the same mistrustful manner. It reminded her, she said, of Freud's *narcissism of minor differences*, but the campaign manager wasn't well versed in psychoanalysis.

'The more you look alike, the more virulently you hate each other,' Sari explained.

He sighed and stared at her. She wore classic black trousers and a long-sleeved pearl-coloured blouse, but her unusual physique had earned her more sneers during these couple of hours in France than she had ever received in Chicago.

Sitting backstage, the campaign manager had introduced himself as Jean-Sébastien Vogel, and pronounced his name as if it were some sort of scandal not to know it already; he was a lean, cool-headed fifty-something Parisian politician, with an expensive blue suit, a shiny silk tie and no time to lose – he was to become France's next prime minister if Chaouch won the election.

'Listen,' he said in English, with an odd accent that sounded more German than French, 'I don't really know what you're doing here, but if you want to be useful there's a very simple way: when you meet him later tonight, tell him that there's nothing for us here, that we'll lose in the South no matter what, and that we should move forward and up north ASAP. Got it?'

'Pardon me, sir, but the race might be tighter than you think, and staying here . . .'

Vogel's jaw was clenched; his nostrils flared.

'It's not an American election, you know. We don't have big fundraisers or crazy ad budgets. It's not all about the money here, *mademoiselle*. What's your name, by the way?'

He brusquely stood up while she was still clearing her throat to answer.

An incident occurred towards the end of the event. The region was famous for its bullfights and hot tempers. A man and a woman started insulting each other – unsurprisingly, the bone of contention was the Islamic veil that some of the women in the Arab crowd were wearing. Chaouch wanted to address the issue, but the argument quickly turned into a brawl; security was on edge; Chaouch was asked to cut his speech short and leave the stage.

The whole delegation was driven to a four-star hotel in nearby Nîmes. Sari Essman was supposed to have dinner with the candidate, but he had instead locked himself in his suite as soon as they arrived. His wife and his daughter Jasmine were expected the following morning. In the hotel restaurant, much of the senior advisers' conversation revolved around Jasmine's boyfriend, an actor who was apparently popular enough to have drawn the attention of the national media when he announced his endorsement. Endorsement was too strong a word – he was merely an actor, after all. But the twelve to twenty-five year olds adored him, as did the eighteen to thirty year olds, and the latter – one fourth of whom was struck by unemployment nationwide – happened to be the main target of the extreme right party. Shallow as it seemed, you couldn't neglect the influence of such support in this complex and unpredictable race. Or could you?

No consensus could be reached around the table about Fouad Nerrouche, who was either referred to as the *boyfriend* or the *actor* – and always in the same condescending tone. The candidate had talked to him several times, behind closed doors; he figured this southern escapade was the perfect time to 'officially' meet him. When one adviser mentioned the candidate's vision of a photo-op with Fouad at lunch, the table wobbled. At last there was a consensus: it was the worst idea of the week! Fouad had the same Algerian origins as the candidate. In the South – in *this* South – it would be considered sheer provocation! Fouad would bring with him a nasty whiff of television hype and Parisian jet-set; the whole of France hated Paris and its success – why would this remote godforsaken town prove an exception? No, no, a lunch with Fouad would send the worst possible message. Big, big mistake.

When the cheese cart arrived, postures loosened and jokes began. It had been a long campaign; Chaouch was still the frontrunner; there was no reason not to open another bottle of this rather respectable local red wine.

Sari hadn't done anything to conceal her surprise and discomfort; but nobody cared about her. Three out of the seven main advisers were women; Sari detected a hint of hostility from them, as well as a touch of mockery. When she returned to the table after leaving to take a phone call, she thought she heard the word *steroid*. Female empowerment had obviously not crossed the Atlantic draped in physical fitness; it was inevitable that they would look upon her with suspicion. Those sophisticated French liegewomen seemed super-thin; and they didn't care too much for outsiders, especially foreign outsiders, and certainly not a month away from the first round of the election – you didn't want one of the vipers embedded in the press pool to churn out articles about Chaouch calling in American muscle for help so close to the finish line.

The bodyguard who knocked at Sari's door raised his eyebrows when she appeared in the doorframe – she was wearing a Superman T-shirt, moulding her impressive chest and revealing bulging biceps and forearms that would most likely defeat his own in an arm wrestle.

'Wait, what time is it?' she asked in French.

She didn't understand the answer – she was still half-asleep and he didn't articulate; his eyes were too busy voicing their own questions: what sort of chicken do they feed women in America? And what was *he* waiting for to go back to the gym on a daily basis?

Sari clumsily stepped back and scrambled around in the dark to fetch her glasses on top of the nightstand. She stumbled upon the alarm clock she had punched and bashed up after waking with a start, less than a minute earlier. It was still functioning and indicated 4.45 a.m.

'What the hell?' she mumbled.

'Monsieur Chaouch wants to see you.'

She put on trainers and a tracksuit top and the bodyguard escorted her out. Then he drove her into the countryside, back in Petite Camargue. The roads were empty and the night was still thick, with no trace of red or orange in the star-spotted horizon. The car eventually passed an ornate wrought-iron gate, and parked in the muddy courtyard of what appeared to be a horse farm. As she stepped out, Sari smelled the odour of dung and thought: eight thousand kilometres east across the ocean to end up in the Wild West – well, a tiny version of it.

She suddenly saw dozens of torches, directed at the candidate smiling on top of a whitish-grey horse, with large limbs and a streak of blonde hair that made his clever-looking head appear as if it had been customized by some dimwitted Valley Girl.

'Do you like riding?' said Chaouch.

She nodded, even though the last horse she had encountered was a coughing pony in summer camp, some twenty years ago – the other kids had bullied her for days after she had fallen off the poor sick animal; the little pricks had even invented a game: who's more awkward? Sari or . . . – filling the blank with anything mean that crossed their minds.

Dawn was now breaking. Bulky clouds prevented the ball of the sun from materializing above the lines of poplar trees; flaming colours still managed to find their way around the misty landscape where two horses and thirty looming and giant-stepping shadows marched together in the chilly air, at a very slow pace, among the loud and invisible early morning birds.

'I'm very glad you came,' Chaouch told his special guest.

Sari heard a toad croaking just below her; she hoped the horse would avoid stepping on it.

'Sir, I'm afraid you're not going to like what I have to say.'

'Idder, please.'

Sari frowned; she sat up straight on the saddle and stroked the neck of the horse.

'Well, Idder, you're going to lose.'

'You mean lose the election?' Chaouch grinned.

'Sir, I have scraped together all the past electoral results, precinct by precinct, census data, Google searches, Twitter feeds, press. And by the way, if you really want the "future to be now" you should think of making more public data readily available in France . . .'

The future is now was Chaouch's campaign slogan. He encouraged her to go on.

'I'm sorry to break it to you, sir – Idder – but having plugged your campaign strategy into my models from all that data, there's little doubt that you're going to lose. Your campaign manager told me about his advice to stay out of the South where most people hate you because of your curly hair. Well, from what I've seen he's right, people hate you here, and you'll never get close to a majority, and that's what the bird's eye view captures: depressingly low scores and depressing postcolonial hatred of Arabs. That's the information your strategists have access to. However . . . that's also where my scourging of fine-grained data and looking at changes beyond levels kick in. Don't get me wrong: you'll never get a majority here, but inching your way up a couple percentage points – from twenty per cent to twenty-three per cent – will make a difference.

In five years, I'll also be able to tell you who to target with what ad, when France finally starts collecting better individual-level data . . . but for now, I just have one thing to say: stay here, stay in the South.'

This piece of advice was to cause a formidable uproar later that day; but for the time being the two riders sat motionless on their mounts: the fireball had torn through the murk and the clouds, and was now burning right above the scrawny naked vines, so close it felt like the enormous face of a blushing beast that they might touch with their extended fingers if they were bold enough.

'You know what I wanted this campaign to be?' Chaouch said quietly, as he looked at the sunrise. 'I wanted it to be like a family reunion.'

He paused. Sari could see the pink light illuminating his lovely face. He hadn't shaved yet and his cheeks looked bluish.

'And what are you going to do about it?' Sari asked.

He smiled and trotted backwards, whistling the first notes of Beethoven's *Pastoral Symphony*. At the end of the famous opening crescendo he made the horse rear and waved at Sari:

'Look! Over there!'

Silhouetted against a blurry grove, a herd of bulls had raised their massive heads and were now clearly bellowing to be part of the concert.

A few hours later, the candidate was sitting in the back of a tasteless fancy restaurant, protected by three folding-screens spangled with lilies. Fouad and Jasmine were late. In the main dining room, security officers whispered in their earpieces while scanning the ordinary diners; sometimes they sternly shook their heads, when one of the onlookers seemed on the verge of drawing out their smartphone to take a picture. Beyond the screens, the bordeaux carpet seemed a bit worn and fluffy. The nicest round table of the restaurant had been laid for five. A large windowpane overlooked a patio hosting an umbrella pine, a hibiscus and a waterless fountain. The walls were salmon-rose, covered with ivy and Virginia creeper. A group of heavily armed bodyguards watched the entrance of the garden, and sharpshooters were hiding on the roofs on top and around the building. The candidate had received too many threats; his security detail numbered as many units as that of the incumbent president.

Unaware of these precautions, Chaouch had taken off his tie and elevated small-talk to a mild, medium level; he was entertaining his American guest with anecdotes from his teaching years at Harvard – his enthusiasm was so genuine it sounded like it really was the first time he was telling them. But his wife, Esther, seemed to think otherwise. She kept glancing at her watch and smiled briskly whenever her name popped up in the conversation. She had a PhD in Ancient History, and was a prominent expert on Roman politics, but there were certain subjects on which she had great difficulty maintaining her scholarly cool: she and her daughter were the targets of persistent innuendos, presenting them as a couple of evil-minded Jews attempting to trick the candidate in the interests of their 'tribe'. These rumours spanned ecumenically from the far left to the far right; the word the latter used to describe them was not Jews but *Israelites*, a throwback to the nineteen-thirties and the Vichy period.

'Idder, you need to speak up about these attacks,' she suddenly said, in French, as though out of the blue, while her husband was ordering a plate of asparagus and kidding around with the waitress in white livery.

'Which attacks?' he asked in English, so as not to exclude Sari.

'*Tu sais très bien de quoi je veux parler,*' Esther Chaouch replied. She raised her glass of white wine, but didn't drink from it.

'We'll talk about it later,' Chaouch offered. He put the palm of his hand on his wife's bare wrist.

'What do you mean, later? After the election? In five years?' she asked defiantly, lowering her glass and staring at the window-pane. 'Forget it. I guess fighting anti-semitism isn't considered the best way to bring in new votes these days, huh?'

Sari thought it would be a good idea to use the toilet now, but a black suit removed one of the folding-screens to make way for the long-awaited young couple. Chaouch stood up and pinched his daughter's chin. He then proceeded to give two kisses and a friendly handshake to Fouad, who was indeed startlingly good-looking, with big dark eyes and an actor's smile that was remarkably neither toothy nor too aggressively fake.

'You're right on time!' Chaouch exclaimed, jokingly. 'Five more minutes and you'd have missed a passionate conversation on anti-semitism and freedom of speech.'

'Oh, you think this is about freedom of speech?' Esther asked, raising her glass again and shivering as if shifting one of the three screens had blown in a draught. She wore a beige cashmere-style shawl, with long sleeves that she rolled back down while her husband was introducing Sari to the newcomers and warning them that they would have to practise their English today.

Esther gulped down half of her wine and squinted her eyes to decipher the tiny inscriptions on the bottle. '*Et on peut connaître la raison de votre retard?*' Chaouch twitched his finger and slightly bent his head. 'Oh I'm sorry,' continued the soon-to-be First Lady, remembering she was supposed to stick to English. 'Was the traffic bad?'

As Jasmine couldn't move an inch without a chauffeur and a police escort, the question was sarcastic. Fouad sat down in front of the window, facing the candidate. Sitting next to her mother, Jasmine feared she might notice her rosy cheeks and make further snide comments; Jasmine would then have a hard time holding back from describing the wild fuckfest that had caused their delay. Since things had become serious with Fouad, she spent most of her time provoking her mother, because her mother had once claimed that her newfound playboy was nothing less than a dowry hunter. Such allegations infuriated Jasmine, of course. They gave her the worst part in the drama; plus, come on, we don't live in Balzac's France any more, there is no dowry to be hunted! 'You can call it fame if you wish,' Esther Chaouch had replied. And they had never talked about it again; now Esther was cautiously avoiding *the boyfriend*'s looks, but she kept him under close observation, and didn't miss any of his graceful hand gestures and timely chortles.

Chaouch was telling him about the singing bulls at the crack of dawn. Esther abruptly shifted the conversation back to the attacks.

'Oh no, really, darling,' Chaouch said, rubbing his hands at the thought of the meal that was arriving, 'I know it's frustrating but if I start replying to every one of these attacks, it'll end up giving them credibility, and that's the last thing we want, isn't it?'

'So instead you'll let it spread, like a tumour?'

Jasmine stepped in. 'The tumour's already there.'

Chaouch backed up his daughter. 'And the more we feed it with outraged condemnations and moral sentencing, the bigger it'll grow. Now, we shall confront all this, but...'

'But in the meantime they have a free pass, and they can spit on your family in front of the whole country?'

'Well, that's what a family reunion is all about. Fighting and spitting and letting the drunk uncles rant on whatever they need to rant on.'

'What do you mean, a family reunion? Half of the country hates us – half of the country thinks you're not even French! These people are not your uncles, they want you dead, for heaven's sake!'

'Listen, I'm running an economics-oriented campaign, and that's why I'm in the lead. What this country needs is ... jobs, growth ... Let the bastards be bastards, nobody will listen to them any more when we've put an end to massive youth unemployment, trust me.'

Fouad nodded admiringly. He leaned towards his neighbour on the left and whispered: 'So, you're the expert, what do you think about the polls? Are they right? Are we going to win the election next month?'

Sari chuckled. 'God only knows.'

Chaouch caught the phrase and sang gleefully: '*God only knows what I'd be without you ...*'

Esther raised her eyebrows and poured some more wine into her glass. 'I hate this place. We're leaving this afternoon, right? What are you doing after lunch?'

A bustle in the main room made everyone turn their heads

16

towards the folding-screens. A little girl appeared in the gap. She was all dressed up and carrying an envelope – pressing it jealously against her bullhorn-print top. The bodyguard let her in after checking there was no poison inside and that it was okay with the candidate. Chaouch opened his arms but the little girl stood silently, fiddling with the corner of the envelope and twisting her ankles.

'*Comment tu t'appelles, ma chérie?* Don't look at her, she's intimidated, poor girl.'

She had long blonde pigtails and two blue ribbons on top of them. Chaouch went up to her and kissed her shiny domed forehead.

'*Tu me donnes l'enveloppe? C'est un cadeau?*'

She still couldn't utter a single word. Chaouch kneeled down in front of her and stared at her until she let out a burst of childish laughter. One of her teeth was missing on the left side of her upper row. She gave him the envelope and pranced out of the room.

Chaouch opened it and smiled. He handed it over to Sari, who didn't smile. Nor did Fouad, nor did Jasmine – and when Esther finally read it she got up, fuming. Chaouch captured her wrist in his hands and asked her to calm down.

'"Go back to your country, you Islamist son of a bitch?"' Esther repeated it over and over, in French. 'Listen, I'm not hungry any more, why don't we leave this shit-hole?'

Jasmine groped for her boyfriend's hand under the table. Behind them, the fountain was now spouting water, albeit jerkily.

Chaouch stood up and addressed the whole table.

'I might as well tell you now that I've decided to stay in the South for a few more days.' He gave a friendly look to Sari while his wife gaped at him. Then he winked at Fouad and added, with an imperceptible sadness in his voice: 'No need to worry, I've already done the heavy lifting this morning and secured the bulls' vote.'

1

Krim: An Introduction

Community Centre, 3.30 p.m.

Soon they would have to decide: who would stay behind, 'nice and quiet', at the community centre and who would leave for the town hall. The bride's family was too large and not everyone could fit in, especially given the fact that the mayor wasn't known for his patience in these situations. His predecessor (a left-wing independent) had quite simply banned Saturday weddings, to spare the town's peaceful residents all the honking, Rai and flashy cars draped with Algerian flags. In spite of his right-leaning tendencies, the new mayor had lifted the ban, but threatened to reimpose it every time an overexcited tribe wreaked havoc in the house of the Republic.

First among those opting to stay put – right on her *couscoussier*, no less – was Aunt Zoulikha, fanning herself with that day's *Metro*, which was missing its front page, bearing the headline: ELECTION OF THE CENTURY. Next to her sat old Ferhat wearing an improbable blue-green *ushanka* hat that made his ears sweat. One of his great-nephews had tried to reason with him, but every time he broached the subject, Ferhat dodged it by pinching the boy's chin and babbling on about the latest polls in a soft, almost professorial voice no one recognized.

Everyone was acting a bit strange that afternoon: the bride's party, it was rumoured, numbered in the hundreds, plus it was too hot outside for early May. The results of the first round of voting had turned *la belle* France into a pressure-cooker and it seemed that cousin Raouf was the only screw keeping the lid from blowing off. He sprayed himself with facial mist while tapping on his iPhone. Granny watched him, mystified, unable to comprehend this new species of men who lived their lives through screens. Following the Twitter feed of an obsessed pollster and the comments thread of a political site, Raouf lit cigarette after cigarette, keeping everyone abreast of the election forecasts that a colleague – a halal restaurant manager like him – posted on his Facebook page from London. Raouf, normally the paragon of elegance in his thousand-euro pinstriped suits, was dressed in the same t-shirt he'd worn the day before. Bearing the face of the smiling Socialist Party candidate, it was badly tucked in, perfectly visible beneath a blazer rolled up at the sleeves. With his agitated-businessman forearms thus exposed, it was as if the pulse of the nation throbbed in his veins.

Granny, who had told him off for not putting on a suit straight away, no longer had the strength or the desire to scold anyone for anything. She sat silently on her throne in Raouf's gleaming Audi, air-conditioning on high with the passenger door open, half-listening to the Kabyle songs that made the other shiny cars hum. She swung one of her wiry legs out of the vehicle and swept her gaze across the car park where her sparse tribe vegetated. About eighty-five (nobody knew her real age), Granny enjoyed a special status in the family: everyone was terrified of her. A widow almost since time began, she had never been known to feel pity or tenderness or to have a nice word to say to any human being past the age of puberty. She stood amidst her frivolous and voluble daughters like the embodiment of reproach, fuelled by an extraordinary endurance that reeked of both a pact with the devil and the certainty that she would bury them all.

In the meantime the tech crew began their sound check in the reception hall and Granny returned to the cocoon-like silence of the Audi.

'But why are you already here?' the head crewman asked Raouf.

'We needed a meeting point,' Raouf replied without bothering to take off his earpiece. 'Before going to the town hall. But we'll leave soon; we're just waiting for everyone to get here.'

The sound guy didn't look convinced. He had a piece of lettuce stuck between his teeth, which were too big for his mouth, and he smelled of onions.

'So, you're the groom's family? Well, if you don't mind, you'd better stop that music coming from the cars. We've been told not to disturb the neighbourhood before nightfall. What's with that woman over there on the pot?'

'What about her?'

'I thought you had a caterer?'

Raouf didn't know what to say. He opened his hands sheepishly and turned towards Aunt Zoulikha, a venerable barrel of pink flesh, stoic and immaculate, breathing heavily beneath a chestnut tree whose budding foliage did little to protect her from the unseasonable heat.

Three other aunts, stamping their feet in the tiny shadow of a poplar, began to speak about their unruly youngest sister, while Dounia, the mother of the groom, went from group to group dismayed that no one seemed to want to join the race to the town hall.

'There'll only be people from that family,' she complained, waving her white veil and her mobile phone. 'It's a crying shame, *wallah*, you just don't do that ... And Fouad!' she exclaimed suddenly, thinking of her other son, the middle child, who was coming down from Paris to be best man. 'I can't even get Fouad on the phone!'

Uncle Bouzid took off his hat to mop his bare skull. He sported a distinctive baldness, rippled and muscular, traversed from end to end by veins that, when bulging, generally announced an imminent fit of apoplexy.

'Hey, calm down, Dounia. The thing at the town hall starts in an hour and Slim hasn't even arrived yet! We're all here, right? We're all here an hour early, actually, so let's keep cool, please! Cool!' He stopped short of shouting before adding with a hint of a smile: 'Do you think they'll turn the groom's mother away? This isn't a nightclub, you know! Ha, ha. *Sorry, it's a private party.* I mean, really. Go and say something to Rab, the poor girl's all on her own.'

Rabia was indeed there too, talking as usual, this time on the phone to their youngest sister, whom nobody could be sure was coming. Almost all the Saint-Etienne family was there, in fact, not least Toufik the Helpful, his burly baby face crossed with its funny V-shaped unibrow – Toufik who, no doubt, would soon be picked on for no good reason but who for the time being kept on listening and smiling, completely out of sync

22

with the other uncles, cousins and sons-in-law who chatted about car mechanics, the presidential election and horse-racing while occasionally shouting at their wives who shouted at their overexcited brats.

And then, right at the back, behind the gym where people would vote the following day, far from the Rai and the malicious gossip, stood Krim. Krim with his sleepy eyes, Krim with his compact, stubborn eyebrows verging on hostility, Krim with his bizarrely flattened cheekbones that everybody said made him look a little Chinese.

Leaning against an election billboard that now flaunted just two posters, he'd been rubbing a silver lighter against the fluorescent stripe of his tracksuit. When his mother, Rabia, came to ask him if he intended to go to the town hall, he stuffed the lighter in his pocket, shrugged his shoulders and looked away.

'I dunno.'

'What do you mean you dunno? What the hell are you doing hanging around here? Have you taken up hash again? Show me your eyes . . . You swore you'd stopped, so what's this all about? Does it mean you can never be trusted? Look at me. Have you been smoking again?'

'No, I haven't.'

'So you're coming along, then?'

'I just dunno. I. Don't. Know.'

'Well, if you don't know, don't come. What is it, you don't want to show support for your cousin at his wedding? You don't have a choice anyway! Do you really not give a damn about supporting him?'

'What are you talking about?' Krim snapped. '*Support my cousin*, as if we're at war? And why are you being so pushy?'

Rabia looked up from her phone and dragged her son over to the changing rooms, which had been opened up by the building manager to store a stash of chairs. She went directly to the showers and raised her voice.

'Krim, you're not going to start jiving with me, are you? Not today, I'm warning you now.'

'Just go away, and get your head checked. And nobody says *jiving*.'

'What?'

'Forget it.'

'It's all my fault: if I'd been a horrid mother you'd be kissing my feet. *Reddem le rehl g'dunit*, serves me right. Too kind, too stupid, as usual. *Chai*, that'll teach me . . .'

She consulted her inbox for the tenth time in five minutes. She may have been only in her forties, but the mobile phone remained a mysterious object to her, to be handled fearfully, her fingers tense and perpendicular to the screen, her full focus trained on not missing a key. She again raised her curly finch-like head towards her son. All those years in municipal daycare centres looking after 'cutie pies' had prevented her eyes and voice from taking things seriously. Volatile, restless and naive, she resembled those little girls with disproportionately large dimples and eyes, those children who adored her almost despite themselves because she had never stopped being one of them.

'Well then, sweetie, are you coming with us?'

'God, you drive me nuts. You're driving me nuts! Don't you get it?'

'Promise me you'll stop the hash,' she begged. 'Think of your sister. If you won't think of your father, at least think of your sister.'

'Whatever, it's fine. I get it.'

'Where do you think it'll lead you if you—'

'All right!'

'Dad was right: you're turning into a donkey, like Pinocchio.'

'All right, I said!'

With his eyes, his shoulders, his hands, his whole physiognomy on edge, he sought the nearest door.

Rabia was insisting on the town hall because Krim (whose real name was Abdelkrim) was not only the second groomsman but also, out of all twelve cousins, the one that Slim had been closest to. Rabia and Slim's mother, Dounia, were the best of friends, sisters bound both by blood and destiny – having both married for love and then been widowed young. Despite their two-year age difference and increasingly divergent lives, Slim and Krim had remained inseparable. They had once nicknamed each other Mohammed and Hardy, and together they had seen it all: games of tag at Granny's; outdoor barbecues where their fathers bet on horses that shared their birthdays; the mock-fearsome *I'll see you at the school gates*, which they marched through side by side at five o'clock, chins up like Western action heroes; the parquet floor of the principal's tiny office; weddings where they tormented their little cousin; and finally and especially the smell of the pine trees in the city centre, at the foot of which they urinated while studying their circumcised willies.

Slim would never forget the day Krim had whooped in the

changing rooms to announce with proof in hand that he, at last, had the dick of a man:

'Pff, what, you're saying that's a man's dick?'

'Come on, then, show me yours.'

'Pff – if I show you my cock, you'll faint.'

But Krim was no longer listening, too fascinated by his long curly pubic hairs, which he could almost count around this new olive-coloured penis whose size was indeed considerable.

Abdelkrim was known as Krim – or Krikri, even, right up to the moment the puberty fairy precociously and rather mischievously doubled the volume of his forearms and drew a threatening tuft of hair on his upper lip. From that moment on, everything had decidedly gone downhill. At the end of middle school, he was advised to concentrate on vocational studies, though not on the basis of his results in such subjects, which were hardly less mediocre than his other grades. They had found his calling, and, besides, it was stupid and downright criminal to discredit the manual trades, etc. It was the same speech that had been given to his aunts thirty years earlier, when they were placed on the vocational track. A lost generation.

His new school was in the middle of nowhere and architecturally depressing: a concrete block perched on a small hill near an industrial park, waving a flag so suggestive of a skull and crossbones that the Eugène Sue Technical School had been nicknamed 'the Titanic'. Indeed, its four chimneys floated in the early morning mist, and the classroom windows were covered with wire mesh all the way up to the third floor, with the fourth housing, as one might expect, the offices of the school administration.

At the start of the academic year, Krim, who would henceforth come to blows with any stranger who dared call him Krikri, met the misfit his kind and frail father dubbed Lucignolo, after the young charismatic thug who leads Pinocchio astray. Krim became his henchman and started to smoke. He gave up his football team and the piano lessons he was now ashamed of. His mother had signed him up for piano because his Year 3 teacher, who played the violin, had proclaimed that he was not only exceptionally gifted, but also possessed what she called, with incomprehensible reverence, 'perfect pitch'. Indeed, it was that same winter that an ENT doctor from Lyon diagnosed young Krim as hyper-acoustic: he could hear more and better than anyone else, which probably caused his terrible headaches. Could he be cured? No. So they bought some earplugs and thicker curtains, and it was never brought up again.

Right in the middle of the Christmas festivities, when snow had fallen for the first time in years, Krim's father died, succumbing to an accident at the factory where he had inhaled toxic fumes. It is a well-known fact that snow stifles noise, dulls pain, and confers dignity upon the world – while it lasts. But in this case it was powerless against this tremendous, cataclysmic, unconscionable event that ultimately cast Krim out to the margins of a system that, when all is said and done, offers very little to those who play by its rules.

Everything proceeded smoothly from bad to worse until the day Krim incurred the wrath of an authority more brutal than that of the State: Mouloud Benbaraka, an elusive gang leader, the 'Bernardo Provenzano of the Rhône', as he had been nicknamed by the local paper. Krim had been a lookout; he kept watch outside the stairwells where deals took place and hooted like an owl when he caught sight of an unmarked police car. At the age of sixteen he was making fifteen hundred euros a month, something his father had never earned. One day he managed to steal fifty grams of the best pot that had been seen in the area for years. Mouloud Benbaraka summoned him and started by tweaking his ear. Krim fought back and received a few punches in the jaw. When Mouloud Benbaraka leaned his jackal-like head forward for an explanation, Krim bit his left earlobe. It took all the diplomatic talent of his powerful cousin, Nazir, Slim's big brother, to calm the fury of the lord of the Saint-Etienne underworld, who nevertheless swore that if he ever happened to bump into Krim again he would rip him to shreds.

Rabia knew nothing about this episode, of course, and neither did anyone in the family. It was, as Nazir said, something between him and Krim – though Fat Momo, Krim's best friend, ended up catching wind of it. For his part, Krim learned to live with this Damoclean sword hanging over his head. In fact, the worst problems tend to disappear on their own if you stop thinking about them 24/7. On evenings of sorrow and anguish, he simply closed his eyes and repeated one of the sonatas he had once played on the keyboard his granddad had given him. The music lit up and purified all the passageways in his mind. It shut out the chaos of the world.

There was, however, another problem: his little sister Luna, whom he had always pampered in his own way, his own rough way, and who wept every time their mother was summoned to the police station for another of Krim's misdeeds. There was no escaping the turmoil awakened by Luna's sadness. Years later, she still spoke to him in the same nagging tone, as if there was something in his face that provoked sermons and scolding:

'Why did you tell Mum I was prancing around naked on Facebook?'

'What?'

All grown up, Luna was decked out in her fanciest black dress, covered with sequins that gleamed absurdly even in the shade of the building. For a moment, Krim thought he had misheard; the sound check was getting louder and louder with each skip to the next Rai track.

He jerked his face away as if to escape an invasive ray of light and moved back a few metres. 'Why the hell are you hounding me about Facebook?'

'You hacked my account? No, you're too dumb for that. You friended one of my friends and you looked at one of my videos? I can't believe it. You know what you're going to do now? You're going to go tell Mum you made everything up. I don't give a shit what it takes, you go and find something . . .'

But Krim had started to smile. The joint he'd hidden in his palm was beginning to seep into his system.

'Loser,' Luna hurled at him before heading into the gym. Her resolute stride broke into a run: fists clenched, arms outstretched like a gymnast charging towards a pommel horse.

Krim had yet to come around to the idea that a fifteen-year-old girl could be more muscular than most boys her age: gymnastics had sculpted her biceps, abdominal muscles, traps and delts. When, like today, she wore a sleeveless top, the veins of her forearms and her triceps popped out, even when she kept them still by her body.

As if she had heard her brother's thoughts, Luna hurtled back and threatened him with her finger cocked at her ram-like temple. 'If you don't tell Mum you made up the thing about my Facebook pics, I swear you'll regret it.'

'Oh yeah? Since when do you even know the word regret?'

'If I were you, I'd watch out.' Suddenly more hesitant, unable to look him straight in the eye, she added, 'I know . . . stuff about you. If I were you . . .'

'Hey, get lost. *Wallah*, I'm not even listening.'

'You think I didn't see you last week with Fat Momo?'

'Okay, leave me alone, you stupid brat.'

But instead of waiting for her to go away, he preferred to do the honours, moving swiftly towards the thick bushes by the gym.

He walked, minding the thorns of holly, the little bay leaves you are not supposed to eat, and the stems of flowers he couldn't name. Near the changing room entrance that held so many memories, a path led up to an artificial turf field, but to get there you had to lose yourself in a maze of greenery. This was where Krim found a spot to smoke in peace. He let his attention drift from sound to sound, from raised voices to chirping birds. A pneumatic drill droned on a few streets away, perhaps at the edge of the motorway. There was also, a little further off, the engine of a leaf-blower stubbornly keeping time, a dramatic accompaniment for a melody that would never come.

Suddenly Krim heard a familiar voice:

'The worst thing is that half the people we're going to see tonight aren't registered to vote. That really drives me nuts . . . But what can you do, force them to vote? . . . Ah, you mean because they're foreigners?'

Krim recognized his cousin Raouf and understood from the silences punctuating his sentences that he was on the phone. Raouf was the entrepreneur of the family. Krim could not see him, but imagined him wearing a brown turtleneck sweater and a striped jacket, flashing a perfect Colgate smile.

'No, no, well, yes, foreigners should be able to vote as well. For the local elections – fuck it, for *all* elections . . .'

Raouf had moved to London and hadn't been seen around for ages. Krim suddenly wondered if he hadn't smoked a bit too much: he couldn't remember his cousin's face. He swallowed a mouthful of saliva and shifted position while trying to make as little noise as possible. Through the branches he could now see Raouf's silhouette, earpiece and all, kicking the air at the goalpost; he was literally a few metres away. Krim listened carefully, wondering above all if he was going to manage to chase away the mental image of his joint's contents, its tobacco-brown crumbs shrivelling away with each passing second.

'Anyway, most of them are *not* foreigners. I mean, what do you call someone who's been living here for thirty years? . . . Give me a break . . . if you pay your taxes here, you vote here, then that's that . . . My Socialist Party membership card? Yes. No, but wait, listen, this is different, this is one of those historical moments when one man can make a difference. Ha, ha . . . Fuck, I've got nothing here, I don't know how I'll survive till Monday . . . What? No, don't worry, fifty-two to forty-eight in all the opinion polls, even the front page in *Le Figaro*. Things look solid. I don't know if the rumour that the Americans helped his campaign are true . . . but who cares if he wins! And come on, he was so good at Wednesday's debate . . . The other guy was so nervous, all that finger-pointing . . . Whereas Chaouch was . . . Chaouch . . .'

Krim was under the impression that if he concentrated very hard, he could guess who Raouf was speaking to. But Raouf scarcely gave the person on the other end any time to catch a breath.

'No, I don't believe that crap. They're driving us crazy with their overzealous caution. "The secrecy of the polling booth", my arse. I mean, fuck, Chaouch won the first round, right? He ran a perfect campaign, completely positive, he hardly ever mentioned his opponent. You know how people talk about "protest votes"? Here it's the opposite! It's a vote for hope, people are proud. At last a little hope, a little enthusiasm and optimism. Chaouch embodies vitality. When people see him on TV they don't see themselves as they are – nasty, hypocritical – they see what they want to be. They suddenly want to have faith in life, in the future . . .'

Raouf seemed carried away by his impassioned vision. His eyes darted around but never settled on anything. He looked around in the same way that he spoke: quickly, so quickly that, from this short distance, he seemed on the verge of taking flight.

'Me, worried about what? The fall from grace? What, "You build a campaign with poetry but then you govern with . . ." No, no, I'm not worried, I'm sick of being worried . . .'

Meanwhile, Krim, in stitches with laughter, had stretched out on the slope and was watching the clouds race each other, graceful and dappled across the screen of a matt-blue sky that actually seemed soft, like a pillow – just as he imagined the sky would be in heaven.

He waited for Raouf to start speaking again and rolled another joint for later. Beyond the bushes, the sun drew the contours of the imperfect triangle of a pine tree on the sloping lawn, so distinctly that you could make out the cross-like point at its top. Krim had sniffed out nothing less than the ideal burrow: something between a hiding place and a promontory, an open-air den.

'Hang on,' Raouf said in a low voice. Then, scanning his surroundings: 'I've got to ask you something, if you have a minute. Do you remember the last time, when we talked about MDMA? Well, there's a girl I know, a friend from London who has taken some and is saying some pretty wild stuff on her Twitter feed . . . The love drug? No, I didn't know. What, like you take it and then love everyone?'

Raouf drew on his cigarette. The sound made Krim shiver: it was succulent and moist, almost like that of a sluice pump, dampening the filter and proving Raouf had just reached a new critical threshold of nervousness.

'Honestly, you've got to help me here. I'm not going to survive two days with the whole tribe if I've got nothing . . . Ah yeah, while we're at it, why aren't you coming? Because of Fouad, is that it? No, come on, your little war's not going to last a hundred years! Hello? Nazir? . . . Yeah, I lost you for a sec, I was saying why don't you come, but yeah, okay, I know. But fuck, I mean, it's your little brother who's getting married after all . . .'

A long silence followed, so long that Krim stopped listening. He only bent his ear when he thought he heard Raouf say his name. But he had no doubt been dreaming because Raouf was speaking about Fouad again, their actor cousin who had been on TV five times a week since the start of the year:

'I know, when I came to Paris in January, there was a party and he didn't show. Another time I was on Facebook at 4 a.m. and suddenly Fouad appears, I write to him and he doesn't even reply. The same thing happens the next week. And what's worse, each time he signs on and there's my name on the list, he disconnects straight away. I mean, come on, don't tell me that he's busy at four in the morning! . . . If it really pisses him off to

33

speak to his cousins, if we're not good enough for him now, then screw him, you know what I mean?'

Krim's mouth felt furry. He stood up with difficulty and went down towards the gym to fetch a drink of water without being seen. But the door was locked again. He was trying to find another entry when Raouf joined him on his way back from the playing field. His cousin winked at him and put a hand on his shoulder to ask him a favour.

There were a few niceties at first – how are you, your health, the family – with Raouf paying little attention to his cousin's monosyllabic answers. When he finally got round to the subject at hand, it was Krim's turn not to listen. He was fascinated by the cocaine addict's tics, how by turns they lengthened and shortened his entrepreneur cousin's clean-shaven face, its complexion whitened by his new life of dinner parties and the company of moneyed, fair-haired human beings.

'Krim, you listening? I was just asking you if you could find something by tonight?'

'What?'

'Some weed, for example.' Raouf hesitated, chewing on his lips, then added, 'Have you heard of, what's it called, MDMA?'

'No. What's that?'

'Forget it. It's Ecstasy, or a compound of it.' Raouf put his hand on his neck and added dreamily, 'People are calling it the love drug . . .' With this he plunged his hand into his pocket and took out a fifty-euro note, which he stuffed directly into Krim's palm.

'In case you find something. And if not just keep it. *Sadakha.*'

Krim said he would let him know. Raouf asked for his phone number and called him straight away so Krim would have his.

34

Then the two cousins disappeared into the muffled activity still floating over the car park.

Montreynaud Neighbourhood, 4 p.m.

A few moments later, in Uncle Bouzid's car, Krim sent a text to Fat Momo asking about MDMA. Bouzid turned the sound down.

'Well, Krim, I promised your mother we were going to have a little chat. You're seventeen. When's your birthday?'

'It was yesterday.'

'Okay. As of yesterday, you're eighteen, so listen to me carefully ...'

Krim knew very well what this was about. He went onto autopilot and chose to nod every fifteen seconds.

As he heard himself being scolded for having resigned from McDonald's after two days, for having slapped his chignonned superior, and for slowly killing his mother, Krim delighted in his uncle's smooth driving, which reminded him of his father's and those evenings when, just because everyone was in a good mood, he was allowed to take the front seat and enjoy the shock-absorbed bumps offered by the road under a full moon. Krim could recreate this feeling whenever he played *GTA IV*: he stayed on the sidelines and kept away from the missions, the cops and the thieves, and just drove endlessly around those tentacular virtual cities where the world stopped, like in the good old days when the earth was flat, at the edge of an abstract ocean beyond which it was inconceivable to venture.

Uncle Bouzid, just like his father and just like Krim himself behind the wheel of his pixelated car, took ample and generous turns. In his uncle's case, this was down to his professional training: he drove the formidable Number 9 for the Saint-Etienne bus service, linking the difficult neighbourhood of Montreynaud with the city centre. The habits of a wide turning radius and a steering wheel three times bigger than average could explain Bouzid's way of forgetting the lines on the road when rounding a corner. Some of his turns made Krim shiver with bliss. He felt beautiful, worthy and important next to a man who drove his vehicle so serenely that you might let yourself imagine the same held true for the way he led his life. But it wasn't the case – quite the opposite: Uncle Bouzid was in fact beginning to get worked up. He was looking in the rear-view mirror more and more often, and less and less at Krim:

'. . . and then the moment comes when you have to have a bit of honour – *néf, tfam'et*? I too did some stupid things when I was young. What do you think? That you're the only one? We've all been there. But hey, you've got to grow up at some point. And then you have to stop hanging around with your homies. People blame the right, what they say about immigrants and thugs . . . But the truth is, they're right! I too would wipe out all those little scumbags with a hose. I see them every day, those *wesh-weshes*, those punks. I'm telling you: if one of them lights up a spliff or bothers an old lady, he's going to hear from me. What do you think, that these thugs are going to rule the place? Well, now you've got to own up to your responsibilities. Especially with Chaouch's election. I hope you're registered to vote? You're eighteen, so there you go, you can vote. Now, there comes a time when . . .'

Krim received a text as the car exited the fast road and pulled onto the winding road that climbed the hill of Montreynaud. He read it, hiding the phosphorescent screen with his hand.

Received: Today at 4.02 p.m.

From: N

D-1, I hope you're ready.

Krim's face clouded over. These last months Nazir had sent him an average of ten texts a day, ranging from 'How's it going?' to philosophical maxims like, 'Hope only makes people hopeless.' Krim had learned to think for himself ever since he'd first been approached by his older cousin – to whom he probably owed his life. Maybe Mouloud Benbaraka would only have gouged out his eyes or cut off his balls. It was rumoured he once burned some guy alive who had disrespected his old mother . . .

Nazir had been able to negotiate with Benbaraka and save his little cousin's skin because Nazir was of the same calibre as Mouloud Benbaraka: he was a man who saw things as they were instead of deluding himself. The texts he'd sent Krim were witness to that and Krim had carefully archived them, even though Nazir had categorically forbidden it. He'd even copied the most important ones on a piece of paper folded in three, which never left his tracksuit pocket.

To this text Krim simply replied that he was okay, that he felt ready. And then the car stopped at a red light, in front of a picture of Chaouch staring Krim straight in the eyes. Krim looked away and added, 'What's MDMA?' which he blamed on the joint and to which Nazir replied in a bizarrely abrupt way:

Received: Today 4.09 p.m.

From: N

Mind your own business. And no
drugs today.

The neighbourhood where his uncle lived was perhaps the most dilapidated in the city. It was also Mouloud Benbaraka territory and Krim unconsciously sank into his seat for fear of being spotted.

The streets on the hill were named after illustrious composers, the buildings after birds with melodious sounds: warblers, robin redbreasts, chaffinches ... Here and there tower blocks sprouted up, thousands of windows bristling with satellite dishes that sparkled intermittently under the blazing sun. The concrete balconies were crumbling, the curtains and the walls were losing their colour. It was roundly expected that at any moment, despite the pushchairs loaded with shopping bags and the mothers who quarrelled with the madwomen on the first-floor landing, the towers could explode just like on TV. Twenty floors suddenly vapourized: no one would have been surprised. The landscape was desolate. It called for demolition like the jungle calls for rain.

'Come on, we've no time to lose,' said Uncle Bouzid, stepping over a twisted door at the entrance to his block of flats, on which a sheet of paper warned: THERE'S NOTHING LEFT TO STEAL HERE.

Uncle Bouzid stormed up the staircase and into his studio flat, where a thick smell of feet stagnated – coloured by that of his musk aftershave, the one he'd been buying since his teenage years in the seventies.

'Try this one,' he ordered Krim, pointing to a grey suit, blue shirt and brown tie that he'd just grabbed from his wardrobe.

On the door to the left were traces of a recent assault that had probably been carried out with fists. To confess his dark secret, Bouzid seized the moment when Krim was changing in the bathroom. He was just on the other side of the door, but thanks to the deafening ventilation system that came on with the lights, Krim could only hear about a third of his uncle's speech.

When he came out holding his jacket, a bit dazed by the hunger that had begun to gnaw at him because of the joint, his uncle stood there staring at him with big brown eyes full of emotion. His chin trembled like Charles Ingalls's in *Little House on the Prairie*: he looked like he was at the end of his rope.

'For the rest of my life, I'll have to pay. For the rest of my life. Five hundred euros a month, all that because of, *zarma*, a fight in a bar . . .'

Krim didn't know how to react to solemn declarations like these. His mother also made them sometimes, with the same dilated eyes that tried to convince you that you were all part of a large artichoke called humankind. Feeling uneasy, he looked down and noticed that he would need some loafers. Had Uncle Bouzid thought about that?

'You've got to stop all that stupid stuff, Krim. For fuck's sake, you're young, you're intelligent, you're in good health *hamdoullah*, you have your whole life ahead of you. Promise me you're going to stop?'

'Yes, yes, I promise.'

'No, no, I'm serious here. Swear you'll stop.'

'Yes, it's okay, I swear.'

'Good,' whispered the uncle, pinching his shoulder. 'I swear that things are going to turn out fine. And look, tomorrow's the election, aren't you pleased, Chaouch's becoming president, *insh'Allah*? An Arab president, just to see the faces of those shit-scared Frenchies I want to see him elected, don't you?'

'Yes, yes.'

'Good, then come here, we'll find you some shoes and a tie. Do you know how to put on a tie? You have to, you know. It's not every day Slim gets married!'

He seemed finally to notice his nephew's odd appearance. 'Okay, it's a bit big, but it'll do. Hey, you've got to eat a bit more, you don't want to end up looking like Slim. *Miskine*, he's as thin as a rake.'

Krim let his uncle plunge head first into the cupboard by the front door, using the chance to look around the place where Bouzid had lived since his 'girlfriend' had left him. He only went out with French girls, and each time it ended in *merguez gravy*, as he would say: they weren't serious, they spoke to him rudely, so much so that he swore every time on Granny's head that this was the last time, the very last time. He would find himself a girl who was good – Muslim, that is to say, sweet and fertile.

'Do you know Ait Menguellet?' he asked Krim, who was checking out a CD whose cover showed the spitting image of his father close up. A man of forty with a face that was long, fine, fair, tragic and moustached.

Krim shook his head.

'Then consider it a present, for your birthday. We can listen to it in the car if you like, a bit of a change from the Rai. After all, our ears are going to be ringing from their towel-headed music tonight . . .'

Krim stuffed the CD into the pocket of his new jacket. It was the first time he'd worn a jacket with shoulder pads, the first time too that he'd worn canvas trousers with that kind of sophisticated fly. The grey, blue and brown top with the smart tie pleased him, but not the bottom part, where his black loafers clashed with the light trousers, as egregiously as a pair of white socks with a dark suit.

Uncle Bouzid pushed him towards the exit and fastened the three locks on the steel door. 'What about the Army?' he suddenly said. 'Have you thought about the Army? No, really, I'm telling you, there are lots of possibilities. Or the Navy! A cook in the Navy! You need plans, you know. The most important thing in life is to have plans.'

Krim let his eyes rest tenderly upon that shiny pate. He soon heard the voice of a little girl at the other end of the landing; she was gearing up to leap down the six steps to the lift, all in one go. The dust in the corridor was irresistibly drawn towards a flood of light, which crossed the stairwell from the broken windowpanes all the way to the little girl's caramel-coloured thighs. When she finally jumped, Krim felt the impression, the premonition, and soon the absolute certainty that this was the last time he would ever set foot in this building.

2

At the Town Hall

City centre, 4.15 p.m.

Twisting his neck, Zoran reached up towards the fourth floor of the narrow building, trying to prevent the little cat he'd spent the morning with from venturing out onto the ledge. He was making grand, useless gestures and whispering pleas, trying to avoid shouting out loud so as not to frighten the animal. For a moment he considered calling the fire brigade, but he didn't know the number, and the cat had already turned back, no doubt frightened by a couple of pigeons cooing on the drainpipe.

Two passers-by turned towards Zoran, whose outfit, which he was wearing for the first time, couldn't go unnoticed in this neighbourhood. He'd decided on it at the last moment, on a whim, in front of the wardrobe mirror that silhouetted his slinky figure against the depressing disorder of the studio flat from which he'd just been evicted over the phone: low-cut jeans faded at the thighs, with studded back pockets, iridescent ballet shoes; and a spangled t-shirt decorated with the Union Jack, which he'd cut away and shortened so people could admire his flat stomach and pierced navel. The jeans were a gift from a guy he'd met in Lyon who liked to see him in drag. As for the top and the ballet shoes, he had no idea who they belonged to. He'd simply taken them in the flat where he had been staying before being kicked out, thinking out loud in Romanian – maybe also for the edification of the cat, with whom he'd spoken at least as much as with his 'roommate' during the previous days – 'If you're going to be taken for a thief, you may as well have stolen something.'

After nodding to a guy who'd stopped dead in his tracks to observe him with his fist on his hip, Zoran took his suitcase and looked up for the last time at the half-open window, which peacefully welcomed the reflection of blue interspersed with an almost motionless white beam, indicating the passage of a plane or other motorized creature in the crystal-clear sky.

He walked along the cemetery that crested the hill, the one he had seen from his window for the past three weeks, then entered the bar where he had arranged a meeting for 4 p.m. sharp. He was late, but there was no trace of the person he'd planned to get together with. His favourite bartender wasn't behind the counter, either, and the red-haired woman who'd replaced him looked like she was in a bad mood. She was dumping a pint of yellowish foam into the sink.

'The barrels are empty,' she immediately warned him.

Zoran hesitated to cross the few metres separating him from the counter. He couldn't stand the tiled floor and the constant squeaking of the chairs.

'Give me whisky,' he said, dropping his suitcase at the foot of a high stool. He rested one buttock on it and repeated, looking her straight in the eyes: 'Give me whisky.'

'Can you pay for it?'

'Yes.'

'Then show me the money.'

'Why me show? Why he not show?' He pointed at an obvious regular at the other end of the counter.

'Listen, if you're here to make trouble,' she spat, 'the answer's no! We're sick of...'

'Sick of what?'

'Of all you lot! When are you going back home to Romania? Don't you see you can't stay here? There's no room here, no work! Are you at least here for work?'

'None work in Romania.'

'*None* work here either. Nothing at all, *nada*. I'm serious...'

The regular, who had been using his thumb and index finger to smooth the ends of his sandy moustache, grunted indecipherably. Did he want to prevent the barmaid from going too far or was he just suggesting she keep her voice down?

Zoran continued to stare at this horrible woman, to show her that they were equals. But his difficulty forming sentences in this impossible language made him stammer and look at the floor despite himself. 'I have meeting man, four o'clock, he pay thousand euros. If I thousand euros, I ten euros. So give whisky, expensive whisky.'

The barmaid looked to the heavens and slapped her thick, flat palm against her forehead.

'What do you mean a thousand euros? Hey, this isn't a brothel, you get me? Get out right now! Out! Go on, out!'

At that moment, a customer appeared, a small man in a suit, sweating profusely. He came down the stairs that led to the bedrooms, or perhaps the toilets. Zoran stared at him until he was out of his field of vision. The barmaid waved at the man politely as he left, and Zoran felt like killing her when he saw her look him over in disgust.

'Right, come on, time to leave now. Or I'll call the police.'

Zoran slid off the stool, insulting the barmaid in Romanian. He asked the drunk, now sprawled against the counter, what time it was – he hadn't seen anyone since early afternoon. It was 4.30 p.m., and his ultimatum had not worked.

He wandered around the city centre in hope of finding the man who was to make him rich. Most of the people who saw him that afternoon turned round as he passed and made rude comments, sometimes mouthed in silence, sometimes muttered quietly. There were also a few who spoke loudly enough for him to hear: a goateed grocer, a young mother smoking a cigarette by her pushchair, some Arab teenagers in tracksuits, two construction workers on their break, and an electrician with hairy shoulders. They all hated him the instant they realized he wasn't a girl, but their hatred was fuelled by the fact that he was in no certain and definitive way a non-girl; he personified sexual ambiguity long after the first impression, from the provocative swaying of his hips to the slightest of his delicate gestures. His carmine nail varnish, which he openly continued to blow on, thus contributed to the hatred, as did his stubborn expression, his air of defiance, his twitching nostrils that asked for trouble. And then there was the mole under his left eye. It happens, when you find someone particularly unpleasant, that all the hostility he inspires in you is focused on one of these moles. Zoran's was bluish, compact and disgustingly round. Through it, his whole unstable character screamed for attention. Because of it, his father had often beaten him. In public, Zoran appeared sure of himself, all-conquering. With his yellow eyes, broad shoulders and dark blemished skin, he wasn't beautiful by any measure. But with the sort of men whose eye he sought to catch, being beautiful wasn't much use; it was enough to be young, well made-up, have a slender body and a hairless torso, and give off an animal warmth, a smell of stables and sin.

After buying some gum, he walked around the cathedral square where children rode an old merry-go-round. Suddenly convinced he was being followed by a man in a beige jacket, he walked towards the centre of the square where nothing could happen to him. Three fountains sprang from an invisible source between the flagstones. When the sun reappeared after a brief absence behind the clouds, Zoran observed the shadow of one of the vertical jets of water, which seemed to flow more slowly. His own shadow also seemed to move on a delay, and he took advantage of that to look at it closely. It was then, while he cursed his shoulders, his stature and his penis, that he heard the honking.

Everyone had stopped to watch the cortège of cars decorated with pink and white ribbons, each vehicle packed with swarthy, smiling faces that sang along with the Arab music blasting forth. Zoran followed the procession and found himself in front of the town hall, among a small crowd of passers-by who had gathered to enjoy the spectacle. When a bloke stepped backwards onto his shiny shoes, Zoran pushed him violently, but the man didn't answer. Maybe he hadn't done it deliberately. He spat out his chewing gum to smoke before realizing he didn't have any cigarettes. No one was smoking around him, except for a tall brute of a man who didn't look very approachable. He popped another piece of gum and amused himself by blowing bubbles.

A few moments later, while the well-dressed people strutted around at the foot of the municipal steps feeling very self-important, a fat blonde girl pointed to Zoran and made her mother lean down so she could whisper something in her ear. Zoran was trying to make her smile by grimacing when in the crowd he spotted the familiar face of the man he had arranged to meet half an hour earlier

'Slim!' he shouted.

He tried to push his way through while avoiding the girl's eyes and saw that he wasn't mistaken. His heart began to beat faster. He wanted to get hold of Slim, but was jostled by a bald man who had seen him coming.

'I know to him,' protested Zoran, pointing to the young Arab.

But the bald guy pushed him unceremoniously back into the crowd, as if he was a bodyguard. And as if he'd had a premonition of what was about to happen to him, Zoran shielded his head with his two hands and crouched down so quickly that he heard his jeans rip. One or two pairs of powerful arms lifted him off the ground and carried him through the crowd. He didn't have time to call for help or make the slightest attempt to free himself: the bloke who'd caught him threw him in the back of a car, which sped off without making the tyres screech, so smoothly that it was easy for any witnesses to the scene to return to their business and pretend that nothing had happened.

Town Hall, 4.30 p.m.

'Do you remember Bachir? Yes you do, Aicha's son! Krim, come over here! Krim, do you remember Bachir? Krim, I'm talking to you!'

Aunt Rabia's *joie de vivre* was a profound mystery the family no longer questioned. It magnetized her nieces, her sisters and their men, and no humiliation ever managed to dent it. The only one who'd ended up immune to it was Krim: the unbelievable flow of words from his mother inspired in him only a vague sense of fatigue. He was writing a text message when Toufik encouraged his Aunt Rabia to go on.

'So, you have to know that Bachir *miskine* is banned from the casino, he's had serious problems, I'm talking two, three years ago, poor dear he was banned from the casino of Montrond-les-Bains, oh yes, yes, I swear it's the truth, but, wait, he was spending hundreds and thousands, too. And there comes a time when it's too much, and then he can't find a nice little girlfriend either. Ah *yes*,' she digressed, egged on by Toufik's astonishment. 'What kind of wife wants a husband who spends his life at the casino? *Wallah*, I like Bachir a lot, he has a good *miskine* heart' – she joined her thumb to her other fingertips and bestowed on them a vehement kiss – 'but on Krim's life I'd never marry a man who's an, what do you call it, addict, addictive? No, really: how do you feed your kids when all the cash is getting thrown into the casino, the *rhla*?'

'No, really, that bad?'

'Yup,' bellowed Rabia. 'Next to him Al Pacino is a choir boy!'

Everyone burst out laughing, even if no one, including Rabia, had understood the reference.

'What was I saying? Oh, yes, so he went to see some useless shrink, and each time he spent one hundred, two hundred euros. I'm telling you it was worse than the casino, *matehn*, and one day the doctor, he tells him: that's it, you're cured. Bachir *miskine* he says, "thanks doctor" and he starts his little life again, his little routine, and then one day he goes to the launderette, this is true you know, he goes to the launderette, he puts a coin in the little machine to start the wash, and there, *wallah*, I swear on Granddad's grave, on the life of Krim if he dies just now, he slips a coin into the little machine like that and—'

She was interrupted by some commotion a few metres behind her. They turned, as did the bride's party, to witness Granny shouting at Dounia. Uncle Bouzid ran up and tried to calm his mother, who was thrusting her finger at Dounia, indifferent to the strangers who pretended not to notice.

'What's happening, Bouz?' Rabia asked.

'There's a problem. Fouad's train's going to be late.'

'How late?'

'I don't know, an hour, maybe even more. He's Slim's witness but the bride's family is saying they can't wait for him.'

'Where is Dounia?'

Rabia wanted to take things into her own hands but Granny was blocking the way. She took her daughter by the wrist and drew her aside, saying in Kabyle, 'Ah no, no, come on, enough with the scandals, we can't have everyone always barging in to take care of everything. Go, go, let her sort things out herself.'

'*Yeum*, *yeum*, let her come here, what are you doing, *l'archouma* . . .'

'Dounia, Krim's the other witness, right?'

'Where is he?' asked Dounia, standing on tiptoe.

While the women were looking around for Krim, Slim showed up. He hadn't stopped grinning all day. In fact, his whole appearance was smiling – his white teeth, his white suit, his beautiful and slender white hands. He was wearing a fat, puffy tie and soft loafers, which allowed him to flutter from group to group and speak to everyone in the same light-hearted, easy-going tone. He had the same large, black, feminine eyes as his brothers: astonishingly long lashes, their perimeter stark as if marked by pencil, and huge irises that reduced the whites of his eyes to a corner that was hardly any lighter.

Leaning against a lamppost, Krim watched the whole tribe arrive in single file. He edged backwards, which made him drop the cigarette he'd just lit.

'What, me?' he replied when asked to step in to replace Fouad.

'Come on, please, don't make any trouble.'

'You're getting on my nerves, I didn't ask for anything! Fuck, I was sure this would . . .'

Slim arrived behind his aunt. He took Krim aside and explained the situation. After a few seconds, Slim managed to sit down, with his back to the town hall. He and Krim were now looking in the same direction, except that Krim, unlike the little prince of the day, didn't keep on crossing and uncrossing his legs.

Slim suddenly changed the subject and looked away. 'Anyway, Mum told me about the job centre. You're in deep shit, you know that?'

Krim raised his eyebrows. He lit another cigarette and began to fondle his tie, wondering if he didn't look like an American actor.

'Do you know what you'll do now?'

'Yeah, we'll see.'

'You're completely stoned again, Krim. When on earth are you going to grow up?'

Krim took his cigarette filter between his thumb and index finger and silently observed its burning end. 'And what about you?' he asked in an impassive tone. 'You still in college?'

'No, I'll have to work, if only to . . . Well, I've got something for you, Krim, but . . .'

Krim kept silent, so silent that Slim felt obliged to say something startling to attract his attention.

'I've told no one, not even my mum, but . . . I'm worried I won't make it with her, you see.'

'With who?'

'Kenza. But you mustn't repeat this, it's too weird, but I feel like I'll never be able to . . . you know . . .'

In a daze Krim stared at the horizon. The world's ramparts were on fire and no one but he could hear them burning.

'Why aren't you saying anything?'

'Well, uh, I don't know,' Krim replied, in a blind panic. 'Don't know.'

'I feel like I'll never manage to make her happy,' Slim persisted. 'I do what I can, you know, but . . . You're not listening.'

Slim stood up and looked at the treetops on the square, anxious to escape the silence weighing upon their neatly coiffed little heads. To his surprise, Krim took the first step.

'Hey, seriously, you shouldn't worry. You're a nice guy, you know, it'll definitely work out.'

'Thanks, Krim.' Slim stepped in front of him. 'Thanks.'

Krim hated that earnest, whiny tone. If that was what it meant to be an adult, if it meant taking things with that kind of stupid solemnity, then he wanted to remain a child to the end of his days.

'Anyway, I've heard about all the shit you've been getting into. Is that why Nazir is slipping an envelope to you?'

Krim was stunned. He cut the conversation short. 'No, it's fine, let's not talk about that stuff, you know, it's your wedding day.'

Slim put his arms around his cousin and Krim gave him the clumsiest pair of kisses he'd ever received.

From the steps where she continued to babble on, Rabia saw the fancy groom hand an envelope to Krim. The latter seemed surprised and kissed his cousin on both cheeks before putting his hand on his heart.

'What was that envelope, Krim?' she asked when he'd returned.

'None of your business.'

'*Zarma.* "None of your business"? Why are you being like that? What have I done to deserve being treated like a dog in front of everyone?'

'Here we go again . . .'

She ran her hand over her son's head. And then her eyes lit up, gleaming with a purely adolescent excitement. 'Come on, why can't you tell me, sweetie?'

'It's just my present for yesterday, it's nothing. Great, and now you're going to tell everyone . . . I swear, you're like a little kid.'

'Yes, and you know what, I'm proud of it! Everyone thinks you're my little brother. You should thank God you've got such a young mother! While we're at it, what's this story about Luna on Facebook?'

'What,' Krim suddenly said in a rage, 'your daughter's exposing herself to millions of people and you don't care?'

'Words of an ayatollah . . .'

'Yeah, okay, whatever.'

'That's just how girls are these days. She's just being flirtatious . . .'

52

'Yeah, flirtatious all right. You'll see the day she gets raped.'

'How dare you!' screamed Rabia. 'What's wrong with you?'

Her anger subsided as fast as it had appeared: she had to greet one of Dounia's French friends. After a few polite words she returned to her son and buttoned his shirt right up to the top, but Krim began to choke.

'It's too tight, I feel like throwing up.'

'No, no, leave it, that's how it's supposed to be worn. Leave it, trust me! What do you think, that the billions of people who wear ties all feel like throwing up? You'll get over it, don't worry.'

While he got used to having a compressed glottis, Rabia looked at him with pride: her big boy (in a suit and tie). But as soon as he turned around to join Slim, her pride turned to sadness, so suddenly that she had to wipe a little tear from her eye before it threatened her mascara.

The bride's clan had colonized the steps of the town hall even before Slim's family had arrived, but the sun now crushed the square with a zeal worthy of a heatwave, to the point that they eventually all resigned themselves to cramming into the measly shadow of the hackberry and sycamore trees.

'There aren't that many of them in the end,' Dounia whispered in Bouzid's ear.

'You'll see later on. This is just the town hall, and they already outnumber us three to one. But don't worry, it'll be okay.'

A woman from the other side came towards Dounia and bowed to congratulate her. She wore an empire-line dress of printed silk, and her black hair had been stiffened with a smoothing iron and highlighted with random blonde, auburn and chocolate extensions. She turned to Rabia, who introduced her son.

'Come on, Krim, say hello, don't be anti-social!'

Krim couldn't stand his mother when she used what he called her French accent. She lingered on her *a*'s, softened her *r*'s, lengthened the diphthongs, and even went as far as to change her laugh.

'My son, Hicham,' said the woman, pointing to a well-built boy proudly fitted into a tight grey satin shirt.

Hicham turned round, his face cut in two by a playboy smile. A mobile phone was glued to his right ear, so he stretched out his left hand to Rabia, who took it to bring him towards her for a kiss – or rather an avalanche of kisses.

'Ah, with us it's four!'

The woman explained that Hicham was studying law with Kenza. Noticing some uncertainty in Rabia's eyes, she added, 'Kenza, the bride.'

'Yes, yes, of course I know. Besides . . . Krikri, you're going to see her soon, no?' Then, ostensibly whispering to the woman: 'Abdelkrim is the groom's best man.'

'Ah, well, bravo, congratulations!' the woman exclaimed, casting her smiling made-up eyes on the best man's motionless silhouette.

Disgusted by the hypocrisy of it all, Krim abruptly slipped away. He wanted to take out his mobile to make people think there was an emergency, but he'd already begun his retreat, now fully delighting in the deviance of his behaviour and the air that his movement created around him.

The bustle was growing on the steps. Bouzid asked his sisters where Ferhat and Zoulikha, the Elders, were. A nephew had

54

stayed back at the community centre to keep them company. Bouzid slapped his forehead with the back of his hand: he'd completely forgotten that some had wanted to stay behind. He went to update Granny, whose stubborn yet energetic figure blocked the way for a whole column of guests on the steps.

'Well, don't just stand there,' she fumed. 'Go and fetch them, you bloody *arioul*!'

'*Wallah*, you're so rude, can't believe it—'

'Go ask Toufik, come on, don't just stand there!'

Bouzid forced his way, running and mopping his brow, through the dense crowd where he recognized no one.

A short distance away he noticed Krim strolling about looking at his shoes. He made a detour to reprimand him. 'What the hell are you doing? You're supposed to go up there!'

'But there're too many people, I can't get through.'

'What are you talking about, even if you can't you have to go up there! Haven't they given you the rings yet?'

'No.'

'Where's Toufik?' Bouzid scoured around, his hand shielding his eyebrows. 'Wait for me here,' he shouted to Krim while he went to give instructions to Toufik the Helpful: 'We have to go back to the community centre. Hey, take my car and bring Uncle Ferhat and Auntie Zoulikha to Granny's.'

His mouth agape, Toufik looked at the keys he'd just received in his palm. Bouzid the Terrible frowned. 'Do you understand what I just said?'

'Yes, yes, but why Granny's?'

'Get on with it. After the town hall we'll all go to Granny's, you take them back there, okay?'

Toufik nodded. He was by far the oldest of the cousins, older than some of the husbands of his aunts, so he should have been called uncle, but there was something too juvenile about him: round, smooth and shiny cheeks, a worried look that tirelessly sought approval, and the hurried movements of a man used to doing what people asked him to do, rarely less and never anything else.

He went off towards the lines of double-parked cars as Bouzid cut through the crowd like a bodyguard to escort Krim to his destination.

A young girl was crouching in front of Bouzid's 307. All Toufik could look at were her endless blonde locks, which took in all the light from the sky. He cleared his throat, not knowing how to speak to her and unable to imagine saying something as ridiculous as '*mademoiselle*' out loud.

'Is this your car? My cat doesn't want to budge from underneath,' she explained without getting up.

'Puss puss,' hummed Toufik, stretching his hand underneath the car.

'He's not called Puss,' she said, corking her head back to face him.

'How should I know what his name is?'

The girl's mood changed for no apparent reason. She had almond-shaped eyes and the domed forehead of youth, but you couldn't say she was beautiful, perhaps because of the way her face and neck were contorted in an uncomfortable twist.

'He's called Barrabas.'

'Barrabas isn't a cat's name.'

'Really, and what's a cat's name, then?'

56

'I don't know ...' He searched his brain unsuccessfully. The girl was not only being unhelpful; she was now giving him a hard stare. 'Don't know.'

'What about Beethoven, you think that's a dog's name?'

Toufik couldn't understand what he'd done to deserve this hostility. What did they all have against him today?

'Beethoven, yes, that works for a dog.'

'And if you had a parrot, what would you call him?'

'Uh, I don't know, maybe Polly.'

The girl burst out laughing, a sharp, dry cackle in which her eyes took no part. Toufik wondered if she might be mad.

He gave up on crouching down again and waited for what she'd say next. Fortunately, the cat ran out the other side. But not before Toufik had noticed that it was black. The poor bloke wouldn't stop thinking about this bad omen until the day was over.

The bells of Saint-Charles Cathedral struck 5 p.m. The little groups that had been pushed back down to the town hall square waited patiently while the photographer meticulously set up his equipment. He wore glasses with big lenses and blinked frenetically, sometimes opening his mouth wide to crease his nose and push the frames back up.

Suddenly the bride's mother appeared on the steps and shouted to the photographer, 'What are you doing? Come and film over here!'

Flustered, the photographer looked around. He couldn't leave his high-tech equipment unguarded. He ran up to the bride's mother with his camera under his arm. The crowd parted to let them through and they joined the party at the head of the group, which was beginning to enter the hall.

The high ceiling, the chandelier, the mouldings, the gilding and especially the shiny floor brought back bad memories for Krim, for whom the Republic had mainly appeared in the form of courtrooms up until now. He took his place next to Slim and held the bride's mother's gaze; in it he could detect a particularly unabashed glare of contempt.

She was quite obviously a nasty specimen, one of those cantankerous women who latch onto any opportunity to humiliate fellow human beings. Krim guessed this from the enormous jewels she displayed wherever they could be attached, but also and especially from the way in which she constantly readjusted the bracelets around her puffy wrist. She wore a dress of pink chiffon with loud stripy motifs spread over three layers of flounces; Krim had heard his mother and his aunts speak of these flounces in very disparaging terms.

Beside this lady, the one who had to be her eldest daughter displayed her fat thighs in a short kaftan-like dress, held together by a belt embroidered with golden pearls through which, sadly, you could see her pistachio petticoat. Krim also observed the oriental twists on a dress in the second row, with its leopard-print silk side panels, and reached the conclusion that all these Oranese women were repellent because they were evil, and not the other way round as he had first thought.

The deputy mayor came in from the left and Krim saw, for the first time close up, the woman whom Slim was going to vow to spend the rest of his life with. He could only see her in quarter profile: her hair was masked by the veil of her long white dress and her eyes were betrayed by the perspective, which made them appear bigger than they really were. But there was no doubt she was pretty.

She probably benefited from the contrast with the fat and vulgar women in her family, but there was also, as he noticed when she was introduced to him later, a real singularity to the prettiness of her face: it was open and generous, simple and clear, with a protruding chin but remarkably symmetrical features, eyes that were almost spherical but lips that were full without being fleshy, and above all a piercing disposition that conferred on the whole a certain boyish charm.

'Okay, let's begin, eh?' the deputy mayor declared.

During his entire speech Krim couldn't take his eyes off the bride. When her name, Kenza Zerbi, was mentioned, he delighted in seeing her look down and smile stupidly like a schoolgirl being praised in front of the class.

When Krim had to sign the marriage register, he was distracted by the sound of a motorbike on the main street outside: the acceleration in E flat was about to become an E natural. First studying Slim's signature, which was supple, elegant, as gentle as his voice, he put his own in the appropriate boxes, in his big left-handed scrawl that hadn't even earned him a middle school diploma.

'I'm not going to keep you any longer,' concluded the deputy mayor after three quarters of an hour, his dry bureaucratic cheer completely out of place amidst the sobs and the sniffling heard throughout the hall. 'I wish only to say that this is quite a special day, on the eve of quite a special day, and that, well, I wish you both all the best. You may now kiss the bride!'

There was a moment of unease that seemed to go unnoticed by the minor city councillor, who was already putting away his papers: it was out of the question for young married Muslims to kiss in front of the entire family. So Slim lifted Kenza's veil, a little clumsily but not without gentleness, and placed a chaste and quick peck on her scarlet cheek.

On the way out, Rabia, who had shed her little tear, found Krim sitting on the arm of a bench, a cigarette behind his ear and thumbs in the hollows of his eyes.

'This all reminds me of Dad. We got married here, you know, in the same hall, just here, all the same, a deputy mayor ... Ah ...' As he wasn't reacting, she added, 'Are you all right, Krim? You look pale.'

'I'm starting to get a headache.'

'You want me to find some aspirin?'

'No, no, forget it.'

'You sure? Come with me.' She took him by the shoulder and eyed their surroundings as if what she was about to reveal was a state secret. 'We'll go to Granny's, okay, and that way we can go directly to the party afterwards. But Uncle Bouzid's going to take you somewhere in the meantime, and you can join us later with him ...'

Krim sighed bitterly. 'Okay, what now? Can't you leave me alone for two minutes?'

For the first time in months, Rabia didn't answer back. Instead, she settled into a silence that took a lot of effort, until it became as comfortable as an armchair from which she could make her son feel guilty without doing anything but wait.

'Okay, go on,' lamented Krim, 'now you're the martyr.'

Rabia took out a tissue and dabbed at the corners of her eyes. It was a revelation for Krim: it had taken him eighteen years to realize that if you gave a tissue to snivelling women at the movies, it wasn't so they could blow their noses; it was so they could dry their tears before they made their mascara run. This small discovery made him curiously melancholy. Everything therefore had a purpose in this sad world, everything its place: there were two witnesses for both the bride and the groom, *just in case*, and handkerchiefs to prevent nature from tearing the female mask away.

'You're behaving weirdly these days, Krim. How come you no longer ask me for money?'

'What, you're telling me off for not asking you for cash?'

'You're not being indoctrinated, are you?' Rabia inquired, grabbing his chin. 'Look at me, are you being indoctrinated?'

'Yeah, that's right, I pray five times a day.'

'What do you do in the cellar with Fat Momo?'

'What do you think, we pray.'

'Watch out. Don't do your *ke'ddeb* about getting indoctrinated. Mind my words, Islam's like a cult, *wallah*, they're all the same. Anyway, what do you think all religions are about? They're cults in disguise, my son, what do you think? Because let me tell you something . . .'

But Krim didn't listen to the probably harebrained explanation that followed; he had gone into *I acquiesce* mode and now only heard the peculiar little music of his mother's chattering, a variation on a minor, Eastern chord, four notes she sometimes sang one after another – lo lo lo lo, D A C-sharp D – in order to criticize someone who had no shame, or a shocking situation that everyone else had chosen to accept.

Krim felt his mobile vibrate. He checked the text he'd just received and had great difficulty in hiding his dismay from his mother, who, thankfully, was too absorbed in her own monologue to notice that her eldest son's knees were trembling and his ears bright red.

Received: Today at 5.59 p.m.

From: N

Good news, bad news. Mouloud Benbaraka will be at the party tonight, had to be expected. I spoke to him just now but watch out all the same. And no silly stuff. This is not the day to get even. OK?

3

Wrong Number

Granny's neighbourhood, 5.45 p.m.

Uncle Bouzid didn't have his car, so Krim had to walk dressed as a penguin through the whole of the city centre. He caught a few smiles that were possibly mocking, but he didn't know exactly what of, seeing as he had more than one reason to be ashamed: his suit, which now seemed atrociously out of place; the way his uncle walked, chest out, chin held high, casting his gaze from left to right like a building site foreman, confident, self-satisfied and haughty, as if enthroned on an elephant.

'We're going to take advantage of you looking all clean and proper, okay?'

They marched back up to Granny's neighbourhood, past the big black silhouette of the theatre, *La Comédie de Saint-Etienne*. Past blocks of Stalinist flats where indefatigable government agencies remained amidst construction sites and rows of low, dilapidated houses. It was less hot than on the square; Krim even thought he could feel a sharp, spring-like breeze on his cheeks. When they arrived in front of the butcher's shop, Bouzid, who hadn't looked at Krim once, took him by the shoulder and encouraged him to enter. The windows were daubed with photos of Chaouch, and inside the butchers wore CHAOUCH FOR PRESIDENT badges on the lapels of their white tunics.

The owner hauled out a headless, footless, skinless hulk of frozen sheep from the walk-in. While chatting up the old couple it was intended for, he began chopping up the carcass with vigorous manoeuvres, using all sorts of knives and even a saw for the bones. He had not even glanced at Bouzid since he'd come in. Krim looked up at his uncle and noticed on the one hand that he was blushing and on the other that he had extremely small ears. In order to look less stupid, Bouzid turned to Krim and pretended to continue their conversation.

'And? How are things?'

'"How are things?"'

'Yeah, what's new? Is it true you're going to be taken off the job centre register?'

Krim turned his head and began to chew his lips. All this meat made him ill at ease, but not as much as his uncle's flushed, hostile, almost hysterical face. There was such a contrast between his angry prophet-like eyebrows and the casual tone he was trying to adopt that Krim seriously wondered if he wasn't a bit mad. His mother said that often, but she would immediately correct herself by invoking the Nerrouches' infamous hot-bloodedness, which characterized his family as surely as the hooked nose and the propensity to make mountains out of molehills.

'And now there's something you need to learn, *dalguez*, you're no longer a kid: your mother, you must understand, is going to start her life again one day, that's the way it is, with a good man, completely honourably.'

Krim deliberately tuned out this last sermon. He concentrated on the tram bell that he technically couldn't hear, given their distance from the overhead tracks, yet it rang right into the heart of his consciousness, like a promise of catastrophe.

There remained only a fleshless carcass on the butcher's worktop. The butcher warmly thanked the couple but downgraded his smile for his next customers. Clearly, something was amiss.

'*Salaam aleikhoum,* Rachid.'

'*Salaam,*' replied the butcher, on his guard.

'You remember, last week at the mosque you told me you were looking for an apprentice?'

'Yes, I remember very well.'

Rachid was a bit older than Bouzid. The shop belonged to his family, the richest Kabyles in Saint-Etienne, according to Rabia ('They've got millions,' she said, emphasizing the *mi*). It was perhaps an illusion fed by this reputation, but Krim found that this butcher indeed had a bourgeois air about him: pinched lips, well-coiffed greying hair, a nose too fine to be honest. His mother also claimed that they were Harki descendants.

When Rachid came out of the little room where he'd washed his hands, Bouzid didn't know what to do other than repeat what he'd just said. 'So last week you told me . . .'

'Yes, I know what I said.' Rachid wasn't even looking at him. He pretended to put away his butcher block and carry out little tasks that you didn't have to be an apprentice butcher to see were pointless.

Bouzid murmured in Krim's ear: 'Go and wait for me outside, go.'

Krim stepped out and lit a cigarette.

Once he was sure his nephew was looking elsewhere, Bouzid raised his voice. 'What's happening, Rachid? Why do you show me no respect in front of my nephew?'

Rachid threw a blank look towards his assistant. There weren't any other customers and the latter understood that it was better if he disappeared into the back of the shop. Rachid waited for him to close the door, then undid his apron. 'I'm sorry, Bouzid, but I'm not going to be able to help you.'

'Yeah, and why is that?'

'I'm sorry, and I'm going to ask you to go and buy *aksoum* elsewhere. You're no longer going to be served here, I'm sorry.'

'Stop telling me you're sorry and tell me what's going on!'

You could sense from the beginning that Rachid's calm was fake and that he could explode at any moment. 'It so happens that I've heard a few things, *that's* what's going on. Listen, we all have our own lives and I don't want to be judgemental, but it just isn't right, *wallah*, it's not right.'

'What are you talking about?'

'The cards! What does all this mean, reading cards for people and ripping them off? My aunt, *miskina*, she's got Alzheimer's and yet your mother, Khalida, takes advantage of it to read cards for her? *Wallah*, I've always respected you, you were a good family, your father – *ate ramah rebi* – was a good man, respectable, as they say, but this is too much, I swear to you Bouzid, it's *haram*.'

Bouzid was dumbfounded. He felt – or at least that's what he'd recount a quarter of an hour later to his sisters in Granny's kitchen – that if he stayed in front of this butcher a second longer he was going to kill him. His sisters clustered around him would have no problem believing him. He'd often got into tussles, and what could be more offensive to a son than to call his old mother a witch?

Without a word he lifted his fist and extended his index finger. He pointed it at Rachid while his lips curled with disgust.

When he stepped out onto the street he couldn't find Krim. He called his name several times, to no avail, and waited on a bench to calm down before calling Rabia.

Krim had escaped to the heights of the Beaubrun neighbourhood. He was walking on the rue de l'Ecole des Beaux-arts when he came across a couple of students. The guy had the big head of a Frenchman with gentle and easy-going features. His laughing eyes met Krim's, who turned towards him.

'What are you laughing at? Got a problem?'

The student's dreadlocks flowed from his borsalino. He looked to the sky, as if this kind of misunderstanding happened to him all the time. His girlfriend, whose arms were around his waist, encouraged him to continue walking but Krim didn't want to let it go. He followed them for a few metres until he caught up with them. His fist was already clenched, ready to land on the student's pale face.

'I'm talking to you, arsehole. I'm talking to you.'

'Come on, chill out, everything's fine.'

The student didn't dare look in Krim's direction. His cheekbones were on fire and his back was shaking.

His girlfriend was more courageous. Her cheeks were covered in freckles; orange tights moulded her muscular calves.

She had the stubborn look of a girl who'd grown up among boys. 'Hey, leave us alone!'

'I'm not talking to you.'

'Get lost—'

Krim didn't hesitate: he punched the rim of the student's hat.

The guy in turn immediately bent down to pick it up.

'Ugh,' muttered the girl. 'Pathetic. Come on, Jeremy, let's get out of here.'

Krim watched them walk away: the girl's hand moved from her boyfriend's waist to his back. She soon began to rub it to comfort him.

A few metres further along, the road reached a fork lined with pine trees. Krim heard someone calling him from the square.

'Leon! Leon!'

It was his nickname in the gang. Why Leon, he'd never properly understood: because he was silent, bizarrely intense, because he was often called a Frenchman, owing to his inability to correctly pronounce Arab sounds – the *kh*, the *ha*, the *a* of Ali – because he possessed something indefinable that distinguished him from Djamel and Fat Momo. They circled around him like vultures and made fun of his suit, pinching its sleeves.

'*Wesh*, the old man. Leon! James Bond! You'd think it was James Bond!'

'Come on, give me a break!'

Krim had no desire to hang around with them, and he risked getting into trouble if he lingered too long before heading back to Granny's.

Djamel stuffed his chin into his tracksuit collar. He pushed his glasses up on his nose and jabbed his face in Krim's direction. 'Who's getting married?' His shaved head was pointy – rigid, even. Like all brutes who wear glasses he felt obliged to make his voice sound harsher.

'My cousin.'

'The fag?'

'Hey, *wallah*, shut your mouth. Say that again and I swear on your mother's life I'll beat the shit out of you.'

'Calm down – what did I say? Isn't it true he's a fag? And I'm not the one who says it,' Djamel persisted. 'It's—'

'Shut the fuck up,' Krim shouted, giving him a shove. 'I'll bust your head in. I swear, I'll bust your head in.'

Fat Momo slipped between them to prevent a fight, but Djamel clearly wanted to have a go. 'Come on, you're a fag too, your entire family is a bunch of fags, what do you think, that he'll get married and he'll no longer be a faggot? You think faggots are, what, part-time cock-suckers?'

Krim got away from Fat Momo and jumped on Djamel. Fat Momo grabbed him from behind and all but lifted him from the ground. The intercessor's bear-like frame made him well behaved and respectable, in any case more than that jerk Djamel, who was miming fellatio as he regained his breath.

Krim walked away to collect his thoughts and ask a small favour from Fat Momo.

'Hey man, you wouldn't have something on you?'

By speaking in codes and euphemisms so much when he was on the phone, Krim had ended up never pronouncing the word 'dope' at all.

'Honestly, it's not even for me,' he insisted. 'I swear on my mother's grave it's for my cousin, remember Raouf?'

'Yeah yeah, but there's nothing around. Maybe later. What are you doing tonight?'

'What do you think? You think I'm dressed like this to go to Mass?'

'All right, how 'bout this: call me around seven or eight and I'll let you know. You got any minutes left on your phone? If not I'll call you, it's better that way. Hey, go on,' he added, giving Krim a friendly rugby player's tap on the belly, 'have a good wedding and *bsartek*.'

'*Wesh.*'

'And wait, about the mac, you want to go training today?'

'Obviously I can't, why are you even asking?'

'Nothing, I was just thinking it's a nice day, and ... Never mind, forget it.'

'Seriously, everyone's being all weird today. I don't know what's going on.'

'No, no,' Fat Momo reassured him, 'go and just take care, eh.'

Krim could tell something was weighing on his friend, but he didn't have the strength to make him spit it out.

As was often the case, Fat Momo told him anyway. 'That other psycho. Benbaraka.'

'Ah, well, I don't give a shit about him,' Krim grumbled.

'Yeah but what are you going to do this evening? He's what, the great-uncle of the girl Slim's marrying? He has to be there, *wallah*, he has to.'

'Well, he wasn't at the town hall. See you later.'

He walked back up the road he'd just come down. His fist was trembling and he felt vaguely like throwing up. Passing a window daubed with grey paint, he noticed a whole section had been replaced with semi-reflective glass. He used it to assess the damage. Minimal, fortunately: a green smear on his thigh and some pine needles in the back.

70

His telephone buzzed: he had five missed calls from his mother. He texted her to say he was coming and stopped for a minute to compose himself in front of the Saint-Ennemond church. It was framed by two streets: the one on the right went up to the library opposite where Granny lived, and the one on the left led to the car park. He took the one on the left and went around the library to be sure no one could see him from the balcony. The wind had picked up and the beautiful clouds of the early afternoon had been stolen by a thick veil of pearl-grey fumes. Something was burning. On the other side of the railway, a man in shorts was torching rubbish in a copper drum. Behind him a cloud of shanties stretched out at the foot of what, in the family, were known as 'the two mountains by Granny's'. These mountains were slag heaps from the mine at Clapier. There was nothing less natural than these piles of coal waste, and yet trees had already thickened on their slopes; only the summits remained bald to betray their status.

Krim remembered seeing them in a different light on the day of his father's funeral. From the cemetery perched high on Côte-chaude, the two innocuous mountains by Granny's had appeared to him then as the outposts of hell. The pit-heads that once swallowed lifts down into the mine lost their harmless postcard stupidity that afternoon. It was no longer the neighbourhood's fake little Eiffel Tower, but the demonic metal structure it had been at the time when its winding-wheel still sent men into the depths of the earth.

Desperate to escape the chill brought on by this tragic landscape, Krim hiked back up to the library through the small park behind it. He couldn't resist stretching out on a shiny little hill that could have been straight out of *Teletubbies*.

His phone vibrated again: another text — from his mother, of course — but it wasn't addressed to him. Krim read it three times to be sure he wasn't dreaming:

```
Received: Today at 6.13 p.m.

From: Mum

I feel like I've always known you
even though we've never met, it's so
bizarre! I can't wait to meet you
this evening!!! I also had a silly
question: how will I recognize you!?
Hugs and kisses, Rabin☺uche.
```

Krim jumped up and took his head in his hands, looking for something around him to destroy, but the bench was obviously unmovable and the first dustbin was at the park exit. The thirty seconds it took for him to reach it had already lessened his fury, so he just stared, in a daze, at the contents of its green transparent plastic bag flanked by a notice some advertiser had not only dreamed up but even convinced an entire galaxy of civil servants to publish. No doubt it was the slogan of his career: YES WE GARBAGE CAN.

Saint-Priest-en-Jarez, 6.15 p.m.

Of the myriad instructions that Farid and Fares hadn't followed, the one that struck Fares as most significant concerned the beige jacket he was now using to prevent Zoran from seeing where they were taking him. But did twins who wore the same jacket not

72

attract twice as much attention as twins with different outfits? It took Fares a good twenty minutes to ask this question, between the intuition of the problem (hampered by his surveillance mission), the mental formulation (always delicate with him), and the pronunciation (which was all the more stilted, thanks to his cold). Their white Kangoo, emblazoned with a logo made up of two *S*'s in the shape of snakes fighting each other, was already entering the residential suburb that housed the headquarters of the security agency that had hired them. All that effort, this whole adventure, just to get the reply:

'Shut up, can't you see we're just about there?'

Farid drove with his nose against the windshield so as not to miss the right street – a regular enough occurrence that usually meant turning back at the roundabout a kilometre further on.

The neighbourhood looked spectacularly uniform: estate houses all made of the same pale concrete, with the same line of pine trees at every crossroads to shield the grounds from curious onlookers.

'We should maybe ask for a GPS, no?'

Fares noticed that whenever Farid said nothing, his eyelid rose in the rear-view mirror. He leaned down a little to see his brother's face but the car braked abruptly.

Farid deliberately skidded onto the kerb and ordered Fares to get out immediately.

'But . . . and . . .'

'I told you to get out.'

Farid put his hands behind his head and stretched. At his feet the Furan River shimmered, emitting a smell of sewage and wet wood. The endless twittering of the birds somehow amplified its murmur. He leaned over to study its depths. He was less brawny than Fares but more menacing. Pumping iron had made Fares more of a spectacle, but Farid took pride in not having lifted so much as a gram to achieve his more than honourable musculature.

Fares, too, began to contemplate the little river but Farid swung around so quickly that he thought his brother was going to tweak his ear. He had certainly done it before – a few years earlier and again just last week, during what Farid claimed was a sleepwalking episode.

'I'm going to ask you a question and you're going to answer yes or no, okay?'

'Uh . . . okay.' Fares hadn't caught on yet.

'Do you think what we're doing is normal? Just answer me, don't think. Yes or no?'

Fares felt this was a trap and half-closed his mouth so as not to come straight out with something stupid. He began to bring his index finger up to his lips when Farid hit him really hard on the neck.

Unlike him, Farid had his father's big eyes, those of an irascible and problematic man – someone around whom everyone, sooner or later, ended up feeling like a problem.

'What is it you think we're doing here? You realize this is no joke, that we could go to prison? Do you realize?'

The silence was intensified by the purr of the river.

'You listening to me, you moron?'

'Yes, yes, calm down. So then why—'

'What? What are you going to say?'

'Why . . . no, no . . . nothing.'

Farid's phone vibrated in his right hand.

'It's him? What's he doing?'

'You can see, he's phoning me! Get in the car, I'm going to ask him when he's meeting us.'

Fares returned to the back seat, where their prisoner began to speak in a mixture of Romanian and French – words that must have been addressed to him. Zoran had an unpleasant voice, a plaintive, whining guttural that sullied the ear, like a small bell that stops you from thinking, a small bell that might somehow also be sweaty and greasy, but here it was as if that little bell was a clot of slime. In the weight room there was a women's body-building champion who had a similar mix of male and female registers: girly intonations and words that came out of a thorax so developed it must have modified the thickness of the vocal cords.

'Shut it!' screamed Fares, slapping the prisoner's head, which jutted out from beneath his jacket.

When Farid got back behind the wheel, he looked pre-occupied. He accelerated and took the first street that climbed the hill. They were no longer in Saint-Etienne, but in the Saint-Priest-en-Jarez municipality. At the end of another dreary subdivision was a half-buried house with a three-car garage, where a pick-up truck and another Kangoo were sleep-ing. You had to look at the rectangle on the intercom to read the agency's name: SECURITATIS. The double *S* logo was nowhere to be seen, which meant that apart from the few com-pany cars that hadn't left the car park since the agency had gone bankrupt, nothing indicated that it was a business headquarters rather than the home of a reclusive pensioner who wasn't very fond of gardening.

Farid backed the car in so he could leave easily. He turned to Zoran. 'Listen, if you say anything without me asking, I'll smash your face. You get it? You've the dirty mouth of a gypsy faggot, get it?'

Zoran was trembling too much to speak. He gingerly moved his head up and down and let himself be taken out of the car.

'I'll smash your face, *wallah*, I'll smash your face,' Farid repeated, more for himself than for the prisoner.

Fares didn't look happy about the turn of events.

Farid threw the keys on the bar separating the American kitchen from the open-plan living room and barked at his twin brother: 'Find the key to the shed. I think it's the red one.'

Fares pushed Zoran into the centre of the kitchen and looked for the red key. On paper, picking a red key out of a dozen was a mission for an eight year old, but, as usual, when it was his turn to carry it out, there simply wasn't one. Feverishly, Fares went through the keys ten times. The closest he could find was circled in orange. When Farid came out of the bathroom, Fares handed it to him.

'I said the red one, idiot.'

Farid had to admit after a few seconds that there wasn't a red key in the bunch he'd given his brother. Perplexed, he went down the stairs, encouraging Fares and Zoran to follow him. An economy bulb cast a lugubrious blue light over the basement. Zoran stumbled and was held back in extremis by Fares. Farid opened door after door of rooms filled with boxes and files, looking for the one that was locked from the outside. But he must have imagined it, for none of the doors he tried had locks. He turned to Fares and pointed to the door with closed shutters looking out onto the garden. This one was completely sealed off, so it seemed obvious to him there was no risk in leaving Zoran in the basement, locked doors or no.

But Fares was obsessing over the room to the left, which also opened out onto the garden and contained weapons, walkie-talkies and the safe. He leaned down to look under the doormat; his white underpants followed suit and revealed the crack of his backside, beaded with two monstrously symmetrical moles.

He was snivelling like a pig when he stood back up empty-handed. When Farid nodded his head in the direction of the cupboard beneath the stairs, Fares shoved their prisoner inside.

Farid got up close to Zoran's face, which was smeared with dried tears mixed with snot. 'You move and I'll break you in two, you dirty fucking tranny.'

Zoran nodded frantically, not daring to look into his torturer's eyes.

Fares went back up with his brother and sat down in the kitchen, sighing as if he'd just returned from a long and satisfying day's work. His mobile began to ring with the chorus of: Born in the USA.

'Who's been phoning you since this morning?' Farid shouted as he rummaged through the cupboards for some booze. 'And I told you to put your mobile on vibrate!'

Fares apologized profusely and switched off his phone. He spotted a drawer that his brother hadn't yet searched. Farid got there before him anyway and in it discovered a box of coffee filters and a grinder. So Fares went and sat down on one of the desks in the living room and played around with the telephone.

There was nothing to do in this godforsaken house. He couldn't watch television; he couldn't go on a PlayStation. The company laptops were in the shed, so he couldn't even get onto

Facebook, where for three months now he'd been chatting up a jujitsu instructor living in the Haute-Loire.

The coffee was rising in fits and starts. Fares thought of the four women he'd known in his life: a waitress who was older than him and enjoyed his candour; a depressed widow who found a way to manipulate him; a sex bomb in the weight room who ended up confessing she wanted to sleep with him and Farid at the same time; and finally the predictable Algerian girl with emerald reptilian eyes, a Machiavellian creature who wanted to marry him for the papers and might have succeeded, making his life impossible with a thousand little schemes, if his brother had not been there to open his eyes.

Downstairs Zoran began to moan. Fares moved to the middle of the room and did a few push-ups. But Zoran's groaning grew increasingly annoying, so he returned to the open space instead, where he waited for Farid to order him to go and see what their prisoner wanted.

But Farid was watching the coffee and typing a text, looking like he didn't want to be disturbed. This, Fares felt, gave him the right to switch his own mobile back on. He briefly looked at the messages he'd received over the last few days.

The one sent by his great-nephew Jibril broke his heart every time he read it: 'Thanks all de seme, uncle.' In a fit of generosity, Fares had offered to take Jibril to watch a Saint-Etienne football match, but he hadn't thought of booking seats and they'd ended up begging for tickets outside.

Two weeks later, the memory of that futile evening still burned his stomach: the stadium crowded with people and none of them there to help them, the aloof arrogance of those in a hurry, the hypocritical concern of those who pretended to be sorry they didn't have tickets to spare. It wasn't his stomach, in fact; it was higher up, at the bottom of the throat, the taste of shame, of waste and insufficiency, the relentless malaise, as if thoughts and seconds alike were burdened with impregnable lead.

Ultimately, the prospect of refreshment had restored some dignity to the evening – even Jibril had a fine time of it, nibbling on merguez frites in front of the big screen at Café des Sports. Now, that was a change of pace from doing your homework and watching *Survivor* – not to mention the fact that, as the kid himself had observed with one of those sage expressions that occasionally visit the face of an excited child, a zero–zero draw wasn't that bad a result given their thirteenth league position at the end of the season.

Slightly intoxicated by his improved mood, Fares went to the bathroom to refresh his face. When he came out, Farid was standing ramrod straight.

'Okay, we'd better get ready, he'll be here in ten or fifteen minutes.'

'And what do we do?'

'Um, I don't know, how should I know?'

'What's this poor bugger actually done? Why was he kid-napped when he wasn't even up to anything?'

When Farid didn't reply, Fares went over to the window and delicately pulled open the curtain. The street was quiet but the road shone like a mirror: had it begun to rain? He couldn't hear a thing. The bowl-shaped streetlights gradually lit up. Fares listened closely in hope of detecting that sound of flutter-ing wings he sometimes heard coming out of them on summer evenings.

A plane suddenly broke the sound barrier. Zoran chose that exact moment to scream. Farid rolled up his sleeves and slowly went down the stairs, staring at his half-wit brother standing in front of the window, as if to teach him a lesson, to make him understand that they weren't there for fun.

The infamous Mouloud Benbaraka stopped his car on the road, in front of the white door of the garage where the vehicles of his bankrupt company were parked. He looked at the back seat where he'd put the cage. While his BMW's alarm clamoured because of the open door, Benbaraka stared at the double *S* logo his associate had designed himself.

'Moron,' he said, spitting on one of the Kangoo's tyres.

Fares was drumming his hands on his knees when Benbaraka came in. Farid ordered him to stop and stood up to salute the boss. Fares felt that it was the right moment to say something, but Farid silenced him, so he looked at the floor instead and ostentatiously kept his peace, as if for prayer.

Benbaraka presented the cage to the twins and placed it at the foot of the table. An enormous brown beast was moving in there dolefully.

Farid commenced his report and rubbed his neck while making his thick left bicep bulge in time. 'You see, like, we haven't bashed him around that much yet. But honestly, I'm not sure he really wants to talk.'

'That's what we're going to find out,' declared Benbaraka, storming down the stairs.

Farid passed the cage to Fares and dragged Zoran out from the cupboard. He slapped him across the cheeks a few times. Zoran was already winded, and soon began to lose consciousness.

A smile split Benbaraka's cruel face in two, his eyes half-closed. He stopped Farid and took Zoran by the shoulders. 'What's with the bad manners? Have a little respect for our guest. Come on, come into the other room. We'll have more space to talk.'

He was referring to the room with no window. It was furnished with a velvet sofa, a fold-up bed, a desk topped with candle holders, and a dust-covered floor lamp. Farid took the boxes off the bed where Benbaraka's associate sometimes slept when passing through Saint-Etienne. Without ceasing to smile and rub his hands, Benbaraka dropped onto the orangey red sofa while Zoran was forcibly seated on the bed. Fares remained in the doorway, ill at ease.

'Okay,' the boss began, 'we're not going to spend hours on this. You're going to tell me what you were doing at the town hall just now, okay?'

Zoran snorted to transfer a lump of snot from the back of his nose to the edge of his throat. He swallowed it noiselessly while Farid shook his head, waiting for the order to smash his face in.

'My two associates here have been following you for a few days, and it's very simple: we just want to know what you were doing hanging around my niece and her husband. You tell us this and we'll let you off the hook and I can go quietly to the wedding reception.'

Mouloud Benbaraka got up and opened the desk. He turned round and cracked his knuckles, his back and his neck. He looked like a snake onto which a spine, extremities, a whole human bone structure had been grafted – a new embodiment that he enjoyed exploring as a child would a new toy.

'Listen, we've got two or three things to sort out upstairs, so we'll give you a moment. But not for long.'

Zoran continued to tremble: his bulging eyes stared at the lamp like two mauve moons, injected with blood and terror.

'We'll leave my little friend here with you, right, so you'll have a bit of company. And when you're ready to tell me how you know Slim, who's just married my favourite great-niece, we can each return to our own lives, to each his own and God for everyone, all right?'

Frustrated at not having been permitted to disfigure the drag queen, Farid put the cage down in the middle of the room and opened the door. A metre-long river rat pointed its nose around, then ran and hid beneath the desk.

Zoran screamed hysterically.

Farid blocked the door with two piles of boxes before joining Fares and Benbaraka upstairs.

Benbaraka had poured himself a bowl of coffee and was concentrating on his BlackBerry screen. 'How do you put those smiley faces in a text?'

Fares leapt up, only too delighted to be of use.

'There's a thingy for smileys, normally.'

'Okay, do it.'

Benbaraka stretched out in his chair and congratulated himself on the texture of his jacket. He watched Fares, who was busying himself, trembling, on the phone's touchpad, perhaps trying to forget poor Zoran's cries. 'Is it true you remember numbers?' he asked.

'Who, me?' Fares felt himself blush.

'Nazir told me. You have a memory like a computer, you're given a number and you remember it. Is that true?'

Fares chuckled and said 'Yes' while looking at the floor, to avoid seeming boastful.

'Do you happen to know what Nazir's up to at the moment?' Benbaraka asked in an unctuous tone. 'He's all agitated on the phone, I wonder if he's up to something. Like planning to take off after leaving us in deep shit . . . What do you think, Farid? Sorry, Fares. I mean Farid. Whatever, one of you.'

'Me? I don't think anything . . . No, no, I don't know.'

Farid looked on keenly as his brother lied.

'I don't know why,' Benbaraka declared as he walked over to the window, 'but I have a feeling that my dear Parisian associate is trying to rip me off.'

Fares kept silent. His ears turned beetroot while he stared at the screen of the phone, no longer seeing it.

Benbaraka's voice made him jump. 'You see, Farid, in this city there are two kinds of people: those who work for me and those who work against me. So listen to me closely, I'm going to ask you a simple question, and I'm even going to leave you a few seconds to reply. All right?'

'But . . .'

'Here's the question, and once again, I insist, think hard before giving me your answer: would you say you work for me or against me?'

Horrified, Fares's eyes sought his twin brother's.

'Take your time, take your time. Think hard about the question.'

Fares forced himself to salivate so that his mouth would be less dry when he replied. Zoran's screams reached them without ever decreasing in intensity. But habit being what it is, they no longer tore at anything, those screams, not even at Fares's attention. For Fares, the only thing that mattered was what he would say to Benbaraka.

'For you, um, I work for you.'

'Good,' Benbaraka declared. 'That was the right answer. Now show me the phone, you idiot.'

Fares joined him, offering him a choice of several smileys for the text that Benbaraka had written and which ended with an unfathomable: 'You will know it's me when I say the word mademoiselle. XO Omar.'

Benbaraka, looking at the dormant engines in the garage and clenching his teeth, impatiently opted for the simplest smiley face: ☺

4

At Granny's

Granny's neighbourhood, 6.30 p.m.

Of the half billion results potentially awaiting him in Facebook's search engine, Krim only cared about one. He turned around to check that the manager was engrossed in his Sudanese songs and typed in the girl's name: A-U-R-E-L-I-E. Several possibilities were displayed, but he chose the photo of the young girl with light hair. Surname: Wagner. Aurélie Wagner.

Aurélie and his sister (password: daddy) had a mutual friend – a little gymnast from Hyères – which usually gave Krim (aka Luna) access to Aurélie's photos, her videos, and most importantly her wall, where she posted snippets of her life and her favourite clips. But today when he clicked on her profile, the photo was still there, but nothing more – just the list of her 647 friends and a banner that announced pitilessly:

Do you know Aurélie? To see what she shares with friends, send her a friend request.

Krim buried his head in his hands and massaged his temples for a long time as he tried to think of a solution. He returned to Aurélie's profile picture and unsuccessfully tried to enlarge it: Aurélie, standing on a lawn, held the Eiffel Tower between her thumb and index finger, enjoying the play on perspective as her other hand covered her mouth in a look of pretend amazement. Her different coloured eyes laughed sincerely, and she was irresistible.

There were three possibilities: Aurélie had removed Luna's gymnast friend from her list of friends; Luna had removed this friend; or – a true vision of the apocalypse – Aurélie had decided to lock her profile and no longer share the highlights of her rose-tinted daily life with anyone but her friends IRL.

Krim pulled himself together and decided to dismiss the third hypothesis. In a genuine act of faith, he spent half an hour going through Luna's gymnast friend's wall, looking for a link that would give him access to the fortress of Aurélie's profile. Unfortunately the only one he found was blocked. The final hypothesis was therefore confirmed: Aurélie had deliberately restricted her profile. Perhaps she was even in the process of deleting her Facebook account.

For diversion from his distress, Krim went through Luna's photos. She had twenty albums, a good half of which were pictures of gymnastics competitions: Luna in a shiny leotard on the beam, Luna in a shiny leotard on the bars, Luna in a shiny leotard saluting the jury with her powerfully shaped body, Luna in a shiny leotard at the edge of the mat encouraging Lea, Margaux, Héloïse, Chelsea, all in shiny leotards . . .

Other photos showed her with a slew of best friends, those she'd solemnly declared to be her 'sisters' in several of the captions.

Afternoon with the Girlz, Gym in the park with the Girlz, Cracking up on the train with the Girlz, strength conditioning, Julie's b-day, Hélo's fifteenth, Me (from the infamous album where she was striking provocative poses on a pommel horse), Jennifer's party on 22 November, and an unlabelled image made up of virtual hearts, in all sizes and colours, where the boys and girls she liked were tagged and accompanied with smiley phrases as mystifying to the profane as they were to the young initiates.

Facebook stalking is like good old channel-surfing on TV: hours can go by unnoticed. Krim felt his mobile buzz in his pocket; he left the dizzying maze of photos where he had no chance of catching Aurélie's pretty little face. But a post on Luna's wall caught his eye. Just yesterday evening, Luna had downloaded an app that showed which of her ten friends visited her profile the most. You might have expected one of her gymnastics friends to take first place, but it was Nazir Nerrouche. Krim wondered what interest Nazir could possibly have in looking at his insignificant little cousin's profile, and concluded that the app was not reliable.

Hunger pushed him to leave the cybercafé, where the boss refused his payment. He was smartly dressed, no doubt because of a happy event, so the tall Sudanese man with deep black skin and kind eyes insisted on giving Krim the hour he had just used up, as a gift.

He arrived at Granny's in the middle of the all-time classic: a big family discussion about the difference between Kabyles and Arabs. His mother's lynx-like eyes (she was, as always, on the front line of the debate) immediately pinpointed him in the crowd of cousins amassed in the corridor.

'Krim, Krim, come, come here, love. The poor boy must be hungry.'

Krim slipped between his aunts and uncles to reach the tiny little space his mother had made for him on the sofa. There were new arrivals: Rachida, the youngest of his aunts, was biting her nails on a chair slightly away from the excitement around the coffee table, shouting from time to time to her children, who were playing noisily with their father, Mathieu. Other cousins gathered in the room next door, as well as the third 'Elder' sister, whose husband had just had a heart attack.

'Say hello, Krim, say hello to your uncle.'

The old uncle accepted the pecks on each cheek without getting up from his armchair. He was a man of considerable stature – almost one metre eighty-five – with a chest like a barrel. His thankless life spent on construction sites had not kept him from showing up in public wearing well-tailored grey suits, polished loafers and clean fingernails. Actually, his fingernails were the only telltale sign that he was getting old: some, Krim noticed, were ringed with black, most needed to be cut, and two or three were even dirty. He took the nape of Krim's neck in his enormous mitt and spoke to someone invisible between Rabia and his son Toufik on the sofa opposite.

'He's grown, eh? Big boy now . . .'

Krim didn't know how to react. He'd been this size for at least four years now, but he understood from his aunt's gentle and dreamy look that the old lion was perhaps starting to lose it.

'Come on, Krim. Here, take some! What do you want, a *zlebia*? A *makrout*?'

Before eating he had to kiss Toufik, which was a genuine ordeal because of the habit his cousin had of kissing four times instead of two, his mouth so perpendicular to the cheek that it felt like a kiss on the lips.

'There's a surprise,' Rabia chuckled into her son's ear, incapable of containing her excitement for long.

At first Krim figured it must be about the old couple's daughters: Kamelia, Ines and Dalia, the joyful trinity, the older Parisian cousins who were each more beautiful than the next and who were the pride of the family, both at parties and at funerals. But Krim couldn't see them anywhere and above all he couldn't hear them. Their habit of shouting at the slightest comment, their madwomen's exclamations, their Parisian accent and never-ending giggles – these created a very peculiar sort of atmosphere even when they temporarily left a room, like a shiver of coolness and *joie de vivre* that lingered in the sixth sense. Krim would have felt it in the core of his being if they had been the surprise Rabia was referring to.

Quite the contrary: in the kitchen he could see Uncle Bouzid's authoritarian head chastising his sisters within reach.

Bouzid came back into the living room, where Toufik got up so his uncle could take his place on the straw chair that was missing half its back.

In the rear room of the flat, Granny was looking after the young cousins and Luna, who gave Krim a dirty look coupled with a cutthroat gesture. Granny really loved only the children in this family; she had installed an Xbox in her bedroom and pulled out some old-fashioned dolls (blonde mop of hair, big royal blue eyes with endless lashes) that she generally kept tucked away in a bureau stuffed with sheets, flannels and towels that no one had used for two decades but which she continued to wash and perfume every week with eau de Cologne.

89

And then right in front of him, Krim suddenly saw Zoulikha, Granny's eldest daughter, who was sending worried looks towards the kitchen where everyone was used to seeing her busy. Old Aunt Zoulikha, who traditionally chimed the first ululation and who always began to soak chickpeas in the early hours the day before, polished her two *couscoussiers* until midnight, and found time the following morning to go and personally choose the bags of extra-fine semolina, which she transported in her cart from the Kabyle shop seven tram stops away, so as not to have to go to the Moroccan shop on her own street, where she had once spotted two cockroaches crawling up the till of the near-sighted shopkeeper. Zoulikha, who prepared the cloths, the ladles, all the utensils that might be needed, and who made sure that the women had their dresses and that the men had bought the right cuts of meat.

But this time she had been unable to do all that because the bride's mother had decided there would be a caterer, full stop.

Krim observed her pink, chubby hands and was sad to see there were no grains of semolina there. Aunt Zoulikha was a spinster but was easily taken for a widow, even though she no longer seemed to care, being the only one of her mother's seven daughters never to have found the right man. After her Uncle Ferhat's wife died (in 1999), she had come to live with him to make sure he would enter the new millennium with his feet stretched out under the living-room coffee table, his *chorba* brought to him on a tray while he watched the familiar faces of his favourite news anchors. This odd couple had people talking for a while and then everyone had accepted it, once it was pointed out that Zoulikha remained and would forever remain that valiant and silent pair of hands, capable of preparing, without batting an eyelid, dozens of dishes for weddings, funerals and circumcisions, and also capable of listening to the most fiery confessions without ever suspecting there might be the slightest bit of gossip to pass on.

And then Krim saw, standing beside her, his great-uncle Ferhat. He realized he hadn't even noticed him come in and, for the first time in months, he felt like crying. The old man hadn't taken off his fur hat all day – he had no more hair on his neck, either – and his eyes were the saddest Krim had ever seen. Ferhat had once been a cheerful and mischievous old man – a musician, no less – gently teased for his stinginess, though he was, according to Krim's mother, less backward than all his nephews put together. Last Christmas he had even taken out his mandolin, the one he once played to pass the time on the benches in front of the Saint-Ennemond church. Everyone who ever shopped at the butcher's on this little square had heard his warm arpeggios. And then one day the butcher's shop was replaced by a prayer room. The benches were ripped up so as not to obstruct the devout on their way out, and Uncle Ferhat, who was known for not being very religious, was asked to go and play his weird-looking guitar somewhere else.

'Take Chaouch!' Rabia cried. 'He's Kabyle, not Arab!'

An uncle made his voice sound conspicuously measured: 'He's Algerian, *rlass*.'

'Yes, but he's Kabyle. In his family they speak Kabyle! He's called Idder, not Mohammed! I hate to tell you . . .'

'Rabia, you don't even know what Idder means,' the uncle said, teasing her gently.

'Idder? Uh, that means Idir, they're exactly the same.'

'Yes and what does it mean?'

'He who lives, no?' Dounia asked. She didn't dare express her certainty in knowing the answer. 'I think it means he's alive, he lives, though I'm not sure.'

'*I'dder*,' Rabia proclaimed with a flourish of her hand. 'Eh, *I'dder*!'

The whole of Algeria was in that twist of the wrist, but not enough to convince anyone in the room.

Rabia suddenly heard the term *elomien*, 'the French', and concluded, only God knows how, that she was the target. But she lost none of her enthusiasm and went on: 'Well, so what? The main thing is that we're not the same, that's all. It can't be denied. You don't have to say we're better or not as good, just that we're not the same. Not the same language, not the same customs. Not even the same music.'

Dounia returned from the kitchen with tea and coffee. 'Doune, tell them!'

'Oh la la, I don't want to start thinking about— No, no, sweetheart,' she interrupted herself, saved by one of the little cousins opening an umbrella in the corridor. 'You mustn't open an umbrella indoors, it's bad luck.'

'It's like whistling,' Raouf joked, leaning over the little boy. 'Granny says that if you whistle it attracts the *shetan*.'

'What's the *shetan*?'

'Well, it's the devil.'

'Shh,' Dounia whispered with a frown.

Raouf smiled apologetically, helped his aunt take away the tray, and cleared his throat to make his own intervention, but his father got there first.

'*Wallah*, it's bigger than that, the truth is that we're all Algerian, that's all, and we have to stand side by side and move forward, together.'

'Like the Jews,' said a woman's voice, swallowed up by the children's cries.

'And what's more, I'm fucking sick of the past,' Raouf added. 'Comes a time when you've got to stop. The main thing with Chaouch is not that he's Kabyle or Arab, it's that he's facing the future, that he motivates young people to create their own businesses . . . And above all, I'm sorry, but Chaouch is neither Kabyle nor Arab, he's French! Like you, like me, like everyone or almost everyone around this table.'

Not everyone laughed because not everyone had listened, but Raouf's father put his hand on his son's shoulder and gave him a long, slanted smile, as if he considered his naivety touching. Raouf poured the tea, exaggeratedly lifting the pot. He had changed his Chaouch t-shirt for a black and blue suit that was worth three times the fake leather sofa on which he had found some room to sit.

The discussion was running out of steam. Rabia sensed this and put in her two cents. 'As for me, during the debate I thought Chaouch was wonderful!'

'Yes, but why was he wonderful?' Raouf asked, challenging the whole room. 'Why?'

It was apparently a genuine question. Toufik couldn't bear the uncomfortable silence, which began to linger in the room as strongly as the smell of coffee. 'He was wonderful because he managed to keep his cool. That's all he had to do at that point. Stay calm and keep winning.'

'No,' Raouf replied, probably without having registered a

word of his cousin's suggestion. 'He was wonderful because he wasn't left-wing! Quite simply! He knows full well that if you keep increasing taxes on small businesses, young people are going to continue to do what I did, and leave for England! Am I right?'

'Yes, well, he also spoke about other issues,' Toufik ventured, blushing right up to his frizzy hair. 'He made it clear he would be the president who would unite the French instead of dividing them.'

'Yes, yes,' Raouf conceded, 'he did show that he placed himself in the continuity of French history, he finally spoke about the rough suburbs and . . . and, you have to admit it was impressive, well, I don't want to sound like Fouad, but we have a candidate who, in the middle of a debate took the liberty of quoting Keynes, Proust and Saint-Simon . . .'

You could count on your ring finger the number of people sitting around the teapot who knew of Keynes, Proust and Saint-Simon.

Aunt Rabia made fun of this without malice by putting on a posh voice to quote from *Titanic*: 'And who is this Keynes, a passenger?'

Everyone burst out laughing.

Raouf didn't wait for the cloud of goodwill to clear before retorting: 'But we don't care about him showing off his education. What matters is—'

His mother gently interrupted him: 'Oh no, we do care, at least he's showing the French that he's as educated as they are.'

'That's not the point, Mum!' Raouf was heating up. 'He doesn't need to show anything to the French – he *is* French!'

'And what's more, he went to ENA,' Toufik murmured,

delighted to contribute an intelligent piece of information in the midst of the hubbub.

For a fleeting moment his eyebrows formed a *V* for victory.

Those three prestigious letters, *E, N, A* – Ecole Nationale d'Administration – filled Dounia and Rabia with pride. They puffed out their chests and looked at each other, laughing, while on the muted TV i-Télé's news bulletin showed images of the charismatic Chaouch speaking without a tie to textile workers who had formed a horseshoe around him.

In a corner beneath the herd of advisers and bodyguards, the camera picked out the inscrutable face of the candidate's daughter; she was a young, pale, hook-nosed woman whom Rabia seemed to dislike.

'She's bizarre, that girl,' she said into Dounia's ear. 'You know why she never smiles?'

Dounia moved her chair in and stared at the TV.

'It's because she has vampire teeth. *Wallah*, I'm telling you.' As her sister didn't react, she added, 'Honestly, you wouldn't think she was Kabyle. Maybe her nose. But she gets her nose from her mother – you know Chaouch's wife is Jewish?'

All eyes were soon on the TV. The continuous news feed indicated that the campaign had officially ended at midnight the day before. Someone turned up the volume and everyone listened as the pretty news anchor explained that the last opinion polls for the second round showed Chaouch in the lead with 51.5 per cent, but that the turnout remained *the* great unknown of the election. Opinion polls had never been so tight on the eve of a second round. As a point of comparison, the previous election had been decided right from the middle of the first week between rounds, a 55–45 that hadn't budged.

An uncle who was thought to be asleep sat upright in his armchair. '*Wallah*, they're not going to elect him . . .'

This fit of defeatism suddenly seemed to be shared by almost everyone in the room. Rabia gestured to Toufik to turn the sound down and asked Dounia for news of Nazir.

Her sister's face clouded over as she thought of her eldest son. 'Eh, I swear those two are giving me a lot of worry.'

'It seems he's got a wedding in Paris, so that's why he can't come?'

'Don't know, he doesn't speak to me much these days. And when he does, he's strange, always asking me if I go to the cemetery, if I go to the Tower from time to time. You'd think he wants me to live in the past.'

'You know what Nazir's like. He's intransigent.'

'He's harsh,' Dounia corrected, her eyes misting over. 'He's too harsh.' Her lips remained half-open, but the rest never came.

'Anyway you can't have three identical sons,' Rabia said philosophically. 'As many sons as personalities!'

Dounia had brought up her three children in the Plein Ciel Tower in Montreynaud, on the thirteenth floor, lift B. Fouad spoke of this skyscraper as if it was a total aberration and regularly got annoyed that it still hadn't been demolished. Nazir believed, on the contrary, that it had to be kept as a symbol. But the two brothers hadn't spoken to each other for three years and had therefore not had the opportunity to debate this, to their mother's great dismay. She was said to be wise, but confessed she was completely overwhelmed by this fratricidal conflict whose motivations she couldn't fathom.

'But they'll make up eventually,' Rabia whispered warmly, kissing her favourite sister. '*Mezel*, be patient.'

'Eh?' Dounia said, indignant. 'Make up? Those two? The enemy brothers? *Wallah*, the enemy brothers. The day they make up, *malat'n g'r' dunit*, will be the day the world ends! Why aren't they more like Slim, easy-going . . .'

Rabia dwelled on this last remark. It was true that Slim was easy-going. Helpful, generous, polite and gentle. Come to think of it, where was he?

'He's gone for a walk with his brother. They don't see each other often, but they'll be back soon, *insh'Allah*. We've got to meet up at Saint-Victor in half an hour.'

Rabia murmured in her sister's ear that she would like to speak to her alone. The two women went out onto the balcony. First they exchanged a few platitudes about the bride, whom they found very pretty, very polite, very lucky also to have found a boy as gentle and peaceful as Slim.

Then Rabia took a deep breath and plunged her big, dark, mischievous eyes into the gaze of the woman who had been her confidante ever since she was old enough to have secrets. 'Doune, I've met someone on the internet. I asked Luna to register me on, what's it called? Meetic? I don't usually like that sort of thing, you know me, but in fact it's just email. You send little messages, he writes back, you answer him . . .'

'But have you seen him?' Dounia was unable to hide her bafflement.

'No, no; not yet. You mean with a webcam? No, no. He gave me his phone number and we send each other little text messages.' Anticipating her sister's next question, she added, 'He's called Omar. Like Omar Sharif.'

'What, another Arab?'

'C'mon, he's not just anybody, he's older. A sort of businessman, really classy, but don't you go thinking . . . no, no, he's a gentleman, I swear.'

'I'm not thinking anything, I'm just listening. Omar.'

'Well, that's not all,' Rabia shrieked, dragging her sister to the end of the balcony. 'Guess what? He's coming to the wedding. I don't really understand why he was invited, but there you go, I'm going to meet him this evening.'

'But how are you going to recognize him if you've never seen him? Does he at least have a photo on Meetic?'

'No, no, there's no need for photos. If you just want to pick up any old *zarma* guy, you might as well go to a nightclub, right?'

But Dounia wasn't reassured: a worrying feeling weighed on her upper lip and kept her from giving her sister the warm smile of blessing that her big eyes feverishly awaited. 'As it so happens,' Dounia said, pulling herself together and stroking her sister's hands, 'I too have a secret to tell you . . . It's about Fouad.'

Krim was staring at his reflection in the teapot, wondering why his father wasn't there. Five years later, it was still just as inexplicable: others learned to turn the page, but not Krim; he didn't want to move on. Could it be called suffering? He wasn't sure. It was more like a sense of unease, like the thought of sinking your teeth into a bar of soap.

Someone put down a plate of little sweets sprinkled with powdered sugar and filled with silvery balls. Krim devoured half of them, much to Zoulikha's delight.

His mobile vibrated in his trouser pocket.

Received: Today at 7.20 p.m.

From: N.

FM can't get through to you. Did you
train today?

Krim saw that his hand was trembling. He stood up and moved
to avoid Uncle Bouzid's camera. Bouzid was relaxing, at last, by
taking dozens of photos of the people gathered on the other sofa.

'Krikri! Krikri, love! Come, come here two minutes. *Allouar!*'

It was, in fact, Kamelia, Toufik's sister, who was playing with
a little cousin. Luna deliberately avoided looking at him when
he entered the bedroom.

'*Wesh* Krimo, so what's up? Come and sit down!'

Krim took his place beside her on the bed while Kamelia
rubbed his head vigorously.

'You all right? You don't look happy.'

'No, no, I'm just tired.'

He didn't dare look at his older cousin and couldn't find
anything to say to her. Suddenly he had an idea. 'Aren't your
sisters here?'

'No, no . . .' Kamelia replied, as if repeating it for the fifteenth
consecutive time. 'They've stayed at home. Hey, you have to
come up to Paris! I'll show you around, I promise, we'll go to the
Eiffel Tower, the Sacré-Coeur; you've never been, have you?'

'No, never. But . . .'

'But what?'

'No, nothing. I'm going there soon, in fact. I . . . I've got my
uncle on my father's side, my Uncle Lounis, you know. He lives
in Seine-Saint-Denis.'

'That's nice, I didn't know you were still in touch.'

'Actually, I haven't seen him for a long time . . .'

The thought of Uncle Lounis always brought back the smell of wood. His father and Lounis – dry, brusque, nervous men – worked as lumberjacks when Krim was a toddler, and even now the strong smell of wood seemed to be the only source of unadulterated splendour in his life: the heady fragrance of the fir plantations encircling Saint-Etienne, the deep, acrid smell of the chestnut groves where they walked in the first days of autumn. One day the men were no longer needed in the forests. Krim's father then got a job with Monsieur Ballerine, a sort of scrap dealer cum bric-a-brac trader who kept an Ali Baba's cave on the side of the motorway. The trinkets his father salvaged from there were the apples of Krim's eye: an old enamel coffee pot with intact white paint, a fat copper Buddha with a shiny gut, an aluminium coffee mill, or that famous sculpture with the three little monkeys – the one who hides his eyes, the one who covers his mouth, and the one who covers his ears.

Krim still owned the scraps of wood his father had used to teach him words as beautiful as *cherry* and *beech*. He'd saved the tin figurines – a couple of flamenco dancers in traditional costumes raising their fingers – as well as a series of paintings that portrayed violet sunsets and boats left at lakesides where each wave formed a crust that could be scratched, cut away and rubbed out as you liked. He had been furious with his mother the day she got rid of an apple peeler and a fluffy orange pouffe that held too many memories for her.

'So you'll have to come and see me?' Kamelia said, jolting him back to reality.

'Where?'

'Are you asleep or what? In Paris, not on the moon!'

Kamelia put little Miriam down and took off her leather jacket. She was wearing a black sleeveless dress with a push-up bra covered by a polka-dot scarf. The scarf was translucent and Krim had to use all his willpower not to look at her full, smooth breasts; only the cleavage, sewn with tiny creases, indicated they belonged to a woman in her thirties.

Ill at ease, he felt two thin trickles of sweat flow from his armpits.

'Well, apart from that, what's new? Do you have a girlfriend?'

Krim turned bright red. Luna, who'd heard it all, decided to take revenge. 'Yeah, he's got a girlfriend, but she's just called N.'

Krim got up to smack his sister, but she was quicker than him and his hand just swiped thin air.

'She calls him all the time on his mobile and he's so afraid they'll discover her that he doesn't even write her entire name. N – who could this be?' Luna was jumping on the bed, hopping from one side to the other to avoid her brother's arm. 'Nathalie? Najet? Ninon? None of the above?'

Krim left the room as Kamelia gave her little cousin a sermon.

'But it's his fault. He tells Mum I'm acting like a slut on Facebook, what do you expect me to do, let him get away with it?'

Saint-Priest-en-Jarez, 7.25 p.m.

Zoran's screams had devolved into endless sobbing. Taking refuge on the top of the sofa, he was on the verge of suffocation. It was fear, the fear that hadn't left him since his abduction, that prevented him from pushing open the door to release the gigantic rat that scampered around and around the room making thin, plaintive, senseless, abominable roars.

A moth suddenly appeared in a corner of the ceiling. Zoran watched its wings beat and wanted to latch onto it so as to breathe more calmly. But the river rat's eyes were staring straight at him, gleaming in the dark, erasing the rest of the universe. Unable to focus on the moth instead of the fat rat, Zoran began to hiccup: his shrivelled lungs were not going to hold out for much longer. He followed the moth's harmonious flight and stopped himself from looking at the monster.

In the rodent he saw Evil incarnate – the devil among the living, with his sinuous movements, his hairy gestures. In contrast the moth was a creature from heaven, who brought heaven into the scents of the flowers, into their colours that breathed life into the weight of the fields of the earth. The moth might be grey, but it was a dense, rich, even luminous grey.

Daring to close his eyes, Zoran heard the murmur of the river flowing a few metres from the house.

The moth found its way to the lamp and settled on its fluffy shade. As he looked at its shadow dancing on the silk of the orangey red sofa, Zoran noticed that he was breathing normally again. He sniffed and kept looking upwards. The beast from hell had no reason to move. Zoran found another way to ignore the rodent: he tried listening to the conversation between the monsters in the other room.

The boss was talking about a wedding, describing the place where the reception would be held: a quarter of an hour away by car, near the motorway exit and the DIY store.

Zoran fantasized that instead of being locked up with a rat, he had successfully extorted the thousand euros from Slim and already fled south, to Marseilles for example, where his sister rented a hotel bedroom by the month.

The rodent suddenly caught his attention by banging against its cage. Zoran couldn't help looking at it again, and therefore couldn't help resuming his frantic crying. But the animal didn't seem to mind in the slightest. It was moving about the small rectangle where it had begun its entry into Zoran's life and had no thought of climbing onto the sofa. It could surely have done so, given its monstrous size and amphibious suppleness, but it preferred to rummage around its cage by the boxes, or under the desk, where it suddenly discovered a little red key, which it examined with its forepaws against its white whiskers.

For the first time, it showed its teeth.

Zoran started screaming again. His previous screams had not seemed to bother the beast, but this time it wanted to defend itself – or the key, perhaps.

Zoran jumped on the bed, shouting, and managed to make the lamp fall on top of the animal. The light cut out, and Zoran realized he had only one solution left: to get out through the door, in the hope that the boxes piled up on the other side were not heavy enough to block it. For if that was the case, if the door was blocked and he had to stay with the beast in total darkness for more than one minute, then there was no doubt his heart would give out before the rodent had even begun to inflict its first bites.

At Granny's, 7.30 p.m.

As he walked past the kitchen, Krim remembered that he was starving. He nibbled on a few pastries and soon felt the need to get organized. He hesitated to open the fridge, convinced that the whole flat was secretly connected to that thick white door and that he was going to attract everyone's attention (which he didn't). Once he'd poured himself a bowl of milk and dipped his *makrout* in it, his hunger grew insatiable and now he wanted something savoury. He discreetly got hold of a tube of mayonnaise and heard, while looking for some bread in the cupboards, the *France Info* radio jingle announcing the evening news. He noticed the old bread basket, which was missing a handle. Granny kept her loaves for several days. She cut up product packages and sent off the coupons to be reimbursed. She spent hours doing this and was reimbursed hundreds of euros a year. But while trying to access the bread that was protected from humidity by three plastic bags, Krim rebelled against the absurdity of the whole process. There was madness in the way Granny tied up the bags. He could easily imagine her tightening knots that only her own fingers, with their ferocious nails, could undo.

Devouring his toast – finally! – and mayonnaise, Krim listened to random interviews of people on the street; everyone, it seemed, was going to vote for Chaouch. Then he listened to a studio discussion featuring an expert on security issues who spoke of rumours of a terrorist attack and of AQIM, which had become, he said, 'a campaign figure in their own right' – the expert was audibly proud of the expression he'd coined. The female journalist interrupted him to remind listeners that AQIM stood for Al-Qaeda in the Islamic Maghreb, after which the analyst, clearly unaccustomed to the way things are done on radio, had some trouble picking up where he had left off. He described the terrorist organization and returned as quickly as possible to current events. The threat was certainly present, but the terrorist alert level had been raised to its maximum since well before the first round of the election.

'And then you must know,' the expert continued, regaining his confidence, 'that the threat is less to the president, as you might suspect, than to the candidate Chaouch. It's a paradox that really isn't one at all, if you think about it: AQIM's last message precisely identifies Idder Chaouch as a – I quote – treacherous dog, who has renounced Islam and deserves death. When you know the Socialist candidate's sensitivity on these issues, his refusal to have too restrictive a security presence, you understand that there are grounds for concern. I would just like to draw your attention back to that resignation on the eve of the first round of the election . . .'

'Quickly, yes,' the journalist interrupted in a curt but smiling voice.

'Yes, the resignation of his security chief, who'd had enough of seeing his team constantly pulled back, well, this move hasn't really been discussed in the press but I'd like to emphasize how important this is, a real first in the Fifth Republic. It really is . . . And then of course we all remember the minaret affair in Saint-Etienne at the start of the year, the message from AQIM even refers to it specifically . . .'

Krim was moved upon hearing his city's name on a national news programme – just like when he was very little, and his mother rounded up everyone in front of the TV whenever images of Saint-Etienne appeared. She always made a terrific fuss over the two minutes of local switch-overs on the evening news – two minutes devoted exclusively to Saint-Etienne, and viewable only by the people of Saint-Etienne, that bestowed on the main street, the town hall or the place Marengo a sort of dignity, a magical and exciting sanction given to banal, everyday things by their appearance, however fleeting, on that mysterious screen.

A scene he couldn't quite date suddenly came back to him: he and Slim in the tram, and some guys who, like Djamel just a few hours ago, were insinuating that Slim was a faggot. Krim wanted to text Djamel to remind him that faggots married each other and not women.

Instead he texted Nazir, as he'd been encouraged to do if he was ever wondering about anything at all. He wrote that people were talking, saying things about Slim. He expected Nazir to reply immediately but he didn't. On checking that his message had been sent he almost tripped over his young cousin, who studied him melancholically while sucking his thumb. Krim kneeled down and showed him his shiny mobile and his beautiful silver lighter, which seemed to spark the little one's interest.

'You want to light it?'

The boy nodded without really understanding, took the lighter in his pudgy fingers and figured out how to open the metal top. But on pressing the button he received a shock and started screaming. It was a dodgy lighter that Krim had stolen after discovering its unique property of emitting a tiny electric shock when you pressed it from the wrong side, which looked like the right one.

The boy's mother, Rachida, came running over. 'What on earth is wrong with you? Go get your head checked, you lunatic!'

In the other room an uncle plugged his ears while his wife

came to calm things down. Understanding the situation in the blink of an eye, she took Krim's side and addressed Rachida in a calm and composed voice: 'Rachida *raichek*, so you're going to start the hundred year war over a lighter, eh? He wanted to play with the little boy, that's all. You've got to let him play—'

'Yeah?' Rachida said indignantly. 'Why don't you tell me how to raise my kids, while you're at it!'

In need of a cigarette, Krim rushed out to the balcony, where Dounia suddenly stopped talking. Her three sons' big black eyes came from her husband, who had died three years earlier; her own were fine, kind, green-brown, and a little sad. Dounia had the most Kabyle face of the family: a strong nose, white skin and clear eyes. She seemed to have aged prematurely from looking after old people in a home in the city centre; her brown hair, tied up in a bun, already had quite a few white strands in it and her skin, ruined by smoke and nicotine, had the greyish pallor of the sixty-year-old she wouldn't be for another ten years.

Rabia encouraged Krim to close the balcony window and pointed out the little corner where he could smoke without being seen by the uncles.

'Go on, Doune, you can talk, Krim won't tell, he's as silent as the grave.'

'You sure?'

'Of course, he won't say a word, trust me.'

Dounia took her young nephew's smooth chin in her hand and shook it affectionately.

'Okay, well, I was saying, he spoke to me about it last week.'

'What's going on?' ventured Krim.

'You sure?' asked Dounia.

'Yes, yes,' Rabia replied.

'Well, there were rumours that Fouad might be going out with someone very . . . how should I put it . . . high up.'

'Who?'

'Jasmine Chaouch.'

Krim nearly fell over.

'Chaouch's daughter? The one we saw on TV just now?'

'Come on, Krim, you mustn't repeat it, hey, swear on your mother's head.'

'Yes, yes, I swear. Wow.'

Rabia's eyes had never sparkled so much. 'But if you think about it, it makes sense. I've always said Fouad is the best-looking one in the family, isn't that true, Krim? Plus he's an actor, women like actors, it's well known, they fall like ninepins! Look, the doctor in *ER*, what's his name?'

'Doug Ross.'

'Doug Ross, exactly! He does ads for coffee now, my dear.'

Dounia turned to Krim and asked for a puff on his cigarette. 'But you shouldn't tell anyone, love, you understand, that'll just make people jealous, people will talk. It's different with your mother, we tell each other everything, but don't repeat this, right? I trust you.'

'Krim, put it out, put it out, Uncle's coming.'

Krim began by hiding his cigarette in the palm of his hand, but threw it out the window when he saw that the uncle in question was Ferhat. The old man appeared lost, and his Russian hat made his face look even more wizened than usual. They made a little room for him while he explained in Kabyle, 'I need a bit of fresh air.'

So as to resume conversation as naturally as possible, Rabia asked him to take off his hat. 'Uncle, it's too hot to wear a hat! *Miskine...*'

'No, no,' the uncle murmured, getting his breath back.

'But yes, yes, it's obvious you're suffocating,' Rabia insisted.

And then Ferhat used all the diminished strength he had left to stand up to the gale of words from Rabia. 'Leave the hat alone, leave it, my son.'

He lost his balance and had to sit down immediately. Rabia looked up knowingly at Dounia, who noticed the moist lines at the corners of the old man's eyes. He left the confined space of the balcony and dragged himself to the living room, where his place had since been taken. Rabia wanted to go in again and ask Toufik to give up his seat for his Elder, but Dounia held her back with a reassuring blink of her eyes: Toufik would think of it himself.

'Hey, give me another smoke, darling,' she asked her nephew. 'I don't know what's wrong with me today, I keep spitting!'

Krim lit another cigarette and skilfully handed it to his aunt. Rabia, delighted by his politeness and perhaps also by the grace in his gesture, leaned in to kiss her son's head. But he drew back abruptly and refused to look at her. Rabia had the sudden impression that he knew.

'We'd better stop there, Rab,' Dounia declared, having drawn a puff so powerful that the filter, reddened by her lipstick, had completely lost its shape. 'This has to stop, we smoke too much. Rabia?'

Rabia, who wasn't listening to her, brushed at her sister's jacket, moistened her fingers and rubbed at a stain on her shoulder pad.

'To think,' Dounia added with a disabused smile, 'that we have to hide on the balcony to smoke, at our age...'

Rabia excused herself with a wave of her hand and ran to the bathroom to rid herself of a doubt. Her face fell as she went through the list of her recently sent messages and discovered, instead of Omar at the top of the list, the first name of her beloved son framed by exclamation marks.

5

Man of the Game

Saint-Victor Boating Centre, 7.30 p.m.

The photographer climbed up the grassy slope to avoid having to round the bend thirty metres ahead. His suit trousers were stained green, but it didn't matter: his instincts hadn't betrayed him and the viewpoint from which they now stood was ten times better than from the restaurant terrace, where two cherry trees blocked the marina from view. He'd had no difficulty convincing the mother of the bride, even if it took a few dubious conjectures such as the quality of natural lighting, the fog and the difference in altitude.

'Okay, well then, we just have to wait for them to arrive.'

Kenza, the bride, had been separated from Slim for less than an hour, and already she felt she'd fallen back under her mother's influence. Plus, she was beginning to feel a bit cold. The gusts of wind wrinkled the surface of the lake and made the tree blossoms flutter. Clutching her elbows to stifle a shiver, she looked in the direction that the photographer was pointing to. The marina was made up of about fifteen mostly deserted pontoons, lazily watched over by a tower with blue-tinted windows, splashed with the last rays of sunlight.

Kenza looked up and noticed they'd indeed better hurry: the apricot sunset would soon disappear behind the cliffs. On the lawn at her feet, the shadows were already lengthening and she really had to squint to identify a silhouette.

'They're coming,' Kenza's mother muttered, looking down towards the car park.

The bride was surprised that there were only three of them (Slim, his actor-brother Fouad and their mother) and disappointed that they gave no explanation.

Still, the photo session proceeded successfully. They had to restrain the artistic ambitions of the photographer, diverting each daft idea spouting out of his mouth every two minutes. The bride's mother supported one of them, which required the married couple to stretch out alongside a flowerbed, symmetrical to one another, head placed on an elbow and a red rose between their teeth.

'Yeah, we don't actually have to keep that one,' Dounia assured them.

The bride's mother heard this and shot her a withering look. After half an hour, the photographer had run out of ideas and there was almost no sunlight left. Slim and Kenza went off on their own as the photographer put away his equipment. The lake below them was not exactly a lake, but rather a particularly wide stretch of the Loire where the residents of Saint-Etienne pretended to be at the beach.

Slim remembered the outdoor barbecues they'd organized when he was in senior school, and he also remembered the day Uncle Bouzid swam out too far and got caught in a whirlpool.

They had to send for a rescue team, and the shirtless bloke who drove the motorboat was very brave.

'What're you thinking, sweetheart?'

Slim took his young bride in his spindly arms and squeezed her with all his strength, until he could feel nothing but the compressed flesh of her breasts. He kissed her passionately as he made a vow, more than a vow, a genuine prayer whose every word seemed to burn the entrails of his brain.

Fouad joined him a few minutes later.

'So, happy with the photo session?'

Slim seemed unusually agitated. Fouad took him by the arm and the two brothers walked along the lookout.

'What's up with Krim?' asked Fouad. 'Last week Aunt Rabia calls and tells me he socked his boss at McDonald's, that he's going to lose his unemployment benefits, that he spends his time doing weird things in the cellar . . .'

'Don't know, I don't actually see much of him any more.'

'I'm going to see him in a bit, to try and talk to him.'

'Yes,' Slim said, taking a breath. Then he shifted to what was genuinely bothering him. 'Fouad, I haven't told you everything about Kenza.'

'What? I'm all ears.'

'I don't know how to explain it, I think . . .'

'Take your time.'

Fouad had stopped and was staring hard at his brother in order to guess, before he announced it, what he figured would be a very unpleasant coup de théâtre.

'Well, I mean . . .' Slim drew another deep breath. 'I'm going to ask you a question, and forget it's got anything to do with me, just tell me, okay?'

'Come on, Slim, just tell me what's going on.'

'Is it possible for a girl to stay with a boy even if . . . even if they don't do it?'

'You mean you've never slept together?'

'Come on – not so loud.'

'But is that it? Never?'

'I can't do it yet, Fouad, I can't do it. I'm with her, it starts out okay, and then I just get these images in my head, I start thinking of something else. It's horrible, it's a total nightmare, but I can't fight it.'

'You're thinking of something else or someone else?'

Fouad could sense that his little brother was on the verge of tears. He took Slim by the shoulders and plunged his dark eyes into his.

'Yes, but . . .'

'What did she say to you?' Fouad asked.

'Well, she laughed, she said it wasn't a big deal . . . that we needed to take the time to get to know each other better.'

Fouad grimaced, not because of his little brother's depressing naivety, but because he was speaking in a thick Saint-Etienne accent, the one he'd shed a long time ago.

'What are you thinking about?' Slim asked.

Fouad's face darkened and Slim knew he was thinking about Nazir. It was a thought he couldn't hide: it opened up his mouth and hardened his handsome jaw spectacularly.

'I knew it,' Slim said, losing his temper and looking down at the ground. 'You think just like Nazir, you're thinking: that little faggot would do better getting fucked up the arse than trying to fool everyone by getting married.'

'Stop talking rubbish and look at things as they are. It's your choice, Slim. It's your life. Do you love Kenza?'

114

'Of course, she's the woman of my life.'

'Well, that's all that matters,' Fouad concluded, feeling like a liar. 'There's nothing else to say. If she loves you back, and I can see that she does, and I'm sure she's a nice girl, then you have to talk to each other – in a relationship you tell each other everything. And then . . .'

'What?' Slim begged, as if his big brother was going to solve the biggest problem in his life with a magic formula.

'No, I mean, in the past, couples used to wait to get married before . . . consummating. Maybe it wasn't that bad, when you think about it . . .'

Fouad turned towards the marina and saw the last ray of sunlight die against the club's blue Plexiglas. He had not felt so powerless in years, probably not since their father's death. When he returned to his little brother's scrawny silhouette, it seemed that the poor boy had no weight in the universe, that he'd been swept away and scattered to the winds. He felt like slapping Slim's face, hardening him, giving him some weight with which to confront the violence of life. Instead he took him in his arms and stroked the back of his head with as much care as he would take with the soft skull of a newborn babe.

At Granny's, 8 p.m.

Krim no longer wanted to leave the balcony. It was starting to get dark, and the windows were turning into mirrors. A vast swathe of clouds where the sun had disappeared merged on the horizon with packs of monotone hills. Behind the library, the slag heaps lurked, sullen and immoveable.

He leaned back against the balcony railing and looked inside at the people who were standing up to greet Fouad and the groom. Lights had been switched on, and only Aunt Zoulikha remained seated, doting on one of the young cousins and approving each of his rolls of fat. Aunt Zoulikha – she confused weight with health and knew only one proverb in French, which she always pronounced incorrectly, with a toothy smile that unmasked the wholesome, shy, charmless young girl she'd been in the middle of the previous century, whom no one had ever wanted.

Fat Momo called his name down the line for the fifth consecutive time.

Krim considered a swearword, maybe muttered it, but then gave up. 'Hey, why do you keep calling me?'

'Come on, calm down, you don't want to go practise in the woods?'

'Where's the nine?'

'Uh, in the cellar, where you think?'

Krim wanted to light a second cigarette but Fouad noticed this and came towards him. It was true he was handsome, and on seeing him, Krim could only think of presidential candidate Chaouch: tall, vigorous without being bulky, with an engaging smile and pleasantly curly hair. A champion.

'Piss off,' Krim spat into his mobile, placing it perpendicular to his chin. 'I have other shit to do.'

'Come on, there's nothing going on over here, I've fuck all to do.'

'No, no, come on, stop, and you've got to get rid of it. Throw it in the Furan. Seriously, on my mother's life throw it in the Furan.'

'What?'

116

'On the Koran, I don't want to hear about it again, throw it in the Furan!'

Fouad had reached the balcony by then, and Krim hung up.

'What are you smoking?'

Krim had to swallow twice before speaking. He didn't like feeling so impressionable, and reassured himself by thinking that it was normal to be impressed by a cousin significantly older than him and who, above all, had been on TV every evening for the past year.

'Camels.'

'Can you slip me one?'

'If you like.'

Fouad looked at Krim's shoes. 'Slim told me you were his witness in the end. Thanks. There was an accident on the tracks and the train was delayed two hours.'

'Yeah, that's fucking annoying. The train, I mean.'

'We're leaving for the community centre soon, but if you want we can chat for a bit later on. I just need to shine my shoes. Sound good?'

He had a clear, powerful voice, and yet Krim was almost moved by the warmth it exuded, which seemed to envelop only him. All the others inside were looking towards the balcony and Krim felt proud.

'Yeah, why not?'

'In fact,' Fouad continued, 'I need to talk to you about your mate, Mohammed.'

'What's he done?'

'Oh, no, no, nothing, I'm just friends with him on Facebook. He friended me, you know. Honest, he cracks me up.'

'*Wesh*, he's too much, such a nutter, Fat Momo.'

'Fat Momo, ha ha. He spends his time hitting on girls, I've never seen anything like it. He even hits on *my* Facebook friends.'

'Dude, you've got to tell him . . .' Krim said indignantly.

'Nah, it's funny, I don't care. Last time he tagged one of his girlfriends and he also tagged himself in the photo, even though she's the only one in it.'

'Ha, ha' – a laugh Krim felt impelled to force out, even though Fouad's story wasn't finished.

'Then the girl asks him: where are you in the photo? And you know what he replies?'

'No, go on, tell me.'

'In your heart.'

Krim looked down, unable to relax and laugh without pretending.

'All right then, I'll go and say hello to the others and I'll see you in the other room, okay?'

'Okay.'

'And wait, one more thing: what has to be thrown in the Furan?' Fouad asked with the glimmer of a grin.

'Nothing,' Krim said hesitantly. 'Some dickhead who does things, I don't know, he wants me to come with him, but, but I'm not into that stuff.'

Krim had no idea what his lie had sounded like. He hadn't heard himself say it and nothing in Fouad's expression indicated that he didn't believe him – not a trace of disapproval. There was only cheerfulness and trust.

Fouad stubbed out his half-finished cigarette and joyfully left the balcony, winking knowingly at his little cousin.

'That's what you call a true film star!' Rabia exclaimed, pressing kisses on his cheeks.

'A TV star, you mean. The star of the small screen . . . that's me!'

'I don't miss an episode, *wallah*, it's so great! Ah, and the other guy, the baddy with the wart. Ah, I can't stand him. You know him?'

'Ha, ha, you mean François! In real life he's the nicest guy in the world.'

All the aunts were soon gathered around the prodigal son. They spoke for ten minutes about *Man of the Game*, the series he'd joined the previous autumn in which he played the manager of the most popular fictional football team in the country. He had quickly become so indispensable that his name headed the opening credits. *Man of the Game* on Channel 6 had even toppled the 8 p.m. news. It was *the* television event of the past year, and attracted both football fans who were curious about what went on behind the scenes – they admired the series' realism – and their wives who were perhaps more interested in the romance.

'So,' ventured Rabia, who seemed to be the most ardent fan in the family, 'are you going to stay with Justine until the end of the series?'

'Well, um,' Fouad joked, 'I've signed a confidentiality agreement, I can't give anything away!'

'*Zarma* – you sign confidentiality agreements now!' Rabia mocked. 'Well, well, well . . . Don't forget I used to change your nappies, so you can't use that confidentiality agreement thing on me!'

Fouad burst out laughing and agreed to reveal a small part of what he knew.

But after a moment, although he was generally at ease and immune to any form of embarrassment, he felt the desire to confess that he didn't think very highly of the series, which he considered a day job above all. He wanted to tell the truth, to share his deepest thoughts, but he quickly changed his mind: his aunts would never have understood why he of all people spat on their favourite show, the one for which they had all sacrificed the sacrosanct evening news bulletin. And it was thanks to this series that they no longer felt shame when their friends showed off about having children who studied medicine or who made so much money in their import-export business that they could build houses back in Algeria and take holidays in Dubai.

A few moments later the fever had died down a bit, or rather, it had moved to Granny's bedroom. The youngest had all gathered around Fouad to watch and applaud little Miriam, who had memorized the choreography of an already outdated Katy Perry track. She wanted to become a professional B-girl. In the meantime, murmuring the words to 'Firework', she threw her arms out in front of her and back to her sides, blowing on the locks of brown hair that got in her way. At the chorus she very convincingly mimed the fireworks shooting from the characters' hearts in the video. Her little brother wanted to take advantage of the aura surrounding the little dancer and do a duet with her, just as she had regularly forced him to do in the secrecy of their bedroom. Miriam blew on him with comic ferocity, as if he was one of her locks of hair.

Krim entered and closed the door behind him at the very moment his sister decided to improvise a game of Name That Tune with Kamelia's MacBook. After what she'd done to him, Krim would never have ventured into the same room as Luna if he hadn't felt the irresistible urge to be in Fouad's entourage, the burning desire to see him and be seen by him, a ferocious, blind and curiously non-violent drive, to which he acquiesced as if he were being carried away by a warm current in a cold sea.

'Go on Spotify,' Kamelia advised Luna, who'd taken her mobile.

She went to sit at the back of the room. Leaning on the cast-iron radiator, she checked to make sure the windowpane behind her, which nightfall had now turned into a mirror, did not reveal the reflection of the photos of the singers she was going to play.

Kamelia and Fouad were sitting next to each other; little Miriam was bobbing her head, sitting on the star's lap. The older cousins were spread out on the bed, where Raouf tried to make a little room for the newly arrived.

'So?' Raouf murmured in the ear of his dealer for the day.

'Yeah, right now it's dead out there, but maybe in an hour's time I'll have something, at the reception hall.'

Krim showed his imperturbable bored face again, the face of someone who would rather not be there despite not actually having anything else to do – but deep down he wanted to be present among his kin, to wait and go with them to the wedding, and for that to never end.

The opening bars had barely started when he shouted out, 'Michael Jackson!'

Everyone turned towards him. The music continued, and indeed, within ten seconds everyone had recognized 'I'll Be There'.

'Wow,' Kamelia offered. 'Krimo one, everyone else nil.'

Luna wasn't very happy with this turn of events. She deliberately chose a song he would have no chance of knowing. A minute passed and still no one recognized it – except Kamelia, who whispered the answer in Miriam's ear. They applauded loudly.

Miriam screwed up her pretty face and twisted her wrists while hiding behind Fouad. 'Come on, next song!'

Luna thought for a moment, deciding to prove that she could be not only the mistress of ceremonies but also a person of taste.

But once again, three notes were enough for Krim.

'Drake.'

In the following round:

'Kanye West, of course.'

And then finally:

'Jay-Z.'

At which point Luna changed her strategy and wracked her brains to find French songs that were so obvious it would be purely a question of speed. The tension in the game gradually disappeared, thanks to Johnny Hallyday and Francis Cabrel, who made you feel more like singing along than moving on to the next song.

Krim, understanding he'd won anyway, decided to let the others sing, even if everyone seemed genuinely delighted that his fifteen minutes of fame hadn't been marred by a single hesitation.

In the other room, the Elders took advantage of Fouad's absence to talk about his older brother. The fact that he wasn't there was regrettable, but you had to acknowledge that Nazir had been very helpful when, a year and a half earlier, he'd returned from a long trip abroad to live with his mother.

'Ah, yes, yes,' said an uncle, who had placed himself in the centre, 'what he did with the Muslim graves of Côte Chaude and Crêt de Roch was really good, *wallah*. And he was fearless, he went to the cemetery services, the town hall, he spoke to them, I swear, you would have thought he was a politician!'

'That's for sure,' Dounia agreed, 'he's fearless.'

The very mention of Nazir often created that sort of silence in the family, a silence that rose in the brain like a black tide and made you roll your tongue seven times in your mouth before speaking.

Rabia rolled hers just twice before giving her opinion on the issue. 'No, and the truth is it's good a thing, what he did for Chakib. No, you have to admit, he didn't have to and he's the only one who . . . I mean it's true!'

Chakib's father, Moussa, was the only of Granny's sons who'd decided, thirty years earlier, to go off and live in Algeria, in Bejaia, where Chakib came of age with no prospects of work. Nazir had managed to bring him to France by finding him a French woman to marry. No one dared say much about her after her photo was passed around; she came from the back of beyond and looked like Droopy, while Chakib was a postcard Kabyle, with light ginger hair, beautiful green eyes, and the sun-kissed skin of a young man who spent most of the time hanging around on the beach.

'The truth is, it's thanks to Nazir that I have a job.'

Everyone nodded gravely at Toufik's remark. If Dounia hadn't been in the room, they could have let loose and talked about the scandal, namely that Nazir wasn't even coming to his little brother's wedding.

Instead, Toufik recounted how Nazir had managed to get a meeting with the mayor by waiting outside his office for three hours.

Fouad, opening the door and hearing his brother being talked about, prepared to return to the surprise party in the bedroom when he saw Mathieu, Rachida's husband, gesturing to him. He manouevred them into the corridor, where they chatted about

Bruce Springsteen and Chaouch's economic programme. Fouad liked Mathieu, the whole family liked Mathieu – they just felt bad about having burdened him with the insoluble problem that was his wife. They had two children now, two beautiful mixed-race children with already sad eyes, so it was now out of the question to advise Mathieu to do the only thing that could be in his interest: to take to the hills.

Just as he was declaring himself in favour of an increased dose of protectionism (he himself, as a skilled worker, had been the victim of unbridled globalization when his business had been outsourced to Shanghai), Rachida wandered over to their little corner of shadow and stood before them, expecting to be invited to join their confab. To avoid the inevitable ire that came from looking at her, Fouad just greeted his aunt with an affable smile and focused more exclusively on her young husband. He had round eyes, thin brows, and that panic-stricken but firm look that clarinettists display when they work through a passage full of high notes. In fact, he looked more like a clarinet than a clarinettist, with his long thin neck and narrow face, spotted with acne and shining with a fine film of sweat, particularly when his eyes lit up as now with pedagogical passion:

'I'll put it this way, that's the problem: why do all the other countries of the world have the right to protect themselves while we let ourselves get screwed?'

'Ah, you're still talking all that rubbish,' Rachida said. 'I'm going, all that stuff pisses me off. And while we're at it, when are we going to the wedding?'

Slim, who had been with the old relatives from the start, came and joined their little group.

'Would anyone like some tea?'

'Slim, are we going to the centre soon?'

'Granny said in fifteen minutes. There's no point arriving before she's there. But I've got to go and prepare the hall a bit and check that everything's ready.'

'Anyway, bravo, Slim,' Mathieu said, patting his shoulder. 'She's very pretty, and she looks like a nice girl, and serious as well.'

Slim thanked him warmly while Rachida began to sulk, hoping to be noticed and asked to explain her mood change. Everything about her was round: round back, round lips, and round eyes that were always on the edge of pity but now shined with a malicious gleam.

'So, Fouad, as soon as we start talking about Nazir you leave the room?'

'Rach, stop it.'

But Mathieu had no authority over her.

'What do you think, that I didn't see you? I see everything. I say nothing, but I see everything.'

'Well, Auntie, I'm sorry to disappoint you but I was in the other room, and I didn't know you were talking about him.'

'You see, you don't even want to say his name!'

'Ha, ha,' Fouad said, unsmiling.

'Come on, say it.'

'What?'

'Your brother's name!'

'But why would I say it?'

'Nazir. Na-zir. He's your brother, after all! Friends come and go, but family ... That's what they say, right? And what's more, he came here two, three years ago, *pshhhhhh*, you should see all he did! Oh yes ... And all on his own as well: he gave cash to everyone, he found work for Toufik, didn't he? I know it's off limits to say it, but you know what, I don't give a hoot about taboos: he even went on a crusade to make the Muslim graveyards bigger. I swear he was a benefactor of mankind, on Granny's life, a true revolutionary!'

'An armchair revolutionary, yes.'

Mathieu was nearly breathless. Then he did in front of Fouad what he'd never dared do in front of anyone: he took his wife by the arm and led her into another room to have it out with her. Rachida was so surprised that she didn't know how to react; her only attempt to protest was extinguished by a severe look from her husband, who was sick of being a wet blanket.

'Hey, let me go,' she whispered loudly. 'Let me go!'

Fouad and Slim remained side by side without hazarding a word to each other. Slim noticed that his big brother's fists and jaws were clenched. But a moment later he was walking towards the living room, making them all fall about with laughter:

'Seniors, I hope you're having as much fun here as they are in that bedroom!'

Before leaving the house, someone managed to persuade Granny to play a home video on her flatscreen. Toufik had to adjust the wiring so the old camcorder could read the VHS tape she'd just found by chance in the bookcase. The setup devised by Toufik – it was his trade, after all – worked perfectly, and all the adults saw Krim appear on the screen, as a child of maybe nine years old, filmed by the late granddad while practising on the keyboard he'd just been given for Christmas.

At first unaware of his audience, he was playing Grieg's 'In the Hall of the Mountain King' from memory, retrieving the notes on his own and having to start again only once, when his left hand failed to hit a bass chord sequence in a dramatic enough manner. When he resumed his playing, intending to apply his left hand more deftly and add some trills, he noticed Granddad's camcorder and hid his eyes with his forearms, smiling, revealing a little boy's shiny mouth from which two front teeth were missing.

'He's too cute,' Kamelia cooed. 'A little Mozart.'

'He's always been shy,' Dounia added, creasing her eyes to fight back the tears, probably moved by her own father's voice.

The adult Krim entered into the family's view, to the right of the TV. The contrast was striking, between the little Mozart bent over the keyboard and the problem teenager with a severely shaved head and a drooping, bellicose bottom lip.

The famous music by Grieg, or rather the wrong notes, had caught his attention. The aunts made a big fuss over him, and his cousin Kamelia moved onto the arm of her chair so he could come and sit next to her, but Krim preferred to remain standing.

On the screen, Granddad, with his warm and gentle voice, managed to persuade his favourite grandson to play something *for the camera*. The scene took place in the living room of the flat where he had been born and raised. A young Rabia could be seen preparing meatballs and, very briefly, her husband appeared reading *Paris-Turf*, the racing sheet, while Luna endured his teasing. She was the most precious thing in Krim's life back then, both mascot and living toy, an agile and explosive little creature whose every funny face, every remark, the slightest cartwheel, the smallest burp, made headlines in that magical newsreel that had been their happy childhood.

While child-Krim struggled away at the keyboard on screen, Rabia, eleven years later, made coffee in the kitchen. Losing herself in the shimmering green earthenware, she pinched her lips and shook her head to keep from crying.

Granny came in. 'No, no, no, why are you making coffee? We're about to leave!'

Krim retreated into the bathroom so that he didn't have to listen to himself massacring Mozart's *Sonata facile*. He locked the door and looked at himself in the three-way mirror on the Formica cupboard above the sink. The wings could be folded like those of a church altarpiece, and Krim enjoyed looking at these other Krims: in profile, in three quarter profile, one quarter profile, all of them more ugly and ridiculous than the last; they had secretly coexisted for years with his normal face, which all of a sudden he no longer seemed to know.

His mother had always told him, with ever so slightly contemptuous tenderness, that he had a 'really small HC', like all Algerians. HC meant Head Circumference, and was one of those medical terms she habitually used, as if she were talking about his nose, foot or forearm.

Krim opened his mouth, pretended to vomit, studied his little Adam's apple and the annoying mole that jutted out ironically between his collarbones. He tried to adopt a serious pose, the look of someone you don't mess with. But his squashed cheekbones, his temples and his smooth cheeks, his feminine jaw and his rounded upper lip – all proclaimed that he was a child, a little Arab of which there are millions, who couldn't even stand his own stare in the mirror for more than ten seconds.

* * *

'Ferhat with his fur hat, we've all told him but he doesn't want to take it off. You want to know what I think? I think it's miserable being old . . .'

The wind was blowing harder and harder, roaring powerfully through the car park. No one could have imagined that morning that it would rain, and yet it was now the most probable scenario. By chance Krim found himself in Dounia's car, with his mother in the front seat and him in the back next to Fouad. Dounia put on a CD by Lounès Matoub, and Krim, who was feeling confident thanks to Fouad's presence at his side, asked his aunt if she didn't by chance have any Ait Menguellet.

'You know Ait Menguellet?'

Krim blushed with pleasure. His lips smiled all by themselves and his efforts to control them only betrayed his vanity. Fouad, who had understood everything, affectionately rubbed his head. Krim felt he was turning into a child again.

Dounia rummaged in the glove compartment while Rabia sought her son's face in the rear-view mirror, in vain.

'What does this song mean?'

Ait Menguellet was singing a cappella or almost (a mandolin played a few notes of accompaniment in arpeggio). The piece was called '*Nnekini s warrac n lzayer*'.

Aunt Dounia strained her ears, stretching her chin towards the car radio. 'Show us the CD. Uh, the title's 'We, the Children of Algeria', but . . . Rab, do you understand this? I just get a few words.'

'But it's in Kabyle, no?' Krim asked in astonishment.

'But not ours. In Bejaia, we speak the Kabyle of Little Kabylia. That's Kabyle from Big Kabylia, my dear, you'll have to ask the aunts.'

'Auntie Zoulikha?'

'Yes, or one of the uncles.'

'Uncle Ferhat?'

Dounia nodded and started to tap on the steering wheel and move her head when the mandolin began a riff. It was soon joined by *darbukas*. They'd had to wait two and a half minutes for the song to really start but Krim already felt like crying at the beauty of that language, his language, which pronounced *th* like the English did and persisted in making everything gentle, uniform, egalitarian and dignified, like a poor neighbourhood ennobled by snow and sun.

'Ah,' Dounia suddenly exclaimed, 'I understand what he means! *Zarma*, we, the children of Algeria, we're the champions of the world, but in suffering, we're the kings of misery, we're like galley slaves, you understand?'

Krim regretted having asked the meaning of the words.

'That said,' Dounia added, 'if we're going to be losers, we should at least be the kings of the losers. *Wallah.*'

'Auntie, has someone cut off your tongue?' Fouad suddenly asked, concerned. 'It's the first time you've been silent for more than a minute!'

'I'm a bit knackered,' Rabia lied.

She turned to her nephew and made him get up in the car to kiss his forehead.

Krim had lowered his head so as not to meet his mother's eyes. He noticed that Fouad's loafers were shining and remembered that he had promised him a private conversation. A terrible thought suddenly weighed on him: what if Fouad was one of those people who made all kinds of promises but ended up never doing anything? Maybe he just pretended to love them all; after all, it was his job to play roles.

He discreetly diverted his gaze towards his big cousin, who was wearing a sort of cool half-smile as the car, which had just climbed a steep slope, descended almost immediately towards Montreynaud. The ease of the descent was comparable to that of a plane before landing. The night smelled of the warm leather interior, from which Krim and his older cousin looked out at the same thing, the city lights spread out below, red, yellow, plural and infinite.

Suddenly Fouad's face came to life, and it was like a revelation: he was thinking the same thing as Krim; it was obvious that he, too, loved this urban night and its promises as happy as happiness itself.

It wasn't possible to fake such happiness.

The exultant Krim couldn't help tapping his cousin affectionately on the knee. To which Fouad immediately replied with smiling eyes, his priceless smiling eyes that narrowed his eyelids, created tiny, kind wrinkles at the corners of his temples. They gave the impression of being in the close company of a prince, and of Fouad being one of the better people in this world – one of the kings, the knights, the bards and the prophets.

Saint-Priest-en-Jarez, 8 p.m.

'Do we get out?' Farid asked angrily as he looked at his mobile's screen.

Mouloud Benbaraka lifted his hand and gave his henchman a withering look.

'*Mezel, mezel.* The longer he waits the better.'

He poured out in three uneven shares what was left of the bottle of Ballantine's, which Fares had been sent to fetch from the boot of the BMW. He then offered the twins cigarettes, but

Farid had just quit and Fares preferred sport and good food to the decadent delights of nicotine.

'Look at me,' Benbaraka ordered, after an intimidating gulp of whisky. 'Tell me what he's asked you to do.'

'Who?'

'Who do you think? The Grand Mufti of Jerusalem.'

Fares was dumbfounded. Nazir must have told him twenty times over the past two days that the mission he'd been given wasn't to be confided to anyone, not even his own brother. And it had taken Benbaraka's one moment of intuition, followed by a hardly insistent look, for all his resolution to waver.

He suddenly had an idea. 'No but, it's got nothing to do with the business.'

Farid frowned.

'Well then, answer the fucking question!'

'No but, well, it's nothing, he asked me to go and get a car and I have to take it to Paris.'

Benbaraka crossed and uncrossed his legs beneath the transparent table.

'And he's paying you for that? How much?'

Fares seemed lost in his thoughts. Benbaraka snapped his fingers several times under his nose. But it was an umpteenth scream from their prisoner that drew him from the strange melancholy the boss's question had plunged him into. An honest reply to that question was even more dispiriting: he didn't know how much Nazir was going to pay him, since there hadn't, in truth, ever been question of payment.

On the floor below, Zoran continued to toy with the idea of escape. Despite all his efforts, he hadn't been able to pick the lamp back up. He'd climbed onto the desk and bent his knees in an untenable position so as not to bang his head against the ceiling. The river rat moved about constantly in the dark. Zoran had got used to it, slightly, but not enough to let him make out what was essential: the distance between door and beast.

The river rat suddenly struck one of the legs of the folding bed. Zoran concluded that it was at the other end of the room. He climbed down from the desk and felt a key under his foot. After picking it up he pushed the door as silently as possible and froze, imagining that his jailers awaited him in the staircase and were about to jump on him.

But there was no one in the staircase: the boss's metallic voice asked questions; one of the twins replied. There was no sign of the other one.

Zoran tiptoed to the room at the back, the one that the twins had been unable to open. He slid the key in the lock and was relieved that the discussion was continuing uninterrupted upstairs.

His hands were trembling like they'd never trembled before when he opened the window overlooking a piece of unkempt lawn. He stepped over the windowsill and felt the cool evening wind on his face, puffy with tears. Instead of running across the lawn, he climbed the low wall separating this property from the one next door and found himself in another garden.

Less than a minute later he was at the riverside, a few metres from the road. Two cars passed, and Zoran burst into tears at the memory of the river rat. A discharge of shivers paralysed him there. It was as if the odour of the beast and its monstrous presence had deposited a nightmarish dust on his skin, which he would never be able to brush off.

The planks of wood that formed the pavement had rotted since the winter thaw, exuding a smell that Zoran associated with the violence of things, the hardness of life, of nature herself, in so much as she was merciless and did not care about us; a baby abandoned in a basket stood a greater chance of perishing against the rocks, drowned in the icy water and devoured by water rats, than of being found by a she-wolf with bronze eyes who would raise it like her own.

Instead of regaining the road and searching for help, he crouched down to pass under the bridge and continue along the Furan, which he'd decided obstinately to follow, far from men and streetlights, to thwart the predictions his pursuers would not fail to make. At the first turn in the river, the bank became a negotiable path lined with pine trees, which zigzagged for two hundred metres before disappearing near a small hill covered in brush. Zoran climbed it while taking care to remain hidden, and it was then that he saw in the distance the infamous Tower of Montreynaud, topped as he remembered by that colossal bowl dripping with the bloody sunset.

6

The Party

Community Centre, 8.30 p.m.

When they entered the hall, the Nerrouche family was
greeted like all the guests by the unavoidable mother of
the bride. She led them over to the three tables that had been
reserved for them, but there was a problem: these three tables
were right at the back, away from the stage. Granny took the
initiative and addressed the mistress of ceremonies in Arabic, in
her language and without an accent.

'Why are you putting us here, away from everyone? We're
the family of the groom, why are you treating us like stray dogs?'

The bride's mother shook her jewellery while pointing to
the tables near the stage. They were occupied by a group of
young men in suits; since the music was too loud over there,
the decision had been taken to place the important families as
far as possible from the speakers. Granny didn't buy this and
wanted to discuss the matter further, but was cut short by the
open palm of the bride's mother, who was speaking into the

mouthpiece of her hands-free phone. She excused herself with an obvious hypocritical smile and ran off to welcome some new guests.

When the whole family was settled at three rectangular tables joined together, Toufik noticed they would have to serve themselves if they wanted to drink or eat anything. He signalled to Raouf and Kamelia, and the three cousins made for the buffet where a spread of sweets, non-alcoholic drinks and Maghrebian pastries were laid out on silver trays.

The main hall had a dome-shaped roof, amplifying a sound system that was already too loud for Uncle Ferhat, who plugged his ears discreetly as soon as he wasn't spoken to. The neon lights illuminating the still-sparse dance floor were enhanced with projectors of all sorts of colours. A glitter ball hung above the stage, which housed four enormous speakers and a complex mixing board managed by the DJ Raouf had spoken to earlier in the afternoon. There was also a mic stand, which stood unused until the bride's mother climbed onto the platform to ask the DJ to turn the sound down.

'Please, please!'

The hall was completely full, now that the Nerrouche tribe had taken its place at the back. Toufik nudged Raouf and nodded towards Kamelia, who was being chatted up by a pretty boy with a gold necklace.

'Oh, wait, I have to go,' the boy suddenly said.

Kamelia replied by flapping the fingers of her left hand with a studied, effective nonchalance.

'Who's that?' asked a worried Toufik.

'None of your business.' Then, realizing she'd offended him: 'The bride's brother, Yacine. Not bad, eh?'

A few moments later the lights went out. It was already difficult for Dounia and Rabia to squeeze through to see the procession pass, and they didn't even try to make room for their alarmed sisters. A few people stood on their chairs, while others didn't hesitate to jostle and crush toes to get through the crowd.

The double throne was held up by eight men, including Yacine, who winked at Kamelia when he passed her. Kamelia was taken aback, not by Yacine's courtly audacity, but by the vision of this throne carried at shoulder height like a coffin.

The bride and groom made their entrance from the room where the bride would have to change dresses half a dozen times over the course of the evening. Slim forced a smile worthy of the Queen of England, which he could manage only on the bottom half of his face, the other half simply paralysed by fear. The bride, though more relaxed, was not quite at ease either. Her Algerian dress was embroidered with so many colours, not a single one could be identified.

Behind them the bride's mother could be heard having a go at the DJ for taking too long to start the music. When the sound finally made the walls and Uncle Ferhat's temples shake, the tsarina of the reception directed the procession personally, receiving the outstretched hands in congratulations and the ululations as if they were addressed only to her.

Suddenly she looked up towards Slim and was aghast: the groom wasn't dancing! She almost climbed onto Yacine's head to attract Slim's attention, and screamed into his ear when he had finally bent in half to hear her.

'You have to dance! Dance, Slim! Move! Move your head, your hands! Come on, come on!' She mimed disjointed undulations that made all the hardware around her wrists tinkle.

Slim made an effort but the result was pathetic: eyes half-closed and face screwed up, turning his head from right to left with his little clenched fists raised up, he looked like a guy setting foot in a nightclub for the first time – or more precisely, given the trajectory of his swinging shoulders, he looked like a *girl* setting foot in a nightclub for the first time, burdened with the obligation to act hot. He must have finally realized this, for he suddenly stopped wiggling his hips in order to adopt a more manly movement, which was, it seemed, universally considered to pass for dancing: hands lifted as if for prayer, then brought back down, again and again in time.

It was soon decided that the procession had lasted long enough. The DJ, observing everything on tiptoe, segued into a softer segment, a recent R&B track that managed to engage everyone. The operation that followed had been rehearsed the day before, but it wasn't any less perilous: it involved separating the two thrones in the air and parodying a temporary breakup. Maybe its purpose was to conjure such a thing away, or perhaps it was just done to take advantage of the mechanical peculiarity of this detachable double throne.

The bride was brought in again, this time by four men hoisting her atop a sort of Arabian Nights altar, which her throne had no problem fitting onto. The groom joined her, to the cheers of the crowd. Their two thrones were then arranged to offer a clear route to the dance floor. Behind a screen pierced with gilded *mashrabiyas*, a direct passageway would allow the bride to retreat to the changing room without difficulty.

A gong was struck and the DJ turned down the sound. A dozen

men in waiter's uniforms stood in the small passageway cleared for them in front of the stage. They carried silver platters with lids they lifted in tandem.

Had they been ordered to adopt such a dramatic appearance? With their shiny shoes, their narrow black ties and their inscrutable faces they looked like Dracula's lieutenants, impatient to show off their massive fangs. Instead they waited, slightly unsure of themselves, for the hundred guests to disperse so that they could serve the hors d'oeuvres.

Krim had shadowed Fouad throughout the procession – had even gone as far as applauding and whistling when Slim joined his beloved. When they returned to the family's tables, he jockeyed for a seat between Fouad and Kamelia. Luna noticed this and made fun of him by staring with one eyebrow arched higher than the other.

'As they say, they've gone to town on the meal!' Rabia exclaimed, calling Zoulikha as a witness. 'You okay, Zouzou?'

Rabia tried to smile, but the uneasiness was perceptible all around the table. The other guests laughed and applauded the waiters, who were obliged to start smiling, in between their complaints that the music was too loud. The windows beside them were draped in thick sheets, alternately yellow and apple green.

Krim went to the toilets, bumping against a woman in a sari. There was already a line and Krim found Raouf again, three guys ahead, screaming into his mobile while nervously slapping his belly with his free hand. Determined to avoid another interrogation from his arrogant chin, Krim hid behind the dandruffed shoulder of the man in front of him. But Raouf noticed him and relinquished his spot to come over.

'So you're avoiding me? In fact, just forget it, I've found some, seems there's a guy coming tonight who's got what I'm looking for.'

'MDMA?'

'Yeah, hush-hush, though. Thanks all the same.'

Watching Raouf elbow his way back into his place in line, Krim caught a glimpse of his sister. 'What the hell are you up to now? Aren't you sick of acting weird?'

Luna was deliberately looking around, moving her head to the beat, as if he were no more important to her than anyone else.

Krim seized her bare muscular arm. 'Come on, I've got something to ask you. No, hold on, it's serious. It's about Mum – tell me what you know.'

Luna tried unsuccessfully to tear herself from her big brother.

'It's Belkacem, isn't it?'

Belkacem was their upstairs neighbour. He had generously repainted their flat the month before.

'Uh, well, Belkacem what?'

'Mum's seeing him, is that right?'

Luna dropped her shoulders a notch and stuck her tongue out. 'Aren't you getting tired of all of this? Can't you let her live her life?'

Krim eyed her with disgust and let her leave. Clenching his fists, he suddenly noticed a small group of children kneeling behind the screen at the foot of the stage. A little girl in a pink blouse was leading the dance and distributing crayons to her pupils for the evening. When she took her turn to draw, four dimples appeared on her small studious fist and Krim felt like bursting into tears again. He rejoined the line and caught the first tingling of migraine: a crowd of shiny stains and spots that moved from left to right and right to left. Just one badly placed thought was enough to awaken the thing: it was like a panther sleeping in his brain, huddling, curled up tight in its minuscule living space beside a white-hot fire, the fire of a headache, which fed on each excessive decibel.

With the aura came several visions that dragged him away, for the tiny period they lasted, from the infernal agitation reigning in the hall. There was a memory of his summer holidays down south, of Aurélie's skin, the gentle cleavage of her young breasts sprinkled with freckles on which an indigo dolphin-shaped pendant danced. And then finally he saw, with those same mysterious eyes of the mind, the silhouette of his shrivelled mother on her bed at the end of a restless night, a band of light running along the ceiling like a steady flow of blood, and Krim was convinced that this was the end and that he had to bid her farewell.

He recounted this last vision to Nazir, who snapped back with advice that sounded more like an order: don't get distracted.

Krim decided he could hold off on pissing and returned to his plate. Well and truly alive, his mother was monopolizing the conversation as she cursed the bride's mother.

'This is just too much! And that music, it's too loud, someone has to tell them, look at poor Uncle, he has to cover his ears! I swear to you, the Oranese . . . the truth is the Oranese are a rotten lot.' Rabia threw her thick curls from one shoulder to the other, revealing the small mole on an angered vein at the base of her neck.

Krim saw some bloke at the next table wave to him. He had just recognized a song, and had rushed onto the dance floor, pointing to his own chest and waiting for Krim to react.

He continued to whisper 'Come on, come on' in his direction, joining his gestures to the words and dancing with his elbows, wrists and neck so ardently that you might have thought the end of the world was nigh. Suddenly Kamelia left the table and Krim realized that she was the one he'd been after from the start.

About ten people were now dancing to the tune of '*Sobri Sobri Sobri*'. Kamelia must have learned not to show off her bosom too much when she shook her hips, but Krim couldn't take his eyes off them: those incredible big breasts and how they transformed their owner, a little piece of flesh and blood with a social security number like everybody else, into a unique and irreplaceable goddess of fertility, of springtime, of love, of all that was most beautiful and terrible in the world.

To change the subject, Fouad mumbled a 'Hmmm' while swallowing his glass of Coke. 'That's funny,' he went on. 'I thought the song went: *chole chole chole Algerians watch out . . .*'

'Pff,' Rabia groaned, 'their Arab songs are crap . . .'

'Rabia, *sesseum*,' her big sister scolded.

'I mean it! It just isn't right. We've been hearing their songs all evening! Don't forget the groom is Kabyle. It should be half and half – half Arab songs, half Kabyle songs! That would be fair!'

'*Wallah*, she's going to get us into trouble!'

Fouad took his aunt by the shoulders before she became the scapegoat of the entire table. He kissed her cheek and invited her to dance.

'But wait, I haven't finished!'

'You can finish later!'

She let herself be pulled towards the dance floor, which was finally getting crowded. Fouad parodied flamenco while an overexcited young man with a frizzy mullet thrust himself forward with each drum beat. He was soon the centre of a small circle where people applauded, shouting 'eh-eh-eh' to the rhythm. An old woman launched into a series of ululations, and the manic dancer knew that his moment of glory was just beginning when the first notes of Cheb Mami's 'In Wonderland' rang out: 'My heart's in wonderland! My heart's in wonderland! *La la la la la, abuma djaou s'habi ou djïrana!*'

'Well, you asked for it, there's your Kabyle song!' Fouad shouted into his aunt's ear.

'Yes, but it's not the original version! It should go: *E y azwaw . . .*'

Rabia stopped talking so Fouad could appreciate the young man's incredible dancing. Fifteen people had just joined the circle around him. They watched him in astonishment, and occasionally with some irony, as he invented before their very eyes what came to be known as the head-butt dance. Indeed, he was re-enacting Zidane's World Cup head-butt against Materazzi, and his whole being glowed as he walked the tight-rope of ridicule: his long laughing face, his big bulging eyes, the curls of his sweat-soaked mullet, the way he dramatically spread his hands out wide each time he changed direction.

'Ha ha,' Rabia laughed, 'this guy is incredible!'

She was the first to imitate him. She was followed by a small group of dancers, a lot of young men and soon some children who wanted to see what all the fuss was about.

A forty-year-old woman suddenly heckled Fouad: 'Hey, I've seen you on TV! Aren't you the actor in that series, shit, what's it called? Hey, Boubouche, Boubouche, come and see!'

Boubouche was dolled up like a stolen car, probably to divert attention from her twisted nose and her heroically proportioned chin. 'Oh yeaaaah! You're right!'

'Yeah, it's him! Man of the game!'

That's when Slim appeared with his wife, surrounded by a cloud of little children all wearing grey sleeveless sweaters. 'Oh yes, it's the great actor Fouad Nerrouche! But above all, he's my brother!' He took Fouad's hand and belly-danced around the children.

It was neither the first nor, probably, the last time Slim showed an embarrassing outburst of affection. Fouad smiled calmly while Rabia went back to their table for some refreshments.

In her excitement, she remained oblivious to the others' gloom. 'Doune, come here! You've got to get up and dance a bit!'

Her good mood finally spread to Dounia, who had the bright idea of tying a scarf around her waist. Rabia grabbed it in turn, fastening it around her own waist and swaying her hips, the way she used to do at parties long ago.

'Krim! Come here! Come dance!'

Krim was slumped in the chair he'd found at the end of the table, between Zoulikha and Ferhat, whose forced smile had become a grimace. Ignoring his mother, he asked his great-uncle if he knew how to play 'We, the Children of Algeria' on his mandolin.

The old man caressed his great-nephew's cheek. '*Umbrad, umbrad*, my son.'

Later. But Krim hadn't been asking Ferhat to actually play it.

'Hellooo, anybody there? Earth calling the moon, do you copy? Krim?'

Krim looked up at his mother and stared at her furiously.

'Yeah, okay, there's no point in even asking, is there . . . Lulu darling, you want to dance?'

Luna jumped up from her chair, immediately joining Kamelia, whom she danced with for at least fifteen minutes.

'Now, who's this little princess?' Yacine asked Kamelia, undoing his tie.

His satin suit continued to gleam in the darkness of the dance floor. Kamelia murmured something in his ear and started dancing with her little cousin again. But Luna couldn't take her eyes off the handsome Yacine. He was about twenty, perhaps even younger, with sparkling eyes and a determined chin.

'Can I dance with him?'

'With Yacine? Sure thing, sweetie, go ahead, it'll give me a break!'

Luna didn't know what her cousin had meant exactly, but she wiggled around in front of Yacine anyway, while he watched the voluptuous Kamelia disappear into the distance.

Saint-Priest-en-Jarez, 9.30 p.m.

After an hour of skidding and careening through the quiet neighbourhood streets around his office, Mouloud Benbaraka slammed on the brakes, drove up onto the pavement and called for Farid's car to join him. It showed up a few minutes later, and the twins stepped out empty-handed.

'I can't believe this!' Benbaraka shouted. 'He can't have just disappeared into traffic like that!'

Farid was paralysed by his boss's anger. He stared at the ground and wiggled his toes to see if the movement showed through his leather shoes. He was about to suggest something, but Benbaraka refused to let anyone speak.

He kicked his tyre. 'Look, I've got to go to the wedding now. Do you understand? So this is what you're going to do: you're going to split up and keep looking for him. You'll

145

stay around here to check all possible paths, as far as the North Hospital, OK? And you,' he added, staring at Fares, 'look at me! You'll go into town, near place Marengo where that fucking gypsy camp was. You'll ask everyone you meet. Fuck, how hard can it be? The fucking tranny stands out like a sore thumb!'

Fares lifted his finger to say something.

'But what about the wedding? Why don't we go straight there and look for him at the wedding?'

Mouloud Benbaraka had exhausted his thin reserve of patience.

Farid took the initiative. 'Fares, how can you be so fucking stupid? If there's one place he won't go, it's the wedding! He knew we were asking him about it, he'd be going straight into the lion's den, you stupid *arioul*! As for the cars, you keep yours, and you take the other Kangoo from the office.'

'And Nazir?' ventured Farid.

Benbaraka didn't reply. He jumped into his BMW and sped off. Lighting a cigarette, he dialled Nazir's number.

A few moments later Nazir called back. Their conversation lasted about ten minutes, until Benbaraka was in the community centre car park. He was seething with rage, and hadn't even switched off the engine when he exploded, roaring into the mobile, 'But that's blackmail! How dare you ...'

One sentence from Nazir was enough to silence him, but once he'd hung up, he pounded his steering wheel, taking no notice of the hoots he sent into the void. A few people who were smoking in the car park turned around. Benbaraka rang Fares: 'Forget the Kangoo and the tranny. I just spoke to Nazir. Go home, have a rest, take a shower and do what he's asked you to do.'

He lit another cigarette and sat silently. People were filing steadily in and out of the community centre, and some were even dancing in the car park. His cousin, Kenza's mother, had called him ten times. He debated whether to put on a tie but ended up opting for an open shirt.

People recognized him as soon as he arrived on the dance floor. He greeted those he had to greet and asked where the groom's family was. His cousin pointed out a far corner and a few people dancing in the middle of the floor.

'*Zarma*, the Kabyles,' the bride's mother added with a disdainful look.

Benbaraka joined the crowd of dancers and moved in close to a woman who looked about forty. Between songs, he reached out to her. '*Mademoiselle?* Rabia?'

The woman shook her head and pointed out another woman with big dark eyes, who had tied a scarf around her waist and was laughing while fanning herself with her hand.

After spotting the small group around her and assessing the calibre of the men who might want to protect her, Mouloud Benbaraka moved towards her and whispered in her ear, 'Can I have the honour of the next dance, *mademoiselle?*'

Rabia stepped back from the gold chain that hung in the middle of Benbaraka's chest like a stolen decoration at the prow of a pirate ship. She leaned towards the intruder's ear and shouted, 'Omar? Is that you?'

Mouloud Benbaraka made a gesture with his head that could also have meant no. Not standing on ceremony, he took Rabia's hand and led her slightly off to the side. Rabia acquiesced but looked back to Fouad and the others. They were dancing a few metres away, the darkness spangled with multicoloured lights zigzagging on moving bodies and sweaty faces, with the exception of Omar's, which was parted in a wolfish smile.

Back at the table, Kamelia noticed that all the young people had left, except for Rachida, who was trying to feed her daughter, and Krim, who looked depressed.

'Krim, Krim, Krim! My little Krim, you're not dancing?'

'No, it's not my thing.'

'You okay? You're all red, you're not too hot?'

Before he could reply she turned to old Ferhat, who was on the brink of apoplexy.

'Uncle, you've got to take off your hat!'

Maybe he didn't hear, or maybe he deliberately didn't hear, but nonetheless Ferhat didn't move until his ear began to itch. He then just readjusted his *ushanka* while Zoulikha, facing the dance floor, offered polite smiles to people who couldn't see her because of her position in the darkest corner of the room.

'Come on, it's just the two of us,' Kamelia whispered. She apparently had the same inability as her mother, indeed as all the women in this damned family, to remain silent in someone's presence. 'Who's this girl, you can talk to me, you know, what are older cousins for?'

'No, but . . .'

'She's called N and what comes after?'

'No,' Krim snapped, 'she's not called N!'

'Then, what *is* she called?'

It was too much. Kamelia's breasts were quite simply too big, too round, too perfect, so he figured she wouldn't notice it if, from time to time, he glanced at them furtively. 'Aurélie. Her name is Aurélie.'

'Aurélie,' Kamelia repeated greedily. 'I'm warning you, I want to know everything about her. Absolutely everything!'

She took up the lotus position on her chair, no doubt like all the girls did at those infamous pyjama parties where they took turns sharing secrets while sucking on a Mr. Freeze.

'Have you met her? Does she live here in Saint-Etienne?'

'No, no, she lives in Paris. But I met her last summer, when I went down south.'

'Oh yeah! That's awesome! Where?'

'In Bandol.'

'And have you been going out for a long time?'

'Yeah, quite a while. It's beginning to be quite a while.'

'And a long distance relationship's not too hard? I've had enough long distance relationships, but then again, you're young.'

Krim was grasping for a reply when he felt his mobile vibrate.

'Who is it? Is it her?' Kamelia's eyes were shining.

He stood up. 'Yes, yes, it's her. Hold on . . .'

'Go on, go and talk to her, you can have some privacy.'

Krim stepped outside for the first time that evening and wondered why he hadn't done so sooner: the wind was strong and it was no longer that warm, but at least he could smoke and avoid the awkward silences and conversations.

'*Wesh*, where are you?'

Fat Momo replied that he was in the area and had something for him.

'In fifteen minutes at the gym. *Sahet*, my brother. No. Wait, not at the gym, just up from it, at that little stadium there. See you.'

149

Krim was on the way to the playing field; he saw a grocery shop with its lights on, overlooking the complex where, in addition to the community centre and the gym, there were two hard tennis courts and a discount store.

He crossed the car park, walked up the road opposite the traffic, and turned onto a street where he remembered there was an internet café. When he stepped in, a bearded man took off his headphones to point to computer 2. On computer 2 Krim launched Firefox and logged onto Facebook. He connected to his sister's account and wrote a message in the dialogue box that had popped up on Aurélie's profile, in one go, and without any spelling mistakes:

Luna: Hi Aurélie do you remember me? It's Krim. I'm on my sister's Facebook account because I don't have my own. Here's my number if you want to call me. Before tomorrow or tomorrow but no later. PLS.

After which he typed in his mobile number and waited seven minutes, seven long minutes during which the counter wouldn't stop ticking, before pressing Send.

He reached the stadium at the same time as Fat Momo, who had indeed brought a surprise: instead of the rotten dope they'd been used to lately, he'd been given some weed, some quality weed that Krim sniffed sensually, plunging his nose into the plastic bag.

'Hey come on, Leon, let's have us one.'

'*Wesh* my man,' Krim replied. His heart had not stopped racing since he'd left the internet café. 'Come on, I know a hideaway in the bushes over there.'

* * *

Dripping with sweat after a frenzied ten-minute dance with his daughter, the bride's father sat down next to Raouf and Fouad, who were busy sparring on the Socialist candidate's attitude towards national identity. Raouf approved of Chaouch's republican values – he was clearly passionate, but didn't want to overdo it. He also admired Chaouch's intransigence on the issue of secularism, and above all he valued Chaouch's 'pragmatism', a word he systematically turned to whenever he lost the thread of his argument.

The music prevented the conversation from developing harmoniously, but after thirty minutes of volleying sentence fragments over the tinny voices and bagpipes, the two cousins managed to express, for the umpteenth time, that which they held closest to their hearts, which would have united them in their division or divided them in their union, even if the argument hinged on the colour of the tablecloth – that enigmatic, distorting phenomenon they sometimes clung to as if their lives depended on it: their *opinion*.

'But anyway,' Raouf said without looking at his cousin, 'you live in a world of fantasy ten thousand kilometres away from reality. At first I, too, thought Chaouch was just that, a yuppie candidate who'd allow intellectuals to ...' – he almost said 'jerk off' but opted in extremis for convention – 'masturbate. Fortunately he's got a good team behind him, and isn't as bad at economics as the lefties who support him.'

'You saw the debate?' Fouad asked. 'When he said, "Democracy isn't when we're all equal, it's when we're all noble"? Didn't you hear that?'

'Yes and so what? That's just a slogan, who cares? It's like support from stars and intellectuals, Zidane and co. It's a load of bull.'

'Yes, I would have said the same about any other candidate. But when Chaouch poses for a photo in front of historical France with its church towers and wind farms with his slogan, "The future is now", I believe it. The future is now. He's not saying we're sick of the past – he knows very well that would annoy born-and-bred Frenchmen – so he says: what unites us is the future, and if you think that's just a slogan or PR, then we may as well stop there.'

'You only care about symbols,' Raouf complained, 'not reality.'

'Yes, but that's what a country is, an idea above all else! And symbols are reality as well. When Chaouch wants to abolish the *legion d'honneur*, for example, it's not just a symbol he wants to get rid of: it's an aberration!'

Raouf rolled his eyes the way he always did when a conversation lingered on a theme where his eloquence lacked the theoretical nails to hammer in. He moved the debate back towards his preferred ground: '*That said*,' he insisted, undoing his tie, 'we're not that far apart. In my view Chaouch is the only one capable of getting the integration machine going again. To make sure that being French is not just about a social security number and an ID card.'

'But that's precisely what it is!' Fouad cried. 'That's it! To be French means having a French ID and the rights that go with it. Full stop! National identity is a purely administrative problem. I can't believe you let yourself be taken in by all this bullshit. If that were explained to Krim, he'd stop living like some sort of exotic creature and harassing his little blonde countrymen!'

'Chaouch,' Raouf asserted, sticking out his chest to process a burp, 'is the man who'll finally get us out of this debate. It's a matter of image, it's about who he is.'

'No, I don't agree.'

'But it is. Chaouch is the one who comes along and says: I'm forty-nine, I'm handsome, I studied at the best schools, I'm charismatic and competent, I'm the mayor of a rough suburb, I'm the only French politician who can speak Chinese, I'm the party's expert on economic issues, I know what I'm talking about and I can do the job. And what's more, given that I have no foreskin and curly hair, my dear friends, fate has singled me out to rid us of the bogus civil war that my opponent and future predecessor has depicted, and we're finally going to move on to serious things. He makes nice speeches, filled with symbols, but he does it precisely so we can get away from symbols!'

Fouad was about to react when the bride's father suddenly appeared in his field of vision. He was an old man with beautiful hands and a profound expression.

'Chaouch,' he declared, pointing to the sky, 'is a great man!'

The way he'd nodded at his own words, his accent from the old country and his air of mystery – these reduced the two cousins to silence.

'Chaouch is a great man,' he repeated. 'I mean it, I'm telling you and I swear by the Koran it's true: Chaouch is a great man.'

Dounia got them out of this impasse. They nodded their heads gravely to leave a good impression and went out to smoke. Fouad felt bad about abandoning him like that: he turned around, smiling kindly at the old man, who kept pointing his finger and moving his head up and down like a prophet of doom.

* * *

153

Out in the car park, Rabia put her arms around Fouad and Raouf. She'd just escaped from Omar when he'd gone to the toilets. 'I hope you're putting the world to rights. What are you talking about?'

'Oh, this and that,' Raouf replied, drawing a puff on his cigarette.

'We're talking about national identity,' Fouad corrected, kissing his mother, Dounia, who'd just arrived.

'Ah, national identity!'

Rabia looked a little drunk. She hadn't had a drop of alcohol since her evening out the previous month with her French friends, but the dancing, the music and the crowd had made her cheeks red, and she wanted to have a conversation with some interesting and amenable young people during which she'd inevitably say more than she'd planned. Happy to find some familiar faces, she set the cat among the pigeons. 'You're another generation, you'll succeed in life. We're finished.'

Everyone protested, except Fouad who gave her a tender, earnest look.

'We don't belong anywhere. Over there we're not at home, and over here we're not at home! Where is home?'

'Oh Auntie, you're going too far,' Raouf whispered without looking at her.

'How is this going too far? You didn't live through all that, but in the seventies, *the seventies*, we had to stand up in the bus and give our seats to the French!'

'Ha, ha, you've seen *Malcolm X* too many times,' Raouf laughed.

Rabia frowned and threw her arms about in protest. 'I've seen *Malcolm X* too many times? I've seen *Malcolm X* too many times? It wasn't that different, my boy. You know what happened to all the Arab girls at school? They were sent to vocational training! Eh, you didn't know that, did you? I've seen *Malcolm X* too many times, well, I swear ... Your mother,' she exclaimed, pointing at Fouad. 'On Granny's life, Dounia was better than all the French girls at school. I remember, the teachers saw it, she got straight As. In French, in maths, everything! And you know what happened? Like everyone, oh yeah, like all the Arabs: sent to vocational training at Eugène Sue! Vocational training the ... *Zarma*, you're going to learn a trade to help your parents. But not a doctor, teacher, lawyer trade, of course. Oh, no ...'

'Yes, but that's all changed now,' Raouf said to calm things down. 'Now almost everyone gets their baccalaureate.'

'And then look,' Fouad said, 'look at Chaouch – for the first time, kids in the suburbs are going to think: this is possible. Someone like me can become President of France, of the French, of all the French. Maybe I'm being a bit idealistic, but ...'

Rabia conceded, pensively, that Chaouch was probably going to change things.

The youngest, Rachida, joined their little group to sow some discord. 'Hey, give it a rest. It's Chaouch this, Chaouch that. But what's that going to change? He's a politician, that's all. He's going to be elected and that's that, the poor will stay poor and the rich will get rich. I swear. The way you lot go on, you'd think Chaouch was God. *Wallah*, you're pathetic. Honestly, you're pathetic.'

'Are you voting tomorrow, Auntie?' Fouad asked.

'Me? No way!'

'I'm going to vote!' Rabia protested.

She took out her polling card, the second she'd ever owned. The first and last time she'd voted had been in 1988, for Mitterrand's re-election.

'And you, Dounia?' Rabia asked.

'My card? It's in my bag.'

'Well, that warms my heart,' Fouad commented.

'Anyway, you'd better stop believing these things,' Rachida slurred. Her mouth felt all furry, as if she'd just swallowed some medication. 'Even if he's elected, he'll be assassinated. Stop . . .'

'Nonsense,' Fouad snapped.

'Oh yeah? Look at his chief of security, who left because Chaouch *zarma* didn't want enough protection. On Granny's life they're going to assassinate him. What do you think the French are going to say? "Well, we've got an Arab president, okay, sure, why not"? Dream on.'

'Wait,' Fouad cut in. 'There's a good reason he doesn't want to be surrounded by an army all the time. He's said so himself, he wants to be close to the people, close to the crowd. He's being trusting, instead of playing on fears. That's all, and it makes sense.'

'We'll see if it makes sense when members of the National Front stick a bomb under his car.'

Rabia scowled at her little sister with disapproval and returned to the battleground on which she had something to say. 'Okay, yes, but how long did it take for this to be possible? And even now, what tells you he'll be elected? You have no clue, you're too young, your generation has had it easy, you weren't around for the attacks against the Arabs. Go ask your uncles how it was back then. No, I swear there's nothing you can do, the French are all racist at heart. They tolerate us but we're still just guests. *Wallah*, we're just guests here!'

'You sound like Puteoli,' Fouad protested gently, in reference to the editorial director of *Avernus*, an online newspaper that had brought together all the right-wing writers in the country at the height of the campaign. 'But I'm telling you, it's true. You'd think colonization wasn't in the past but happening now, you'd think we're the ones threatening France with colonization!'

'Our hair!' Rabia exclaimed, calling her locks as a witness.

'Yes,' Fouad sighed.

'When we were little we were told that we shouldn't have curly hair! Oh yeah, you don't know everything! We were told that curly hair was for lice. On TV, you never saw newscasters with curly hair, they always had straight hair!'

Dounia, who was less interested in these debates than her sister, couldn't keep herself from laughing at the last sentence. Fouad placed a kiss on her forehead.

Rabia took a phone call and launched into an excited monologue about the jewellery belonging to a woman in the neighbourhood who'd just died, about those stupid Arabs' taste for gold, and the deceased's youngest daughter's greed, who had rings and necklaces popping out of her eyes just like in a Walt Disney cartoon. A few moments after hanging up, in great sparkling form, she moved the conversation over to their late granddad, whom she claimed wasn't being spoken about enough. She had called her nephew Raouf as witness, he who had the same nervous-little-man morphology, but was good at heart all the same: 'You know what they used to call him? Alain Prost! Because he drove faaaaaast! *A vava l'aziz*, he drove so fast.'

'Yes, and not very well either,' Dounia added.

'Eh? He didn't drive very well? You mean he was a reckless driver? He'd how many accidents? Ten, twenty?'

'Ha, ha, he had two. You exaggerate so much!'

'Hold on,' Dounia interrupted, 'something's happening around the bride over there.'

Everyone turned to look. The music had stopped for the first time in at least an hour, and the crowd had gathered around the throne.

'That must be the henna,' Rabia commented, turning to her sister. 'You know that the mother's not even an Algerian. She's Moroccan!'

'*Wallah*, you sure . . .'

'On Krim's head if he dies right now! She's Moroccan; her father's the Algerian one, from Oran. And I've seen him, the poor soul made me sad. But she's Moroccan. Which explains everything.'

Dounia and Rabia disappeared into the hall to see the henna ceremony. It was applied to the bride's hand by a woman who then slid the hand several times into an enormous red glove. The two inseparable sisters returned almost immediately – there were too many people.

They never knew that what they were missing was in fact a completely different ceremony. The DJ stopped the music, and the neon lights shone again on the sweat-drenched crowd, where most of the men had taken off their jackets and opened their shirts. The bride's mother appeared on the platform, all the while sending emotional looks to her daughter's throne, reading out the list of cheques that had just been given out by the guests.

'The Boudaoud family, two hundred euros. The Zarkhoui family, three hundred euros. The Saraoui family, two hundred euros!'

The first three families had no luck, unlike the following ones who were congratulated by applause and cheers, so much so that the size of their cheques could not always be heard.

Slim was suffocating in his second suit, which had an excessively thick waistcoat. He wore the look of a condemned man whose punishment was to smile while the soles of his feet burned; with his mouth half-open, he neutralized any movement in his cheeks by keeping the corners of his lips still.

'You all right, dear?' Kenza asked him.

'Yes, yes, I'm suffocating, that's all.'

After a burst of feedback, Kenza's mother restored the microphone to the right distance and continued: 'The Naceri family, five hundred euros. And the Benbaraka family, *one thousand five hundred euros!*'

'Bravo! Bravo!'

Kenza shook her head disapprovingly.

Slim took her hand. 'Kenza, I think we have to talk,' he said, stopping three times to swallow. 'There's something, there's something I've got to . . .'

But the sentence died in his gullet. Sweat had stuck his black hair to his temples and terror prevented him from putting his thoughts in order: at the back of the hall, a little bit away from the guests who had started to dance again, Zoran, dressed in a strange, dirty outfit, was glaring right at him, completely motionless in a pool of multicoloured light.

7

We, the Children of
Algeria

Community Centre, 1 a.m.

Mouloud Benbaraka strode towards the buffet to the tune of loud applause, where he shook hands like a president on a walkabout. He was undoubtedly wearing the most expensive suit at the reception, with a shirt open at the chest to display an enormous *hamsa*. Hanging from a gleaming chain that matched its owner's golden canines, the amulet disappeared into his torso swathed in greying, curly fleece.

He observed a precise yet mysterious ritual as he made his way through the crowd. Every fourth handshake was enhanced with an impromptu visit from his other hand. When Benbaraka reached the buffet, this same second hand took the unsuspecting Toufik in a neck embrace.

Toufik thanked him profusely and began to blush.

'Why do you thank him? *Saha rebi saha!*' his mother said indignantly.

Rabia came up behind her, putting her hands on her eyes and shouting, 'Guess who?'

Her sister was not in the mood. 'Will you stop all this child's play for a bit?'

Rabia sulked and ran in Luna's direction; she was sitting at a table with the young man who'd been flirting with her. She kept her distance, seeking in her daughter's demeanour the teenager she herself had been twenty years earlier. Physically, it wasn't obvious – Luna was too athletic to look like her – but mother and daughter shared an undeniable *joie de vivre*.

While Luna poked at a bowl of melted ice cream, Yacine looked at her ironically, his fist crushed against his jaw and his right eyebrow raised. When Luna began to noisily suck up the last drops of ice cream through her pink straw, Rabia suddenly had a bad feeling – one of danger and scandal.

'Well, well, are you all avoiding me?'

Omar was standing motionless behind her. Rabia gestured to her sister who was also returning from the car park, but she didn't see her.

'No, no, not at all,' Rabia replied in a voice that couldn't help sounding childlike when she pronounced *all*.

The bride's mother appeared between them.

'You all right, Mouloud? Everything going okay?'

Rabia frowned. The bride's mother didn't even glance at her and headed back towards the throne.

'Why did she call you Mouloud?'

Benbaraka took no pleasure in playing this little game. But this woman's voice and her mysterious youthfulness excited him.

'I'm going to tell you the truth, Rabia, my name isn't Omar.'

Rabia gestured again to Dounia and was preparing to join her when Mouloud Benbaraka's hand clasped her naked wrist.

'What are you doing?' Rabia protested. 'Let go of me right now.'

'Come on, can't we fucking talk?'

'Yeah yeah, that'll teach me not to play at child's games on the internet.'

Rabia freed herself from the imposter's shackles and ran over to her sister.

Benbaraka shook his head disapprovingly and texted Nazir to explain the situation.

Dounia was listening to her nephew Raouf, who was showing off in front of his cousins:

'Yes, sure, I've seen Chaouch, several times, even. At a meeting. And at a debate in Grogny, where he's from in the suburbs, you know. But that's normal, as a young entrepreneur you have to meet people in high places.'

Toufik's unibrow arched in admiration.

'But did you speak to him?' Dounia asked, to egg Raouf on a bit.

'Of course!' her nephew replied before stopping to check his phone's screen. 'I've shaken his hand and everything. Wait, I'll show you the photos. Look, Chaouch's bodyguard took this one. And that one, see? Seriously, he's a good guy, and incredibly accessible. Honestly, he'll make a good president.'

Intimidated by his cousin's proximity to the most important man in the country, Toufik found nothing to say except, 'Don't the bodyguards have anything to do but take photos?'

Dounia saw Rabia appear in her field of vision. She looked worried, but Dounia didn't let her open her heart straight away.

'Raouf is such a show-off!' she exclaimed with a flippant wave. 'He won't stop talking about how he met Chaouch, and how he manages restaurants in London, and so on and so forth. It almost makes me want to tell him who Fouad's going out with . . . But anyway, I'm holding back, as Granny says – what does she say? Like, boasting attracts the evil eye or whatever . . . You all right, Rab? What's going on?'

Faced with her sister's good mood, Rabia decided not to say anything about her disappointment with 'Omar', aka Mouloud. Above all, she felt horribly ridiculous for falling for such a disgusting man online. How had she not anticipated such a pre-dictable letdown?

Dounia understood from her favourite sister's uneasy silence that she was hiding something, and she didn't have to deploy great powers of deduction to figure out that her virtual fling had not lived up to its promise. She took Rabia by the arm and forced herself to dance so as not to keep talking about the only subject that came to mind, namely their nephew Raouf's constant boasting.

Far from the sound and fury of the reception, Krim, stretched out in his lair, hesitated to ask Fat Momo for another favour. By now Momo had taken ten hits on the joint, and when he passed it over, voluptuously exhaling his last puff, Krim didn't even notice; he was too absorbed in the grey of the evening clouds, which he could almost hear mumbling on the sky's floor.

'*Wesh* you want the last of the joint or not?'

'It's weird all the same, *zarma.*'

163

'What?'

'They always say *zarma, zarma* it's a true marriage, *zarma* we're going to the beach, *zarma* you're doing your James Bond act. *Zarma*, they always say *zarma*. Can I ask you a favour?' he finally asked, apparently waking up.

'If it's got anything to do with Djamel, that's not my business.'

'No, no, it's not that . . . it's . . . can you give me a shotgun?'

Fat Momo stared at him, trying not to laugh.

'A shotgun, what, are you nuts? We aren't kids any more!'

'Come on, a shotgun of smoke.'

Fat Momo finally coughed out a laugh, but he wasn't stoned enough to fail to see that Krim wasn't. So he turned the joint around and placed the lit end inside his mouth. He then put his open hands around the corners of his lips, and closed them to direct his smoky breath into Krim's mouth, so close it was almost as if they were kissing.

'There you go, happy now?' Fat Momo got up and looked around. At his feet Krim was lost in his thoughts. '*Wesh*, you all right or what?'

'I really shouldn't,' Krim sighed to himself. 'It's not good for reflexes.'

'Reflexes? Dude, what are you talking about?'

Krim got up and hugged Fat Momo, who had no idea what was happening but didn't stop him.

'This is because of the girl, isn't it? The girl from down south, eh?'

Fat Momo's round eyes stayed still, and Krim imagined that his entire body moved in relation to those eyes, like in a Tahitian dance. '*Wesh*, I think it's all over with her.'

'Why?' Fat Momo was only too happy to have crossed the

threshold of the sole taboo subject between them. 'Did you guys hook up?'

'Yes, yes,' Krim lied, 'but there's another guy, a posh little twat called Tristan. They're from the same world. She lives in Paris, you see.'

Krim stopped talking, the way only he knew how: all his body stopped, and all light suddenly disappeared from his eyes.

'Hey,' ventured Fat Momo, 'see you tomorrow. And don't do any silly stuff, okay?'

'You going to vote?' Krim asked him before it was too late.

'Vote for what?'

Krim lifted his hand one last time to wave goodbye and watched his friend walk away, his hands in his pockets, shoulders slightly stooped, glancing like a spy from left to right as if to make sure he wasn't being followed. Fat Momo was walking in a bubble and would walk that way until the end of his days, but Krim was grateful that he didn't try to lock anyone else up in it.

When his best friend had left his sight and his thoughts, Krim stretched out on the bed of twigs again, massed together a few clumps of grassy earth and remembered that day the previous summer when he and Aurélie had gone boating from Bandol to the calanques of Cassis in the South.

They'd spent all morning walking along the pier in companionable silence, without any plans or obligations. She smoked Stuyvesant Lights, one after another, stubbing the ends out on the trunks of the palm trees after three or four puffs. Later on she'd had the idea of heading out to sea, so they'd decided to rent a Suzuki motorboat. The rental manager – who was himself taken with Aurélie – had given it to them without even asking to see their licences.

The sun shone high in a cloudless sky and the sea was still. At the back of the boat, Aurélie looked delighted, running her fingertips along the engine's aerodynamics, while Krim tried to concentrate on not missing any of the instructions that the young sailor reeled off in a southern accent he deliberately exaggerated for tourists.

'If you hit a snag, check under there ... nine times out of ten it's a plastic bag that's got caught in the propeller.'

The boat was white and had six seats, but there was nothing smaller. Once the eight blue bumpers had been brought inside, they were ready to go. Krim manoeuvred the boat skilfully beyond the pier and accelerated to maximum speed, on course for La Ciotat, enjoying the purr of the engine beneath his feet. Aurélie said nothing but she seemed content. The sea was 'oily', as the rental guy had repeated twenty times, and there wasn't a breath of wind to disturb the air. As they distanced themselves from the green and blue coast, the horizon shone as if caught in a rectilinear halo tinged with violet mist. Aurélie had settled in near the engine, where she was protected from the headwind, and she had put her sunglasses on to shield her eyes from the glare of the sun. They didn't utter a word until the cliff overlooking La Ciotat came into view, but as the boat passed by Les Lecques, Aurélie raised her voice to remark on the mountain of Sainte-Baume.

'What does this cliff make you think of?' she asked, taking advantage of a deceleration to change positions.

Krim replied without hesitation that it made him think of a fish. He cursed inwardly as soon as the words left his mouth; he'd meant to say a bird.

Aurélie didn't buy his slip of the tongue for a second. 'It's called the Eagle's Beak,' she explained, bursting into laughter.

The boat was soon running along the port of La Ciotat, with its long line of abandoned rusty harbours, full of enormous cranes that had been left unused for too long and taken on the sad and stupid look of historical monuments. As they passed by, continuing onward, the Eagle's Beak lost the face the young couple had first discovered in it. It became in turn the head of an old man, a foot covered in warts, and finally just a wart.

It was almost 2 p.m. by the time they reached the calanques of Cassis. The cliffs' stone, at first ochre in colour, became light grey, then totally white in places. As they approached the coast to find a suitable place to drop anchor, the cicadas' song grew more intense. Krim chose a remote-looking creek that ran along a cliff bristling with umbrella pines; Indian summer or not, the sun at its zenith wouldn't do them any favours. While he secured the boat, Aurélie unfolded the green awning and took a water bottle out of her handbag. Krim took a few sips and then decided to go for a swim.

He did a few breaststroke laps around the boat, which looked majestic from the green water. He could hear the cicadas as distinctly as if he'd been on the cliff itself. After clowning around a little on the surface, he splashed Aurélie's face and listened to her laugh. Diving down, he seemed to bring it with him underwater, as fresh and clear as the sea.

'Over there,' she said, 'is Algeria. Crazy, right? I can almost see it from here. Can't you?'

Krim creased his eyes, but saw nothing.

An hour later they decided to go back. But before lifting anchor and switching the engine back on, Aurélie put her hand on Krim's and asked him if she could tell him a secret. Krim took a seat next to her. A premonition kept Krim from beating her to it and making a silly declaration. He was rarely that inspired.

'It's about Tristan.'

Krim wanted to drown her, and went so far as visualizing the red safety wire encircling his pilot's wrist as it wrapped itself around her beautiful tanned neck. He could see her pale body and inert legs floating underwater, surrounded by fleeing fish, skirted by rays and jellyfish, and her contorted face that would never again give him false hope. And it was only half an hour later, when the harbour of Bandol was back in sight, that Krim understood that this was why she'd jumped for joy on the palm-tree-lined promenade: she was in love with him, she was in love with that damned blonde-haired boy whose father was a longtime friend of her own father.

Krim clenched his fists and looked up at the tops of the car park's chestnut trees waving about in the wind. It was no longer the masts of invisible yachts that swayed in the distance; it was a patch of heavy, tormented sky, draped with dark clouds and blocked by the slab-concrete corner of the gym. Krim closed his eyes to see only Aurélie's eyes, lost in the foam of the boat's wake, in silvery hoops sparkling under the five o'clock sun. In a voice as clear and salty as the turquoise water that licked the coves, he had called her a bitch. He'd never known if she'd heard him or if the hum of the engine had saved him.

Community Centre, 2 a.m.

Fouad was going around the room in search of Krim. When he asked his Uncle Bouzid if he'd seen him, he found a face seized by a look of disapproval that bordered on disgust: the word *irredeemable* could be read on each of his changing features.

'What's wrong, Uncle?' Fouad asked, risking offence with his tone.

'It's that guy over there,' Bouzid replied, pointing to Mouloud Benbaraka. 'That damned thug, I wonder who invited him.'

Fouad shrugged and narrowly escaped a conversation with Rachida, who was wandering like a lost soul at the foot of the stage. He dodged a few other winks and returned to the car park. He didn't have Krim's number and couldn't see himself sending a text to ask for it.

As he looked around the car park, he came across Luna, who was prodding her finger into the insistent chest of a guy who was clearly older.

'Hi, Luna, have you seen your brother by any chance?'

Luna seemed embarrassed at being seen by her cousin. She stood up on tiptoe to scan the ranks of cars. Her tiny head contrasted with her powerful neck, where two veins bulged as she pretended to look for her brother. How was such a strong neck needed to support the head of a small mouse?

The pretty boy – Fouad suddenly remembered having seen him flirting with Luna – held his hand out to him. 'Hi, I'm Yacine. I saw you on TV the other—'

'Fouad.' He shook the guy's hand and spotted Krim by the gym. 'There he is, I'll have to leave you ... and ...' Usually he would have said don't do anything silly, but here he just stared at his little cousin. 'I think your mum's looking for you.'

He jogged over to meet Krim, who was not walking in a completely straight line.

'I've been searching for you for over an hour, where were you?'

'I was walking around. Honestly, that music gives me a headache.'

'Yes, it's getting worse. And they've turned up the volume. Granny'll be losing her temper soon.'

'Oh yeah?'

'Yeah, they've been playing only Arab songs for the past hour, and each time someone from the family asks when they're going to put on a Kabyle song, the DJ says "Yes, yes it's on the playlist, two or three songs from now" . . . Anyway, have you eaten?'

'Uh, a few little things at the start.'

'But have you had a plate of chicken?'

'No. It's all right, though, I'm not hungry.'

'Okay.' Fouad cut to the heart of the matter. 'I told you earlier that I wanted us to have a little conversation. It's very serious, Krim, come with me.'

He found a bench at the far side of the gym. Two slats were missing so Fouad sat on the back, imitated by Krim, who stopped just short of mimicking his older cousin's entire posture, crossing his hands and dropping his head down.

Fouad was about to speak when Kamelia and Luna made a spectacular entrance, bringing with them all the energy of the party – strident bagpipes, inaudible conversations, marathons of elated dancing, bursts of laughter and fragments of harsh, shrill voices.

'Come on, what the hell are you guys doing there?' Kamelia railed. 'Come on, come and dance! You've got to come *now*, it's not going to last forever!'

Fouad broke into his winning smile.

'By the way, honestly, I wanted to tell you, Fouad' – Kamelia stuck her hair clip between her teeth to reset her sophisticated chignon – 'I don't know how to thank you but honestly, *wallah*, thanks.'

As she thanked him for having set her up in Paris and putting her in touch with people from the hip-hop scene, Fouad let his eyes roam over the bruises on her beautiful arms, hardened by freezes and pirouettes.

'That's what family's about,' Luna chimed in, kissing her cousin.

'Oh yeah, and you'll also thank you know who,' Kamelia added with a wink.

Fouad's open secret was buried beneath a small heap of laughter. Except for Krim who hadn't taken his eyes off his older cousin.

When the two girls had gone their way, Fouad cleared his throat and continued as if nothing had happened. 'Well, I'm not going to beat around the bush.'

'Come on, I swear I won't say anything.'

'What?'

'That you're going out with Chaouch's daughter. That's what you wanted to talk to me about, isn't it?'

'Ah, um, no. But . . . but hold on, how do you know?'

'It's no problem,' Krim replied, smiling feebly. '*Bsartek*, cousin.'

'No, but it's not that. It's . . . Fuck, so everyone knows.' Fouad suppressed his annoyance and continued, 'Slim told me he received a letter from Nazir, with instructions to pass it on to you without opening it.' As Krim didn't reply, he added, 'I don't want to piss you off, Krim, and I'm going to tell you . . . you've always been my favourite little cousin, even though I'm sad you stopped playing the piano and all, but . . . you can trust me. What's in the envelope?'

Krim got up and cracked his joints. If he rubbed hard he could feel the back of his knee through the fabric of his trousers, that bizarre area in the human body that made him think of a snake's throat. 'Honestly, Fouad, I don't think I can tell you.'

'Of course you can! Have I ever betrayed you?'

'But he told me not to talk about it, to anyone.'

'Listen, I'm going to tell you something. It's no secret that Nazir and I don't get on, but it's not just a little fight between brothers. Believe me. Slim told me you often speak on the phone, that he sends you texts, that he's even given you money . . .'

Krim was furious. 'You think that's all right, I tell Slim something, and he repeats it to everyone?'

'It's not the same, here, you've got to understand, Krim. Nazir isn't just strange, he's . . . he's mad, he's evil. I'm not joking, he's mad and even worse than that, he's dangerous, he's a dangerous madman. He's filled with hate and . . .' – he hesitated at the next word, figuring Krim most likely didn't know it – 'resentment. There are people like that, evil people, and you shouldn't let yourself . . .' It was the one phrase he'd sworn he wouldn't pronounce in the course of this conversation. The words *be influenced* were surrounded by red warning lights and, when he dropped them, Krim indeed started to get annoyed; he seethed, and stopped listening.

'But no one influences me! On the contrary, I have my own ideas, I'm not there to . . . to . . . believe just anybody, anything—'

'Hold on, hold on. Believe just anybody? I'm telling you, whatever happens . . . I don't know how to explain this. Look me in the eyes.'

Krim sulked like a little boy.

'Life is suspenseful. People put you into little pigeonholes, and you think it's definitive, that it'll be a prison, a nightmare till the end of your days, but that's not true. Whatever people might say, no one, I mean *no one knows what's going to happen next.* No one. And believe me, things usually sort themselves out, you just have to learn to free yourself... from the present... from... It's as if you'd been programmed to be someone, and your duty, your duty towards yourself is to deprogram yourself, to escape from the fatality of... And then when you lack the energy, tell yourself it's the situation that creates the energy, and not the other way round.'

Fouad knew, from the way his words sparkled and burst like bubbles around him, that he'd assumed, despite the precautions, his most beautiful and warm actor's voice, the one that coloured every last molecule of space and which had earned him so much success in good society. But Krim always heard too much and too well, and what he heard in his cousin's speech were notes that were harmonious but wrong. Another tune for the Pied Piper.

'You understand what I'm saying?'

'Yes, yes, but it's all right, there's no need to say all that, I'm not a victim either—'

'For example, the piano,' Fouad interrupted. 'You've got talent, more than that, a true gift, don't you agree?'

'But what's the point of that?'

'You hear the world! It's an exceptional stroke of luck! *You hear the whole world!* I don't hear anything, I forget a melody as soon as I hear it, but you remember all the notes! And hey, listen, a gift brings on responsibility. Like in *Spider-Man*: with great power comes great responsibility. If you don't exert that power, it's as if you'd never had it.'

Fouad had begun to look away as he developed his speech. The volume of his voice had dropped imperceptibly, as if at some point while he was talking he'd noticed the ineffectiveness of his coaching.

'Life is suspense,' he continued despite everything telling him not to. 'Think about that when you're depressed. Don't let yourself be pushed around, Krim, don't let yourself be manipulated by guys who want to make you believe everything is written down ahead of time. You've got a mother who adores you, a father, God rest his soul, who adored you as well. No, *mektoub* is for the Bedouins, it's our ancestors who believed in *mektoub* and look where that got them.'

'Where?'

'Don't even look at the old folk, just take Kamelia. Thirty-two, a stewardess, she lives at the airport, she spends her evenings in Paris and Hong Kong and she thinks a bad spell's been cast on her and her sisters! For fuck's sake. They've been cursed and all of a sudden they'll never find husbands. And they believe it! Why didn't Ines and Dalia come? Why do you think they never go to weddings?'

'But that's not *mektoub*.'

'Yes it is, look . . .'

But Krim was now only looking at one thing in the midst of Fouad's umpteenth tirade: the vague silhouette of someone who was checking something in the boot of a car less than twenty metres from their bench. Krim struggled to undo his tie and stuffed it into his pocket, still staring at the silhouette.

No longer paying attention to Fouad, he walked towards the man until he was sure it was their upstairs neighbour. On seeing him arrive, Belkacem held out his arms, smiling in that slanted way of his, both seductive and sly.

'Krim! I hadn't yet—'

He didn't have the time to finish his sentence: Krim had jumped on him and was grabbing him by the throat. Before Belkacem could get his wits back, Fouad tore Krim away, who was stuck to his target like an oyster to its rock.

'Are you crazy?! What's wrong with you?'

Krim tried several times to charge back, but Fouad got in the way. Suddenly Krim pretended to tear out his hair and put his head between his knees. He took the silver lighter out of his pocket, the one he'd stolen from Belkacem two weeks earlier, annoyed at seeing him roaming around his father's house.

'Leave her alone!' he screamed at the intruder.

'What are you talking about?' Fouad whispered to calm him down.

'You go near her again and I'll kill you!' Krim screamed again, throwing the lighter at Belkacem's face. 'Rabinouche. Pff, I'll kill you! I'll tear you to pieces!'

Fouad tried to take his cousin by the shoulder, but Krim freed himself and ran towards the community centre, where he joined the crowd of partygoers.

The music was so loud, Krim could feel it weighing on his shoulders. He could already see himself falling face down, vanquished by the Rai, his cheeks stuck to the tiled hall floor. He weaved his way between people, muttering firm, resolute excuse-me's, the excuse-me's of a man who knows where he's going. This was, of course, far from the case, and he soon had to turn back: he was about to reach Mouloud Benbaraka's prowling zone. If the boss saw him, he'd surely smash his face in, in front of his mother and the entire family. Some people might try to separate them, but no one would dare kick out the great and mighty Mouloud Benbaraka.

In his efforts to avoid him, Krim ended up in a corner of the hall he'd thought was unreachable – at the edge of the narrow corridor leading to the room where the bride got changed and the cheques and presents were hidden. Seeing that no one was watching its entrance, Krim rushed into the room and closed the door behind him.

He left the light off and used his mobile to find his way. The cash box containing the cheques wasn't even shut. Krim took the envelopes one by one, until he finally found the one from Mouloud Benbaraka. Krim slipped the fifteen hundred-euro cheque into his boxer shorts and walked out, loaded with the desire to pick a fight. If he saw Belkacem again, he told himself over and over, puffing out his chest, he'd kill him on the spot. But he didn't see Belkacem again.

He went out into the car park and managed to escape Fouad, who was chatting with a small group once again. In this group Krim soon spotted his mother, and he jumped when he saw Mouloud Benbaraka approach her. Could he have already noticed that his cheque had been stolen? Krim wanted to go over there, but was frozen by fear.

Benbaraka was speaking to Fouad and to his mother, smiling. He looked around him, as if he was looking for Krim, and mur-mured an amusing word into Rabia's ear; she pushed him away in an exaggerated shove, like a scene from a bad sitcom. After which Benbaraka walked off, caressing the shoulders of each of the small group's members, whose conversation he'd interrupted.

Krim ran towards his lair. On crossing the car park he felt like breaking a wing mirror with a kick, but he was too afraid. He was about to return to the centre to speak to his mother, to warn her against that monster Mouloud Benbaraka, when he suddenly felt tears rising. He knelt down to control them and heard the violent screech of a car skidding off just above the stadium.

Through the curtain of tears brimming at his eyelids, he heard two voices confronting one another at the foot of the goalposts, in the exact spot where he'd overheard Raouf's phone conversation that very afternoon. He walked towards them, refusing to admit that he recognized the voice that had started a pathetic explanatory tirade. And yet at the edge of the stadium, with his loafers planted in synthetic turf already damp with dew, he had to acknowledge that it was indeed Slim talking to that awful gypsy dressed as a woman.

'Slim, what's going on? What the fuck are you doing with that guy?'

'Leave it, Krim, leave it. Go back, I'm taking care of this.'

Zoran addressed Krim with an inscrutable gesture and a phrase in Romanian, then put his arm round Slim's shoulder.

Slim shook himself from this embrace and turned to the goalpost, as if he was about to throw up.

'Come on, Slim, tell me what's going on. Who is this guy?'

'He's nobody, it's nothing.'

Zoran intervened. 'He to give money me. He to give thousand euros.' Detecting the twitch of Krim's upper lip – he was now just a couple of metres away – he widened his stance.

'Slim, why does he say you owe him money?'

Slim could no longer speak. His throat could be heard twisting and resisting the appeal from his stomach. The nausea shook him relentlessly.

'I had fuck with him,' Zoran murmured, defiant.

Disgusted, Krim turned to this interloper and took in the sight of him – the English flag on his t-shirt, sparkling under the cruel moon of the streetlight – and punched him in the chest.

'I had fuck with Slim, I had fuck with him!'

Zoran let himself be dragged towards the mini-clearing, where Krim's glare immobilized him no doubt more effectively than his shaky headlock.

'Who is he?' Krim screamed. 'Who sent you?'

Zoran was too terrified to reply. Through a superhuman effort he managed to push Krim aside, though in truth he probably wasn't that much weaker than his opponent.

'Slim, Slim, I had fuck with Slim! Not marriage, not marriage, he faggot!'

There were a few moments of clumsy wrestling in which Krim had to pull Zoran's hair to release his jaws from his wrist. He looked at the wounds the dirty teeth had left on his skin. There were also traces of make-up, but it was the thought that this creature's saliva had been in contact with his skin that drove him mad. He clenched his fists like Fat Momo had taught him to do in full-contact. And he brought them down one after the other, and more and more quickly, on the face of this thing of undefined sex. In the distance he saw Slim collapsed against the goalpost at the foot of the streetlight, shiny traces of vomit at the corner of his lips. Krim had never fought in these conditions. Usually he had to bring down the opponent, master him, throw some punches, kicks, put up a struggle. For the first time ever, he met with no resistance, none except for that one phrase repeated obstinately between tears:

'I had fuck with Slim, I had fuck with Slim.'

Krim inflicted blow after blow methodically, without ever

178

thinking of switching technique, even though his bloodied fists were in more and more pain. The other guy had stopped crying for a few moments when Krim decided that he'd punished him enough.

He grabbed his head by his shoulder-length hair and crushed it against the mounds of earth he'd lovingly gathered an hour before. He gave him one last kick in the ribs, a second last kick in the back, then ran and threw up in front of the changing room doors.

One of the twins – Farid – appeared in the darkness across the stadium. On seeing him Slim dashed off towards the gym. Farid pursued him and noticed Zoran's inanimate body in the bushes. He approached on tiptoe, as if afraid of waking a ghost. Anonymous reflections danced from one pool of blood to the other on that motionless head lying in the unkempt grass.

Farid grumbled and continued on his way. Zoran regained consciousness a few seconds later. It took him more than a minute to remember what had happened. And in that aching yet serene interval, all the strange, dazed awakenings that had punctuated his life in exile passed by in single file: freezing hotel rooms, inhospitable floors, sofas too small, then the tents, the trailer berths, the back seats of smoke-filled cars, and the naked ground, the violent earth and especially the concrete, concrete worn down by decades of moisture that it was sick of absorbing. It warped around him, as clumsy and as brown as a pernicious living thing.

Zoran smelled the grass and felt the pain in his face. He got back up and stumbled towards the stadium lights, and then far from them, and then farther from the other lights, as far from them as possible.

Farid thought he heard something beside him move but then noticed a stooped silhouette a little way beyond the gym: a young bloke throwing up into a green rubbish bin. After about ten seconds Krim tore his head from the waste bin and shot Farid a long stare that was wild, yellow and chilling.

Farid rushed back to his car. He tore out of the car park, failing to prevent his tyres from screeching: a few guests smoking at the entrance to the community centre turned around and insulted him, and some man even threw a drinks can in his direction. Two streets down, a police car went off in his pursuit. He had nothing to fear, his papers were in order. Zoran might not be dead and if his fingerprints were on the body, that meant nothing, because the forensic police would never be called in for a dead Romanian tranny. But the panic, the fatigue, the stress scrambled his ideas as much as his vision. The street was one-way and Farid had about five hundred metres to make up his mind. He wearily punched the steering wheel and accelerated. The police car caught up with him five minutes later, soon joined by two others. Farid had just enough time to send Fares a text that included the words 'police', 'all on my own now', 'leave quickly' and 'don't call me'. He switched off his mobile, hid it under his seat and got out with his hands up. Half a dozen police fell upon him.

It was four in the morning and the reception was in full swing. The DJ now only played hip-hop and electro: it was the young people's turn to dance and he had transformed the ballroom into a real nightclub. Standing in front of the buffet, Bouzid told Kamelia how Rachid the butcher had humiliated him earlier in the afternoon.

'But I've always told Granny, it's not right to read the cards, it's *haram*, but she just doesn't care. And now look, afterwards, who pays for it? Us, we've got a bad reputation in all of Saint-Etienne, *l'archoum*!'

Kamelia had a hard time containing the rhythmic pulse in her hips. Two overzealous men danced right into them. Bouzid took it upon himself not to make a fuss, but Kamelia could tell that one nudge would be enough for his bald pressure-cooker forehead to explode.

They both spied old Uncle Ferhat passing behind the buffet, almost hugging the wall trying to get to the toilets. Kamelia wanted to help him, but to do so would require going around the tables and Bouzid would no doubt have taken offence if she'd suddenly stopped listening to him. She watched the sickly, stooped old man make his way with difficulty between the ragged dancers who almost all, by now, had the half-closed eyes of sleepwalkers.

What she didn't see was that, instead of going to the toilets, Ferhat passed behind the stage, right next to the deafening amplifiers, and stood in front of the DJ waiting to be noticed. The toothy DJ turned towards this surreal apparition and asked what he wanted with a nod. Ferhat took a cassette tape from his jacket pocket and presented it to the young man.

'What. . . But I can't play cassettes, sir!'

Old Ferhat seemed not to understand. He bowed a little and shook the tape. He looked as innocent as a little boy, and the DJ couldn't refuse him.

'What track do you want?'

'*Ruh ruh*, go on, play the cassette.'

'Yes, yes I'll put it on, but which track?' He tried to say it in Arabic (*ashral?*) but Ferhat replied in Kabyle:

'*Nnekini s warrac n lzayer.*'

'I don't understand Kabyle, I don't understand.'

'Four, number four.'

While Ferhat hobbled away, the DJ rifled through the CDs he'd been given to see if there was something by Ait Menguellet. He decided to do a good deed for the poor old man and looked online.

Krim had gone to clean himself up at the fountain on the other side of the stadium. He walked in front of the cars asleep in the car park and caught sight of another wing mirror asking for a kick. But his legs hurt and it worried him to hear his heart pounding in all the veins of his head. An Algerian flag was attached to the mirror he'd wanted to vandalize: it was the car of an old uncle who was actually sleeping in the front passenger seat. He had put the seat back as far as possible, but his head moved uncomfortably.

Krim entered the hall again to the sound of partygoers complaining because of a too-lengthy interruption in the music. Suddenly the first mandolin notes of 'We, the Children of Algeria' echoed in the hall. Krim's heart fluttered: it was as if all the projectors had been pointed at his soul.

The crowd had stopped dancing, stunned. People exchanged sarcastic looks. Krim came and sat down next to his Aunt Zoulikha, who was studying him with her piercing eyes high-lighted with kohl. His grey suit was torn at the sleeves and his jacket, though buttoned, failed to conceal a bloodstain on his shirt's front pocket.

Aunt Zoulikha put her hand on Krim's clenched fist and

brought it towards her to give it a noisy kiss. She then searched her blouse for a ring, which she slipped on her great-nephew's finger. It was his father's ring, the one that his mother had wanted Krim to keep after his death.

'You'd lost it under the table, my son.'

Krim saw that she was holding Ferhat's snuff box in her other hand. She was the lost property fairy, Aunt Zoulikha. He got up and went to the toilets, noticing along the way that the Kabyle ditty was beginning to annoy the guests.

'*Wallah* – what is this, a wedding or a funeral?'

There were even a few whistles, but Krim stopped himself from looking at any one of these particular savages, for fear of losing what was left of his composure.

At the same moment, Bouzid had stopped talking to listen to Ait Menguellet and his smooth accent, that perfect Kabyle he would never speak half as well as the singer. Suddenly he noticed a pair of hands groping Kamelia's breasts from behind. Kamelia turned around and threw her glass of Coke at the man who'd dared touch her. Bouzid pushed his niece aside and landed a first punch on the guy's face. The groper's companions jumped on Bouzid, whose rage easily conquered the two boys. He kept hold of the one who'd disrespected Kamelia, engaging him in a full-on fight. They were tearing at each other's clothes, screaming before the horrified eyes of the women who yelled for them to stop.

The jostling that followed propelled itself like a wave and finally engulfed Ferhat, who fell to the ground and lost his *ushanka*. Fouad and Raouf, who had run up to see what was happening, helped their old uncle back to his feet. They didn't see at first what he had on his scalp and therefore didn't understand why a woman had fainted on looking down at their great-uncle. The only surprise for them was that he no longer had any hair. How many times had they exalted the curly mane that aroused the jealousy of every uncle and brother-in-law bald by the age of thirty?

Raouf picked up the *ushanka* and offered it to Fouad, who refused it with trembling hands. On Ferhat's shaven head had been drawn, in indelible ink, two swastikas, one of which was in the wrong direction. Just at the nape of his neck they'd added a circumcised cock with a fat pair of hairy balls.

The music had stopped and the bride's mother tried to make some space around the profaned old man. Krim slipped through the crowd and stood motionless before his uncle's vanquished body.

Fouad took charge, put the *ushanka* back on Ferhat's head and helped him towards the exit. There was talk of going to the police straight away. Krim wanted to take Ferhat's other shoulder, but Fouad looked at him darkly.

'Krim, this is not the right time!'

Krim stood dumbfounded in the midst of the disaster. The sweat-drenched crowd looked at him as if it was all his fault. Someone had the bad idea of filming the passageway cleared for Fouad and Ferhat. The image was eminently cinematic, but Krim didn't care: he snatched the digital camera from the young man's hands and threw it onto the floor.

There was more unrest a few metres from there: Aunt Zoulikha had just passed out on hearing the news. While the other aunts rushed over to her, Krim noticed Mouloud Benbaraka's motionless face observing him from the stage, just heads away. From afar, Benbaraka seemed to have two glass eyes.

He finally nodded towards Krim and made, with his extended index finger, the same cutthroat gesture Luna had given him a little earlier in the day.

L'Eternité Neighbourhood, 4.20 a.m.

Krim ran towards the car park. He sprinted his way back up the bend and then along the road that descended towards the former industrial park, now pompously renamed a high-tech business zone. By the time he slowed down to catch his breath, he was on the verge of tears. So he ran even faster, through the residential areas and the already outdated futuristic buildings that sprouted like mushrooms throughout these former industrial sites. Half an hour later he was in front of 16 rue de l'Eternité. He vomited again and ran up the stairs leading to the third floor where he'd grown up. The key was in the rubbish chute, attached to the piping as usual. He went into the flat and straight to his bedroom. He made his bed, like his mother had been asking him to do for a week. He swept up the tobacco crumbs that dirtied his computer table, and even went so far as to dust his green pillowcase.

In the kitchen he used the last drops of washing-up liquid to clean the few plates and cutlery that had been waiting for him since the day before in the silence of the stainless steel sink. Then he sat down on a chair and looked at his bloody hands, looked at them for so long that he seemed on the point of unravelling their mystery.

He found the vacuum cleaner in the junk room and opened it to empty the bag into the rubbish. He swept the corridor, picked up the visible litter in Luna's bedroom and entered his mother's, which still smelled faintly of paint. The conjugal bed where she had slept for years was made. Krim sat down in front of the dressing table and observed the make-up set and, above it, the little poster of Chaouch that read: *The future is now.*

He tore down the poster and threw it in the bin.

A lamp and three books stood on the bedside table: *Anna Karenina*, which Fouad had recommended to her; *Not Without My Daughter* by Betty Mahmoody; and *Choosing Dawn* by Chaouch. Krim opened the drawer and examined a few photos of his father, especially the one from the Christmas when he had died and seemed to weigh no more than forty kilos. He put the ring away in the back of the drawer and went off to his bedroom to roll a joint. After smoking it he felt like masturbating. He switched on the computer, avoided Firefox so as not to be tempted to go on Facebook, and found his favourite video, which he'd downloaded from YouTube, converted into .flv format and hidden in a fake file cleverly called Job Centre. In the video two fifteen-year-old American girls wiggled around to a rap song while trying to lip-synch between fits of giggles. The one on the right was round, brown and insignificant, but the one on the left, with light brown hair and green eyes, was tall, white, with wide shoulders. She shook her enormous bosom in a skintight yellow t-shirt, apparently unaware that when her friend moved her hips in the same way, no one even noticed her.

But Krim couldn't get hard. After tugging away in vain for a quarter of an hour he gave up and catapulted his faithful sock against the screen.

The computer's puritanical purr ended up lulling him. Slightly stoned, he meditated on his obsession with tall, big-breasted girls. It wasn't the breasts themselves he craved, but the undeniable and more or less spectacular physical event they constituted: instead of there being nothing in that space there was something, two mighty globes of flesh that beckoned inwards. In fact, Krim preferred their cleavages above all else. He liked it when there was something going on; who didn't like it when there was something going on?

He threw the sock and the tissues from his pockets into the rubbish and checked his watch for the first time. As a precaution he hadn't switched off the computer, which could take ten minutes to reboot. He returned to it briefly and logged into Facebook with a sigh. Slumped against the back of his chair, he didn't immediately see the red notification that was going to change his life. His eyes were open but he couldn't see a thing. He was thinking of the Chaouch poster, of Uncle Ferhat lying on the floor, and it was while remembering that he needed to delete the message he'd sent Aurélie from Luna's Facebook page that he realized she'd replied.

He sat up in his chair and read:

Aurélie: Krim!!! I tried to find you on FB but it was impossible! Of course I remember you! It was so much fun on the boat! For the friend request what should I do? Should I accept even if this is your sister's FB? Whatever you like. If not I'm at home in Paris, so if you stop by one of these days give me a shout. My number: 06 74 23 57 99.

Krim trembled, reread the message ten times, and paced around his bedroom. He looked up at Rihanna, Kanye and Bruce Lee. He didn't know which of these divinities to thank for the immense warmth that had just filled him. He'd completely forgotten how much his hands hurt.

A text from Nazir tore him from his bliss:

```
Received: Today at 4.45 a.m.

From: N

Your train's in an hour. Hope you're
not sleeping.
```

Krim wondered if Nazir knew what had just happened at the community centre. Apparently not. He texted back that he was ready, that he wasn't sleeping. And then he put on his second tracksuit with the fluorescent stripe, the one from which he'd torn off the Coq Sportif logo. He found his finest Lacoste polo shirt and decided at the last minute to wear a leather jacket. However, he made the mistake of choosing the pair of new trainers he'd bought with Nazir's money, but which were the wrong size. His feet mysteriously continued to grow: he was now a size 11 when the previous summer his size 10 trainers had been slightly too big.

His mobile indicated that he'd received eight calls from his mother since he'd left. Not one from Fouad. After one last look at the highest C-sharp note on the keyboard he'd hidden beneath the bed since Fat Momo's visit, he took the envelope from his inside pocket and looked at the train ticket. It left Châteaucreux at 5.48 a.m., there was a long transfer at Part-Dieu, and he would get to Paris at 9.27 a.m. A yellow Post-it on the ticket indicated what metro line to take once he got to Gare de Lyon.

He took out the rubbish, tying the black bag up nicely, and then went to the bathroom. When he flushed the toilet he was overcome by emotion, a feeling of finally being free from the weight of things, one that he felt again while tossing the rubbish bag into the long vertical bowel that led to the bins in the cellar.

When he left the building and made his way to the station, he could hear the birds singing in the trees. The desolate wind had finally subsided without giving way to more than a few minutes of drizzle an hour earlier. There remained a few playful gusts that no longer promised storm but sun, renewal, and dew on the lawns.

Krim passed through the city centre in slow motion. He listened to the fluttering foliage of the poplars, the weeping willow and the plane trees. Some shoots of pruned branches suddenly emerged at the edge of the streets, and Krim was astonished to see them covered with buds where all the others had leaves.

He stopped in front of the railing of a little square. The sprinklers were still, the trees stripped of blossom, the sand damp. Why did an empty square always seem to him to have just been deserted?

When he arrived near the station he lit a cigarette, in the midst of the arrogant lunar décor. The ultramodern façade had ten, fifteen, twenty long strips of mirrors folded in pleats, which reflected the immense sky where Krim could still see nothing of the breaking day.

The station was vacant. Whether on the platform, at the ticket desk or in the waiting room, there wasn't a soul in sight. No travellers, no uniformed employees, no families there to say farewell to early-rising passengers. The lighting was faulty, and entire areas of the station were lost to darkness. In the vending machines, long metal hooks were empty of their snacks. The revolving billboards were devoid of posters.

The SNCF train jingle rang throughout the station – C, G,

A flat, E flat – and a recorded voice announced the train for Lyon. As the loudspeaker went silent Krim could hear only one thing: the quavering neon lights of those screens that would soon be praising the morning radio programme on France Inter, or Luc Besson's new film, or advocating the consumption of five portions of fruit and vegetables a day.

He switched on the spell-check function on his mobile and thought about what to write to Aurélie.

Community Centre, 4.50 a.m.

The bride's mother tore out two strands of hair with each hand when she saw the police arrive, just a few minutes after the ambulance carrying old Zoulikha had left, followed by her sisters in Bouzid's and Dounia's cars. The blue flashing lights drove the point home and confirmed her worst fears: this stupid Kabyle family had managed to ruin the most important day of her life.

Slim bumped into her while trying to join his brother, who was negotiating with the police.

'What are you doing?' the bride's mother said indignantly. 'You're not leaving as well, I hope?'

Slim remained still, unable to focus on finding the right response.

Fouad, who'd overheard some of the conversation, asked the policemen to wait a moment and went over to the bride's mother: 'Now that's enough from you!'

The bride's mother took a deep breath and prepared to make a scene.

Fouad stopped her by raising his finger and shooting her a dark look. 'Slim, you can stay if you like – I just want to file a complaint at the station. But tell me, do you know anything about this? Ferhat says it happened ten days ago, the attack, but he's not really making sense.'

'I don't really know,' Slim replied. He was having trouble breathing, trying his best to live up to the situation. 'He's been acting strangely for a while, yeah, maybe ten days. You'd have to ask Zoulikha.'

'Yes, well, that's not possible right now. So, what are you doing?'

Faced with his brother's bewildered face and knowing he was incapable of making a decision alone right then and there, Fouad decided for him. 'Stay, stay with your wife, it's better that way. The reception will soon be over anyway.'

But a deafening burst of music contradicted him, a heavy beat Rai song, which seemed to have been put on specifically to make them forget Ait Menguellet's 'We, the Children of Algeria'. Fouad closed his eyes in acquiescence for a second, to show Slim that he didn't mind if he stayed. It was his party; he couldn't leave while the guests still wanted to have fun. And he would be useless at the station in any case. Slim wiped a tear from the corner of his eye and joined Kenza, who put an arm around his neck and kissed him generously under her mother's nose.

Toufik and Kamelia hadn't followed the ambulance cortège: they asked to ride with Fouad. Fouad agreed, but Toufik no longer had a car. The police, who had recognized and were consequently well disposed towards Fouad, agreed to take everyone in the back seat.

At the same moment, the ambulance arrived at North Hospital. The on-duty nurse and a small, red-eyed ER doctor transferred Aunt Zoulikha from the stretcher to a gurney waiting for her at the entrance. Rabia's older sister, who was having trouble breathing, pointed at her.

'You have to let her breathe a bit,' the doctor said, putting his stethoscope on Zoulikha's deathly pale, shrivelled flesh.

'Where is Krim?' the old woman asked between two breaths of oxygen.

They put a mask on her and led her into an exam room. The nurse asked one of her colleagues to look after the family. Rabia wanted to follow her sister, but the nurse was firm.

'No, no, Madame, your aunt . . .'

'My sister!'

'Sorry, your sister is having a minor heart attack, you must go to the waiting room now.'

'A heart attack?' Rabia's eyes filled with tears.

Dounia took her sister by the shoulders and led her to one of the seats by the coffee machine. 'What did she tell you?'

Rabia was on the brink of explosion. Luna came and took her mother in her arms and began to sob, thinking more of the kiss that the bride's brother Yacine had stolen than of what had happened to her great-uncle, the significance of which she didn't quite grasp.

'She was asking after Krim,' she replied to Dounia.

'And where is he?'

'I don't know! I called him ten times, but he isn't picking up. I'm telling you this is going too far, he's not going to get away with it!'

She was speaking about the skirmish with Belkacem, whom Krim had thought was Omar. But on thinking about it for more than a second, she knew that she would no doubt never see Omar again after what had happened, and then, suddenly, her unbearably intense thoughts overflowed from her inflamed eyelids and she launched into a litany intercut with sobs. 'My children mean everything to me, my children are my entire life. Who do I live for? For myself? Do I spend my money on clothes and jewellery, for myself? No, since their father's death, God rest his soul, I live only for them, I live for my son and my daughter, and I'm telling you now, *wallah, cerfen tetew, rebi,* may he shoot me the moment they touch a hair of my son or daughter's head . . .'

Dounia, who seemed to have inexhaustible reserves of composure, took her sister's hands and covered them with kisses to make her smile and calm down.

'He must have gone home. He has his key, doesn't he? So you see. Everything is going to be okay.'

'Poor Zoulikha. What happened? One moment, things were fine, people were dancing, and then suddenly . . .' She began to cry again.

'The nurse says it was a small heart attack, you'll see, and she's made of solid stuff, *wallah,* she's tough, Zoulikha. You remember in Saint-Victor when she helped Granddad put up his tents?'

'Saint-Victor,' Rabia repeated in a murmur.

'That lazy Moussa went off to sun himself and pick up girls, and during that time we sisters had to do all the work.'

'And *yeum,* where is she?'

Dounia replied that Granny had long since left with Rachida, who was very angry about the reception, which she had known was cursed from the start. 'You're right,' she added when Rabia didn't answer. 'I have to call her to let her know. It's not like I can wait till tomorrow morning.'

'And Kamelia? Raouf? Toufik? The great-nephews? Are they okay?'

'Kamelia and Toufik went to the police station with Fouad,' Dounia reassured her. 'Come on, stop fretting, have a rest.'

Rabia looked up abruptly and searched for her brother Bouzid. She rushed over to him and asked what had happened to Ferhat.

'Hey, calm down, Rab, calm down!' he shouted. He began to explain what he'd seen on their uncle's head.

'And what are you going to do? You're going to find them, I hope! You're not going to be like good little Frenchmen and wait for the police? Bouz, look at me! If the men in the family don't find them, I swear I'll deal with it myself. Attacking an old man like that . . .'

The horrific vision of a head shaven and tattooed with obscene signs stopped her from going on. She almost vomited and went back to sit next to Dounia.

Raouf had stayed in the background and now went to stand under the TV, which since early evening had been repeating the urgent non-news that was typical of the dawn of second-round elections. The TV hung from the ceiling so that everyone could watch. But no one did. Those who waited for medical care or bad news were generally not in the mood for TV. Raoul undid his tie and without really watching saw the images he now knew by heart: Chaouch glad-handing the elated crowd at his last event. Some panning shots worthy of a Hollywood blockbuster swept across the hysterical faces and their bulging eyes. It occurred to Raouf, while he ran his hand over the stubble returning to his chin, that this was what Chaouch had done for this country: he'd enlarged people's eyes. Like in the Japanese cartoons that he watched in the small hours of the morning, since he could no longer sleep more than three or four hours at night: immense, unreal eyes. Eyes enlarged so you could draw more tears from them.

On the motorway, 5.15 a.m.

Fares had never, of course, driven a car as powerful as the Maybach 57S, which he was under strict orders to take to Paris. Night and day during the past few weeks, he'd watched over the garage where Nazir wanted it kept. Fares and another guy took turns pampering it. But it was Fares who'd got to screw on the red and green licence plate. This christening may have tamed the Maybach into a faux diplomatic car, but it didn't make it any less of a marvel.

Since that winter afternoon ten years ago, when Fares had felt the power of a twin turbo engine for the first time, he had dreamed of one day driving a car such as this. A smile of serene satisfaction made his eyes close halfway. When he reopened them, he was racing at top speed along a wall covered with mirrors. The chromed wheels of his tinted-window meteor sparkled in the abstract night across the motorway.

He glanced at his telephone, which would soon be charged, and switched on the stereo. Only classical music seemed a worthy match for the magnificence of this masterpiece of European civilization at whose wheel he flew over the landscape. A Beethoven sonata ended, and the female presenter's soft morning voice told him he'd just listened to the first movement of 'L'Aurora'. Indeed, some bluish beams set fire to the horizon on his right. Pleased with this happy coincidence, he switched off the stereo to take full advantage of the musical silence of the Maybach's engine.

His daydream did not last long. When he consulted his text messages, he discovered his twin brother's and decelerated dramatically. There was no car behind him, so he switched to the right lane and checked the road signs for a petrol station. Nazir had forbidden him from going over the speed limit or stopping the car, but Fares considered that this was a case of *force majeure*. Getting out of the vehicle, he took great care to put on his suit jacket and do up his tie. The driver of such a car could not loaf around in jeans and a t-shirt.

His first reflex should have been to call Nazir to inform him of the situation, but he didn't want to have to justify the stop. He therefore dialled Mouloud Benbaraka's number, which he'd memorized earlier that day. It took three tries before he picked up. He was in Saint-Etienne, right in the middle of an overlit car park, stretched out in his BMW driver's seat, reclined all the way to block out the combined beams of the neon lights.

Fares shared the message he'd received from his brother.

Mouloud Benbaraka sat up. 'When did he send you the message?'

He didn't listen to the reply.

'So that's why he was no longer answering, that stupid fuck.'

'So what do we do?' Fares asked, worried.

Benbaraka let out a nasty, two-toned laugh. 'What are *you* going to do, you mean? I've got enough problems as it is. If your brother gets caught, that's none of my business.'

He hung up in the middle of Fares's reply and shifted to the passenger seat. There was some commotion by the ER exit. After a few moments of confusion, a small part of the groom's family made for the cars, leaving Rabia and her sister behind, still dressed to the nines and lighting cigarettes, as they rubbed each other's arms to warm up. 'What do I do?' he asked Nazir, who'd answered immediately.

'You stay away for now.'

Nazir didn't hear Benbaraka's sigh, or the dull thud of his clenched fist as it hit the dashboard; he'd already hung up.

On the Train, 5.45 a.m.

Krim saw the day break between Saint-Chamond and Rive-de-Gier: an irradiation of reds that were more and more orange, and of blues that were more and more pale. But the sun's disk didn't appear, hidden as it was behind the hills and the train's trajectory.

A woman in Capri pants entered Krim's carriage at Givors-Ville. She had her cheek pierced, and the ring looked like a shiny mole that spoilt her dimple. When her eyes met Krim's she walked to the back of the train and dropped her head against her fist, pretending to be tired.

On arrival in Lyon, Krim chose the same spot in the waiting room as the one he'd occupied the previous summer, when he'd taken the TGV to Marseilles and the local train for Bandol. Though his mobile showed twenty-seven missed calls, Krim allowed himself to doze off. He briefly dreamed of the South and woke up just in time to catch his TGV. There was no one sitting next to him, or in half of the carriage for that matter. He stretched his legs out on the seats and heard a man in a grey jacket and red shirt speaking about the campaign on the phone.

'Well, I'm going home just for that,' he explained, rubbing the base of his neck. 'Who cares about the opinion polls in the end: people faced with the ballot paper are going to be reasonable, there's no doubt about that. And then if they're not, I'm sorry, if he's elected I give up, I'm going to live in England with my niece. There's only so much you can take.'

During the fifteen minutes that followed, Krim couldn't work out who the man was going to vote for. What tipped the balance in favour of the hard-right candidate was not his phone conversation, but the surreptitious, panic-stricken, contemptuous look he gave Krim after realizing he was being watched – that way the French had of never attacking you face-on but always from the side. A nation of cowards, Nazir had written in a text. Genetically cowardly, he'd said. The ruddy guy with his double chin, with his red-checked shirt and shifty eyes, seemed to be living proof.

The morning mist on the farmland made Krim feel like smoking a cigarette. He went to the toilets between the two carriages and took the opportunity to count the banknotes left over from Nazir's last envelope. He had enough to eat on the train if he wanted to, but he wasn't hungry. The stress of the last few hours had ruined his appetite, and as always when he wasn't hungry, he desperately wanted to smoke.

He put his cigarette between his teeth, the way his father used to do to amuse him. He was about to text Nazir to recount the last developments when it suddenly seemed more urgent, more necessary, more crucial for him to write to Aurélie.

Hi Aurélie, it's Krim. I'm in Paris this weekend. Can I come and see you?

Krim dropped the cigarette and jumped up and down. He

went to the buffet bar and bought an ice tea. While he wracked his brains to figure out if his message was suitable, too much so or not enough, the TGV crossed the first suburbs of the south of Paris – red-brick buildings, narrow and dirty apartment blocks, rectangular factories placed like so many bits of Lego on a long, inhospitable wasteland that the sun was gently waking.

He returned to his seat and listened to Kanye West's 'Family Business', one of his favourites, which he'd introduced Aurélie to that previous summer. He knew the melody by heart without actually understanding the words. Each note seemed to contain Aurélie's beauty. Each note was an extra freckle on her sun-kissed breasts.

He pressed Send.

The Frenchman in front of him had fallen asleep. His arms were crossed and he snored softly. Krim noticed the silver watch he'd taken off and left on the seat beside him. When the train exited a short tunnel, it began to gleam provocatively; Krim grabbed it and changed carriages. He was very pleased with himself for not attracting attention by lighting his cigarette earlier in the toilets. Taking refuge in the second-class carriage the furthest from his own, he heard the announcement that they were arriving at Gare de Lyon and texted Aurélie that he was now in Paris. He was the first to step out onto the platform, where he sprinted off to the square dominated by the Clock Tower.

An unusual number of soldiers were patrolling in the stations, machine guns slung over their shoulders. Krim stubbed out the cigarette he didn't want to finish and suddenly thought of Fouad, at Granny's, who'd thrown away the Camel he'd offered him after drawing three pathetic puffs, as if he was bored with him and in a hurry to speak to more interesting people.

He checked his mobile: fifty-five missed calls and twenty unread messages, the most recent of which was from Nazir:

```
Received: Today at 9.29 a.m.

From: N

Train on time? Meet you know where, hurry.
```

Nazir had insisted he wear a watch on arrival in Paris. Krim had found an old Swatch in his sister's chest of drawers, but, as he replaced it with the Frenchman's from the train, he thought he remembered winning the trinket with his father at a fair and decided he didn't want to get rid of it. So he put the other one on his right wrist and took his first steps into the capital, wearing two watches that, miraculously – as he discovered while a beggar woman threatened him with her miserable gibberish – were only seven seconds apart.

Paris, 10 a.m.

He followed the directions and after five minutes found the metro entrance to Line 14. Nazir had insisted he not travel without a ticket, but he hadn't gone as far as putting any in the envelope. Krim bought a ticket and sat down at the back of the driverless train. The infernal corridors snaked away from the back window as the long car swallowed them up.

Krim's eyes lingered on a girl in a striped sailor's t-shirt. She had sat down in front of him and was tapping frenetically on her white BlackBerry. Krim was captivated by her beauty, of a kind he seemed to have encountered only with Aurélie. She had black hair, a long, fine nose, dark eyes and above all a porcelain complexion that seemed to be centuries old and that contrasted with the red of her faintly painted lips.

The most beautiful women in the world were all equally inaccessible.

On the second train that would take him to his destination, Krim found himself across from a large black woman who was busy knitting. An accordionist entered their car and began to play a very personal rendition of a Joe Dassin song. The black mamma came to life on recognizing the tune and began to sing at the top of her voice, seeking the enthusiastic approval of those sitting next to her.

'Oh Lord in your heart my life is just dust! Oh Lord in your heart my life is just dust! Ah ah it's incredible! Oh Lord . . .'

When he left the metro his head was swimming. In Paris the sky was bigger, the buildings richer, people's gestures more lively, and their eyes incomparably harder. The air molecules also seemed larger, and Krim felt that he was not going to be able to hold out for long in this rarefied atmosphere where everyone looked at him with disdain. He didn't recognize anything anywhere. The boulevards abounded with intimidating brasseries; the Haussmann-era buildings were adorned with gargoyles and moulded cornices.

Nazir sent him another message while he looked for the address on his Post-it:

Received: Today at 10.07 a.m.

From: N.

You're 5 min late. What the hell did I tell you? You in the area? This is no time for fooling around Krim.

'Relax, give me a minute,' Krim muttered.

He stopped at the foot of a smart building and tapped in the security code. A staircase led to a second door protected by another code. Krim climbed it without hearing the sound of his feet, muffled by a red-brown carpet embroidered with pale gold bands. The lift that took him to the fifth floor began to rattle about. Krim thought the cables were going to give way.

Arriving on the fifth floor, he didn't dare get out of the lift. Nazir's voice came through one of the doors on the landing and frightened him. He was screaming, and Krim couldn't understand what he was saying. He thought of Aurélie and had the strange premonition that he might not see her for a long time if he joined Nazir straight away.

He had only to switch his priorities around: Aurélie now, Nazir later. He couldn't risk not seeing her. He needed time; all he had to do was take it. And Nazir would understand he was in love. The way he'd understood everything else. And if he didn't understand, too bad.

He texted his mother to tell her that his mobile had almost run out of battery and that there was no point in calling him: he was in Paris as planned, earlier than planned, and he was going to sleep at Uncle Lounis's place – there was a good chance she would not call Uncle Lounis to check on his story because of the terrifying likeness of his uncle's voice to his own father's.

Aurélie's reply beeped in the F-sharp tone of Nazir's loudest scream:

Received: Today at 10.13 a.m.

From: A.

Come to my place, I had a party
yesterday, I'm a little out of it
but it's cool.

The message ended with her address. Krim pressed the ground-floor button in the lift and ignored Nazir's enraged calls setting fire to his mobile, whose battery was comfortably showing three bars out of four.

The fifteen minutes that followed were spent suffering in his undersized trainers. Loosening his laces had no effect: he had to stop every twenty metres and began to consider walking around in socks for the rest of the day. But Nazir must already have been really angry with him to call fifteen times in a row; it would be an unconscionable slight if Krim not only turned up late, but infringed on what his cousin had often called the golden rule of that Sunday morning: *do not get noticed*.

He searched desperately for the entrance to the metro he'd come out of a moment ago. There had been a map there, where he could figure out the quickest way to get to the Buttes Chaumont stop, where Aurélie lived.

At the end of a side street, exhausted, he noticed a small building with no front window. Given the appearance of the men waiting at the entrance, he gathered it was a mosque. When the last worshipper had gone in, Krim saw that the door wasn't closed. He left his observation post and heard a voice chanting prayers behind the unguarded vestibule's door. Among the dozens of pairs lined up on the cardboard shelves, Krim spotted some cream loafers, size 11: he replaced them with his own trainers and made his escape.

He walked for half an hour until he found the Seine, which he decided to follow while he worked out what to do. He soon made his way across the bridge leading to Gare de Lyon. The fresh and sunny air cleansed his brain. His head was full of trumpet calls and glorious thoughts. Halfway along the bridge he saw a metro train crossing the sky on the bridge opposite, at the foot of the high-rise buildings. His own passageway suddenly seemed to have been built just to allow him to walk on the Seine.

He decided to take the first taxi ride of his life.

Saint-Etienne, 11 a.m.

Fouad left the room where his aunt had been admitted a few hours earlier and called Jasmine back, who'd been trying to reach him for a little while now.

'My God, Fouad, I'm so sorry! Is your uncle better?'

'Yes, yes, don't worry. He's gone home, my cousins are looking after him. Everything's going to be okay now.'

'And your aunt . . . this is terrible, I'm so sorry, I so wish I were with you right now.'

'Yes, yes, things are going to be sorted out, don't worry. Where are you all?'

'You all' was the entourage that had constantly surrounded Jasmine since the start of the campaign, a campaign in which she had ferociously refused to participate and which had caught up with her only after the first round. She'd been seen for the first time at her father's side the week before, in the front row of the audience at the debate.

The young woman gave a long sigh. 'There have been some problems with polling stations in the Cantal – why in that area, I have no idea – where ballots with Dad's name have disappeared.

He's talking to his lawyers, but people won't be voting before this afternoon.'

'I thought it was bad form not to vote in the morning?'

'No, no,' Jasmine replied distractedly. 'I don't know much about all that. I don't even know who I'm going to vote for . . .'

She had a beautiful voice, which was mischievous, childlike and piping when she talked in conversation, so much so that it was hard to fathom the vocal power she managed to display on stage. She was part of the forthcoming production of Rameau's *Les Indes galantes*, the most keenly awaited show at the Aix-en-Provence festival, though awaited for non-musical reasons, which exasperated her.

'When can I meet your family, Fouad?'

'Soon, soon. Although, I'm rather glad you didn't come to Slim's wedding. It was . . .' He stopped because he couldn't find a sufficiently strong adjective, but also because he had another call.

After hanging up with Jasmine, whose life he'd been sharing intimately for six months now, he called the number that had just left him a message.

'Hello, did you just call me?'

'Yes, is this Monsieur Nerrouche? This is Claude Michelet, Assistant District Prosecutor. I've just been informed of last night's events, and I wish to tell you that this odious act will not go unpunished, on any account.'

It was the sentence he'd prepared. His flow of words slowed considerably when Fouad remained silent at the end of the line and he had to keep going.

'So then, I'm going to be personally in charge of finding the culprits, and I will make sure that they are punished in an *exemplary* fashion. It is truly and absolutely intolerable to attack a man, a man of mature age, I mean old, in this . . . *odious* way. So, I hope you will send my words of support to your family. And believe me, we will find them.'

'Thank you, thank you, sir.'

Fouad returned to Zoulikha's room. All the sisters had taken turns at her bedside, even though the on-duty nurse continued to claim that it was just a minor heart attack.

Rabia drew down the blinds and switched on the TV. She changed channels to LCI, which showed images of Chaouch from the day before at the Socialist Party headquarters on rue de Solferino.

'No, no, switch it off,' Zoulikha suddenly said in Kabyle.

'What?'

'Switch it off! *Raichek*, switch it off!'

'But why?'

The old lady moved her head frantically on the pillow. Her sisters looked at her in terror. She seemed possessed.

'Switch it off, *raichek*, off!'

It was the first time since their teenage years that they had seen her hair dishevelled, and the first time they'd ever heard her raise her voice.

Fouad entered, smiled at his old aunt's wild hair, and asked to speak to his mother in private. But then the doctor arrived and the whole family got up to greet him. He was a tall, narrow, unflappable man with little round spectacles and an immaculate white shirt. He looked like he hated nothing more than having his time wasted. Without once looking up at the family, he examined Aunt Zoulikha's file and gave a few instructions to the nurse behind him.

'Everything will be fine, Madame,' he declared, making for the exit.

Rabia stopped him and wanted to know more. While the doctor explained that she'd had an angina pectoris that wasn't very serious, Fouad watched his aunts humbly drinking up the medicine man's words. The immense respect he inspired in them, that fear mixed with superstition, repulsed him so much that he had to leave the room before the end of the speech.

Dounia soon joined her son, who was stretched out against the wall.

He looked at his mother's darkened eyes and lost his temper. 'You should go and sleep a little, there's no point in staying here, she's fine now! You heard the doctor, there's nothing to worry about.'

'What?' Dounia exclaimed. 'You think she's fine? Have you seen her?'

'I mean she's stable, nothing's going to happen to her.'

Dounia shook her head.

'Krim's in Paris, by the way. At his uncle's,' she added. 'Rabia's going to kill him when he returns, I swear she's going to kill him. This is the last straw.'

Fouad remained silent. He'd completely forgotten about Krim and was now very angry with him.

'What did you want to tell me, my dear?'

Fouad hesitated and stared at the white window at the very end of the corridor. 'What the hell's he doing in Paris? It doesn't make sense, something not right's going on. What the hell's Krim gone to do in Paris?'

'How should I know what's going on, Fouad?'

'Mum,' Fouad said, drawing a breath. 'It's him, I'm sure.'

Dounia's eyes filled with tears. Her pain instantly turned to rage, and she slapped her son, who came closer and grabbed her shoulders.

'Mum, it's horrible but I'm sure of it. I can feel it. He's the one who did that to Ferhat. I know you don't want to confront the truth but he's mad. Mum, he's mad, you don't realize. Mum, listen, Mum, he's a monster. Fuck, I'm sure of it now, he's the one who brought Krim to Paris. He's preparing something, he's preparing something even worse than—'

'Stop!' Dounia screamed. 'Stop! How can you say that? Your own brother. How can you say such a thing? Ah . . .'

She nearly collapsed against the wall. Fouad held her steady and took her in his arms. Sensing that something was wrong, Rabia came to join them and suggested they go and have coffee on the ground floor. Fouad looked up at her and, so as not to give in to the dark impulse taking hold of him, did the opposite of what she commanded: he included Rabia in their hugs and, stroking the hair of the two women who'd watched him grow up, murmured: 'That's the best idea of the day so far, let's get some coffee. And after that we mustn't forget to go and vote, okay?'

But over Fouad's shoulder, by the corridor, Rabia noticed a man in a black blazer staring at her; his face was impossible to identify because of the backlighting, but his stature and appearance seemed familiar. She turned around, hoping to discover someone signalling to her, but there was no one but him in the long pink corridor. And when she made a step to one side to make sure that it was indeed her he was looking at, Rabia saw the man disappear with measured steps, hiding half his face with a ringed hand that shone with an evil gleam.

8

The Election of the Century

Socialist Party Headquarters, rue de Solferino, Paris, 12 p.m.

Police Commander Valérie Simonetti calmly crossed the blue-carpeted space of the press room. At the start of the millennium she had been the first woman to join the SGPR, the Security Group for the President of the Republic, which also ensured the security of all candidates for the highest office. Chaouch had done everything to reinforce her role in the campaign; he wanted her in the car and in the front row during walkabouts. She had blonde hair tied up in a chignon, but her face was open, juvenile and crafty. She was tall, at one metre eighty, and her pulse never exceeded sixty beats a minute; but that didn't stop her smiling and being close to the people. All of this pleased Chaouch, who detested the square-jawed heavies at least as much as the expert snipers. On the eve of the first round he'd sacked his head of security, who had wanted to put men like that everywhere, and hired 'Valkyrie Simonetti' in his place, to give a more human face to his protection team and to promote a woman to a position where it wasn't expected.

Chaouch's communications director motioned her over and extricated himself from a jungle of phones. Serge Habib had the hollow cheeks, weak neck and slack skin of a man who has just followed a draconian but successful diet. He had lost his hand in a car accident a few years before: his stump, combined with the extraordinary energy he expended to make you forget it, had become one of the most singular images of the campaign. He explained to the security chief that the candidate had decided to delay his departure for the polling station.

'And what about the one o'clock news?' she asked, already preparing to announce the change of programme to her men.

A secure telephone was handed to Habib, who began to bellow, 'What can I do about it? Yes, I told him, but he doesn't give a shit about the news! He says that this "I get up early to set an example" masquerade means very little to him . . . Look, we can take advantage of this – after all, Martine's voted, Malek as well, everyone's voted, it might not be as disastrous as it looks . . . What? Right now? He's with Esther, we're forbidden to enter . . . Listen, Jean-Séb, I've already explained all that to him but then again he's not wrong in that the big community gatherings are going to kill us, we need to keep full control on the visuals. Hold on, hold on, they're already announcing thousands of people at Charléty Stadium, all the Arabs from the northern neighbourhoods in Marseilles are heading into the Canebière, fuck, you know how many people are expected by the Grogny town hall?'

The chief of security thought he was asking an actual question and made two times ten with her hands. Twenty thousand people. She had reconnoitered the place herself a week earlier and based her estimate on the enormous – though probably lesser – crowd that had taken them by surprise on the morning of the first round.

'Calm down,' Habib continued. 'What I mean is that the image of Chaouch acclaimed by twenty thousand Arabs on the square of his town hall is a total catastrophe for the one o'clock news. What's the silent majority going to think when they see Chaouch being applauded by overexcited Arabs on the street at siesta time? No, this can't happen, people are going to think: he's the Arabs' candidate, imagine what it will look like ... Hold on, calm down, listen to me, this may well be the largest gathering of Arabs ever seen in France, we need to do some damage control ASAP. He's going to visit the war monument for the one o'clock news and will vote this afternoon, around three, three-thirty. I've got security here, we'll get organized ... Anyway we can't make him change his ...'

Jean-Sébastien Vogel, the campaign director, had hung up on him.

Commander Simonetti held an emergency meeting in the adjacent room and confirmed role distribution. Her grey-suited staff generally avoided looking her straight in the eye. They were hard, sharpened men: the best. The bodyguard operation hadn't changed since the new chief had taken over: Luc on the left side, Simonetti herself on the 'shoulder' – the right side, closest to Chaouch – and Marco as 'Kevlar', named for the armoured briefcase that was, in the event of an attack, to be unfolded from the head to the knees of the VIP under protection. Around this first circle were two other concentric circles, while from the mobile division there was the hulking 'JP', whose bass voice made their earpieces tremble.

A few moments after the briefing, young Major Aurélien Couteaux went to see his boss to notify her that he had agreed to change positions with a colleague. It involved being Kevlar in place of Marco, who was having some gastric issues and didn't feel well.

Valérie Simonetti, who was simultaneously listening to a report from JP in her earpiece, asked him to repeat what he'd said. She'd understood the first time but she wanted to be sure that the tiny twitch in Couteaux's left cheek wasn't accidental.

'No, no,' she finally decided, removing her earpiece, 'this is not the time to make last-minute changes.'

Couteaux was the youngest in the group, the most recently arrived, with excellent grades and all the possible and imaginable recommendations – a bit too many for Simonetti's taste. All the more so as he'd failed the driving tests but had still been kept on at the SGPR; he was the only one of the policemen in the group who possessed neither of the special red and green driver's licences.

The young major stifled his frustration with difficulty and threw out his last argument, veins bulging at his temples: 'Chief Lindon had no problem with . . .'

She cut him down with one look and assigned him to the second circle of bodyguards and the second car following the cortège.

'Very well, boss,' Couteaux said, bowing, his eyebrows furrowing to process his punishment.

He disappeared into the toilets and made a call on his private phone.

Valérie Simonetti knocked twice on the door behind which the candidate was sharing a private moment with his wife:

two discrete, resolute knocks, to which Chaouch replied, 'No!' with a smile in his voice. She pushed the door open and saw the Socialist Party presidential candidate with his shirt open, standing close to his wife, who was in high heels, hair undone. They were dancing to the words of an old song that Chaouch apparently knew by heart:

'*Darling, je vous aime beaucoup, je ne sais pas what to do* . . . *You've completely stolen my heart* . . . Do you know the singer Jean Sablon, Valérie?'

'No, sir.'

'Well, you should!' he retorted, plunging his shining eyes into the bosom of his wife.

'Yes, sir.'

'How about you, Mrs Chaouch, do you like Jean Sablon?' he laughed, drawing his wife towards the bright spot by the window.

Simonetti stepped gingerly ahead of Deputy Chaouch to make sure that the curtained window posed no threat, as he began to sing again in his beautiful, full, grave voice, exaggerating his French accent:

'*Oh chérie, my love for you is très, très fort* . . . *Wish my English were good enough, I'd tell you so much more* . . . Valérie, relax, this may be the last time that we can breathe for a while.'

'The last non-bullet-proof window,' Esther Chaouch murmured, her beautiful grey eyes fixed on the incandescent light blowing through the curtains.

While buttoning up her husband's white shirt a few moments later, she had the unpleasant premonition that it was their love life she was closing up in a straitjacket. It was the first time in a year that she'd found herself alone with him in broad daylight, the first time she could button up his shirt without half a dozen advisers barking from the four corners of the room. She looked down at the cufflinks that shone like his big hazel eyes. He'd switched his phone off and formally forbidden entry to the pack, but Esther could hear them whispering, pressing against the door, fighting for a front seat at history in the making.

On slipping the tie under her husband's collar, she understood that it would be worse, considerably worse, when he was elected. But he didn't worry about that: he looked at her without fear, but rather with his usual assurance, his simple, mischievous, joyful air.

To prolong this exceptional moment, she made a double knot in his tie. 'Well, see you, darling. I fear I have to let in the *dogs of war* now.'

'*Cry our last havoc,*' he recited in suave and now perfect English, '*and let slip the dogs of war . . .*'

'Go on, Shakespeare, go find your *dogs of war.*'

Esther kissed him and stepped aside. Valérie allowed herself an über-professional smile to respond to the irresistible one the candidate gave her, and announced that everyone was waiting for him. Chaouch checked his personal smartphone and beamed: he had received a message from Chicago – Sari Essman, the American election expert, was telling him that she would have to call him *monsieur le président* from now on.

'Everything all right, sir?' Valérie Simonetti asked.

He clicked his tongue. 'Yep. Let's go and win this thing now.'

She preceded him in the corridor while confirming his exit into the earpiece. Before regaining the cortège, she inquired about Marco's gastric problems. Marco didn't understand what she meant, but confirmed that Couteaux had asked to be Kevlar, to which he'd replied that it wasn't for him to decide.

Baffled, Commander Simonetti heard the voice of JP in her earpiece:

'We're taking the decoy car. I repeat: we're taking the decoy car.'

She put Chaouch and his wife in the second Volkswagen SUV with tinted windows. There was no particular reason behind the choice of official vehicle or decoy; to foil the predictions of eventual criminals, the decision always had to be made at the last minute.

The procession set off. It consisted of about twenty vehicles. At the front were the motorcycle escorts in full dress uniform, who had to clear the path and make sure the motorcade didn't stop. Behind them was a marked car from the local police station, its lights flashing. A dark blue vehicle from the SGPR set the tempo, followed by an identical car transporting the officer in charge of the team. A second flock of seven motorcycles in V-formation protected the most sensitive part of the lineup: two heavily armoured Volkswagen Touareg SUVs, one of them housing the candidate, flanked by a Ford Galaxy and three more motorcycles. At the tail-end of the procession rode various vehicles carrying the campaign staff and medical personnel, trailed at last by a minivan hauling the Tactical Support Team, comprising four heavily armed men with helmets, body armour and assault rifles ready to counter a commando attack.

Chaouch was not supposed to know the details of the meticulous organization that had accompanied his every move since he'd received threats from AQIM. He was even less aware that Valérie, sitting on the passenger seat and always quick to smile at one of his jokes, hid a full arsenal under her multicoloured suit. She wore a Glock 17 automatic pistol on her right hip, and, just in case it jammed, a Glock 26 in an inverted holster, its butt vertical to allow the weapon to be drawn more quickly. Harnessed to her reinforced metal belt was a torch lamp, a small tear gas canister, and a stun grenade. In addition, she sported the radio harness, which delivered one wire along her arm to her wrist microphone, the other down her back across the strap of her bra and up to her earpiece, which had been moulded to measure after a visit to the otolaryngologist.

It was through this earpiece that Chaouch's guardian angel learned that the clearance team sent to secure the route had nothing to report. She allowed herself a second's rest and studied the candidate's body language in the rear-view mirror. This was the strangest part of her work: she had to know every slightest twitch of the man she protected, she had to know him even better than his inner circle, in order to adapt his protection to potential unexpected movements. The anticipation of his every move pertained to a form of magical, or at least inexplicable, empathy. And so, that afternoon, while the motorcade sped along the banks of the Seine, Commander Simonetti couldn't help noticing that, for the first time, Chaouch's right knee began to tremble as soon as the two-toned sirens of one car called to another, erupting into a cacophony of whistling. He was supposed to be used to this by now . . .

Quai de Seine, 12 p.m.

A good hour had passed since Krim had decided to hail a taxi. He didn't dare signal them the way he'd seen it done in films, and those whose windows he'd knocked on had refused to take him, supposedly because they were taking a break or didn't have the right to take customers near a metro station, but more likely because Krim's appearance wasn't very reassuring.

One finally stopped at the edge of a road along the Seine. Krim looked up as he got in. Cars were stopping at a green light to let pass an armada of official vehicles escorted by a swarm of armed riders. Passers-by claimed it was Chaouch on his way to vote in Grogny. Krim felt moved at the thought that everyone was stopping to let him pass. He embodied the Republic, the State, Sovereignty. Krim remembered the day when his father, who'd stopped at a red light, had exceptionally been authorized to cross it for a few metres to let a wailing ambulance through. The endangered life of another person was more important than traffic laws, as was the passage of the king. Noble things still happened in this incomprehensible world.

Not daring to sit alone on the back seat, Krim asked if he could sit in the front. The taxi driver shrugged and asked him where he was going.

'To the Buttes-Chaumont,' Krim replied before looking at his mobile and noticing with astonishment that Nazir had stopped his frantic calls.

'Yes, but where at the Buttes-Chaumont?'

Krim gave him the piece of paper scrawled with the address. The driver switched on the meter and set off again. 'Let's hit the road!'

His father used to say exactly the same thing. All those men, Krim thought, all those men who weren't his father. It was an outrage – more than an outrage. There was still no word to say what it was.

The radio spewed out figures for the voter turnout overseas, and soon, thanks to a leak, those for mainland France: just over thirty-nine per cent at midday, a substantial twelve-point increase on the first round. An absolute *record*, one journalist effused before cueing a satellite link-up to Tulle, where one of Chaouch's defeated rivals at the primaries reminded everyone in a cheerful voice to what extent this day was historic, 'whatever the result'.

'Well,' the taxi driver exclaimed, 'if someone had told me that I was going to live long enough to see an Arab President of France!'

Krim couldn't manage to work out his origin: he had sallow skin, a strong nose and dark eyes; his greying hair was curly and his accent sounded like his uncles'. Yet he looked French. Krim concluded that he was a Jew and realized it was the first time he'd ever met one. He looked at the chain bracelet on the driver's wrist, hoping to see a Star of David. But there were only the letters of his name, too many bizarrely configured letters that Krim, whose sight was blurring from lack of sleep, couldn't put them into order.

'... that said, it's not over yet either,' the driver concluded.

Six euros and thirty cents later, Krim set his ecru loafers on the pavement of a street that smelled of fish. A bit embarrassed by his appearance (tracksuit and dress shoes), he hesitated.

But Aurélie sent him a text, and not just any text:

```
Received: Today at 12.45 p.m.

From: A

Are you coming, my little Kabyle
prince?
```

It took Krim four tries before he successfully entered the building's security code. He climbed the stairs, also carpeted with red velvet, one by one, holding on to the gilded banister. There was only one door for the entire second floor. Before ringing the bell, Krim pressed his ear against a peephole made of simple metal hatchings. He'd expected to find Aurélie alone, but he could hear at least two male voices and a female one.

There were some footsteps in the hallway. Krim stepped back and prepared to retreat down the stairs, but the door opened.

She was wearing denim dungarees with a long white t-shirt underneath. Her hair was fairer than he remembered, her swimmer's shoulders wider, her collarbones less prominent.

Krim thought of the jokes she'd made about her ability to carry small quantities of water in the hollows of her clavicle. Her defiant look hadn't disappeared, but it was tinged with amusement, with an irony that made him ill at ease. She was holding the end of a joint in her right hand.

'It's so awesome you could come. Come on in. What've you done to your hands? Fuck, that's blood, isn't it? You been fighting?'

'Yeah.'

'For a girl I hope.'

Krim shrugged and let himself be ushered in. The ceilings were high, the floors polished. In the large smoky sitting room where Aurélie led her surprise guest, a fully lit chandelier gave off the unpleasant sensation of artificial daylight. But Krim didn't care about the light or the outdoors. The sun was in the apartment, astride the sofa, lustily kissing a half-empty bottle of whisky and Coke. Her freckled cheekbones were dazzling, as were her almond-shaped eyes, as insatiably intense in their crafty mischief as in their difference in colour.

None of the three blokes slumped on the carpet paid any attention to Krim. On the coffee table some flutes of flat champagne sat alongside bottles of wine with labels yellowed by age, probably *grands crus* taken from their parents' cellars. Through the glass tabletop, Krim also noticed an open poker box, lined with black foam and filled with red, blue, green, black and white chips.

'Tristan, Tristan!' shouted one of them, sporting sunglasses and a cigar in his mouth. He was leaning on his elbow. 'Get over here, man, you've been getting ready for an hour.'

Krim turned his head and saw a shirtless guy, helmeted with a shock of blonde hair. He had fine, slender limbs and thin, sarcastic, princely lips. He was holding out a silver tray, filled with little chalk-white crystals, which he set down on the coffee table. Tristan then jumped on the sofa and put his arm round Aurélie's shoulders while gawking at Krim's shoes. His own were Dior, embellished with a touch of gold. 'Hey, come on,' he said to Krim, accepting the joint, 'take the divan.'

Krim didn't know what a divan was. He muttered something incomprehensible and didn't even try to stop the rush of blood that made his heart and temples throb. All eyes were soon on him, including Aurélie's green and brown ones. Her mouth agape, she didn't understand what was happening.

Krim slowly turned his tongue in his dry mouth. A mirror hung above an unused fireplace to his left, and he nearly fainted at the sight of his reflection.

He looked like a camel on a staircase.

Saint-Etienne, 1 p.m.

Dounia didn't want to drive, so Fouad took the wheel. Luna was yawning on the back seat. But when the car arrived at her place to drop off Rabia, who wanted to take a shower and rest for a bit, Luna chose not to go with her.

'Well, why are you going with them?' Rabia asked her. 'You can't even vote so what's the point?'

Luna insisted, and Rabia rolled her eyes and closed the door. Dounia's tired head appeared in the open window: 'Rab, you sure you don't want to come? Can't we rest after?'

'No, no,' her sister replied. She was teetering from fatigue and the gusts of wind. '*Wallah*, I don't feel like it, maybe later. And then I have to phone that little *sheytan*, you just wait, I'm going to strangle him . . . I swear I'm going to strangle him,' she repeated before yawning her head off. 'Fuck, I don't know what's wrong with me, I'm exhausted. I think I'm going to take a nap . . .'

'Anyway, you've got till this evening to vote,' Dounia stated, sending her one last worried look. 'Go with Bouzid, he gets off work at five.'

In the rear-view mirror, Fouad noticed a silhouette standing in front of a silver BMW double-parked at the end of the street. He didn't give it another thought as he went off to fetch Kamelia, who was staying with her parents.

Although based in Paris for several years now, Fouad still voted in Saint-Etienne, in the northern constituency. On entering the community centre car park, he remembered Uncle Ferhat's fall and gritted his teeth. Slim was waiting for them next to the astonishingly dense line at the gym entrance.

'You see that?' he said in amazement as he kissed his brother. 'He's bound to be elected with all the people who've come to vote!

221

And look, there are only Arabs.' Realizing he was showing a bit too much enthusiasm, given the previous night's events, the young groom lowered his voice and asked for news of Ferhat and Zoulikha.

Fouad took care not to lay into him in any way.

Fortunately, the ever-joyful Kamelia arrived behind Slim, slipped her arms around his stomach and lifted her featherweight cousin off the ground.

'I hardly saw you yesterday! Mr "Groom" ... *Zarma*, look at him,' she said to Luna, who had joined them. 'Little Slim's a real man now. So where's your wife?'

'Same, she's gone to vote. She's voting in the south of Saint-Etienne.'

Fouad looked for his mother and spotted her at the foot of a poplar tree that shivered in the wind like a gorilla. He didn't join her straight away, thinking of those nights he couldn't sleep because of her, because of both the small and the big threats that hung over her. No immediate threat, in truth, just that little leaden fact, that little fact that was too heavy to bear for a normal human conscience: that one day his mother would die.

He went to kiss her and was angry with himself for having made her cry earlier at the hospital, by mentioning Nazir. 'Sorry, Mum,' he whispered in her ear.

'Come on, love, we're going to vote. At least there's one good thing in this nightmare. I mean honestly,' she continued, joining the line, 'how can you do that to an old man? *Wallah*, I don't understand how such monstrous people can exist.'

Fouad remained silent.

'Take me back to the hospital after, okay, love? I don't want Zoulikha to be left all alone.'

'But isn't Granny with her?'

'Even worse if she is.'

Fouad made sure that the whole *smala* had an ID and polling card. Luna came up to him and grabbed his hand like a little girl.

'What's up, cutie?' asked her big cousin.

'I'm worried,' she said, frowning.

'But it's just a polling station, come on.'

'No,' she smiled, 'it's not about that, it's about my results. I may be getting on France's junior national team. Well, fingers crossed . . .'

'I didn't know, that's fantastic!'

Fouad rubbed the future star athlete's shoulders while looking at Slim, who was fluttering among his cousins, all excited despite the circumstances, unless – the thought made him pinch Luna's trapezia too hard and she cried out – it was because of them, because of the tragedy of the previous night, and because of the power that tragedies have to bring clans together. Fouad shook his head to chase away these strange ideas, which were very unlike him. He decided to set an example and was the first to put his paper in the ballot box. A voice boomed out confirmation that he had carried out his civic responsibility:

'Voted!'

At the same moment Mouloud Benbaraka found the key by the rubbish chute on Rabia's landing. He inserted it very carefully into the lock and found himself face to face with Rabia.

'Om . . . ar . . .'

She was holding a glass of grenadine, which she dropped on seeing the intruder reach out with his long muscular hand to stop her from screaming.

Aurélie took Krim by the wrist and led him through a series of crisp, bright rooms.

'Here's my father's office.'

'What does your father do?'

'He's an investigating judge, but he's away in Rome for the weekend with my mother. You've never heard of Judge Wagner? He was almost killed a few years ago by some Corsicans. So now my father always carries a gun and has two bodyguards at his side, at all times. They were there in the South, don't you remember?'

Krim took in the room, whose panelled walls were covered with books. Aurélie invited him to sit in her father's swivel chair and spun him around at top speed. Krim stopped the movement by catching the edge of the desk. The chair screeched, and he got up and looked at the buttons gleaming in the intimidating dark green padding.

'What kind of piece does he carry?'

'You know about guns?'

'Totally,' Krim stupidly boasted. 'I know how to shoot, and everything.' He didn't dare speak in longer sentences, fearing she'd notice his accent. Whenever he was in the presence of foreigners – that is, of people not from Saint-Etienne – he couldn't stop hearing the accent and found it abominable.

Tristan shouted from the living room. It was ready.

'What?' Krim asked.

'The MDMA ... You've never taken any? You'll see, it's crazy. Ecstasy gets rid of all the shitty things inside you. It's the love drug, you know? While it lasts, you're in paradise, and afterwards you don't even feel like you're coming back down. It's sweet,' she whispered, eyes closed, 'it's so sweet that it's sweet even when it stops being sweet.'

'Yeah, yeah, I know it. I think I had some once.'

Krim had the sneaking suspicion that she'd taken some the night before, at the party, and that she was still under the influence. Was it because of the MDMA that she'd replied on Facebook? Was it because of the love drug that she'd invited him to her place and called him her little Kabyle prince? The thought depressed him.

But he merely had to look back up at her breasts swelling under her t-shirt to regain faith in her, faith in love, faith in life.

He followed her like a ghost from room to room. She always walked in the same jaunty way, even though they were no longer on shiny sand or flagstones sprinkled with pine needles magnified by her little feet.

When they reached the living room, Tristan left the coffee table to kiss Aurélie on the lips. She rejected him and lay down on the sofa, one leg above the edge. She stretched out like a kitten, her bosom doubled in size, making the metal buttons of her dungarees click.

Krim saw her misty, loving eyes and realized she was stoned.

'Who are you going to vote for?' Tristan asked provocatively.

'Who? Me?'

'What do you think, Nico, who's he going to vote for? Go on, tell us about the sociology of elections, show us there's a point in spending three years studying political science!' His narrow eyes closed when he spoke. It was as if a demon was speaking through him.

Nico refused to play his little game, and Aurélie came to Krim's defence.

'But that's meaningless, Tristan, you can be so stupid sometimes. I'm too young, but I would have voted for Chaouch. For sure.'

'Because he's the most handsome,' Tristan replied. He had the power to silence the gathering without even opening his mouth. 'You'd vote for the one you felt like fucking. You little slut. I remain loyal to my convictions.'

'Your convictions, my arse.'

'Hold on, I've been with the young conservatives for two years now,' Tristan said with his wolf-like smile. 'And you know what? I wouldn't mind voting for a candidate from an ethnic background. So long as he can do the job, that is. You have to judge someone by their ideas, not their origin. We've never said anything else.'

'Yeah, right,' Aurélie said sarcastically.

But Krim didn't understand who was mocking whom. Appalled by Tristan's tone, he stepped back and knocked over a halogen lamp.

'Do you mind putting on a bit of music instead of smashing everything?' Tristan pointed to an iPad on the marbled mantel-piece of the fireplace.

Krim obliged, hoping the conversation would stop there, thanks to the music. But once he was standing in front of the expensive gadget, it took all his mental energy to avoid his own reflection in the mirror.

'Hey, come on!' Tristan said impatiently. 'Put on something cool, some techno . . . Come to think of it, just play whatever you like. And watch the computer, right.'

Krim considered taking the precious tablet and smashing it on the blonde bastard's head. He went onto Spotify and almost typed 'Ait Menguellet' into the search box. Instead he put in 'Kanye West'.

On the first cello notes from his favourite version of 'All of the Lights', he heard a few sighs of disappointment. But not from Aurélie, who had roused herself and was staring at Krim's reflection, hoping to catch his eyes. Krim looked up and tried to communicate to her his distress, his utter distress.

She was going to react when Tristan forced her head towards the tray.

'Hey stop, you idiot,' she protested before she burst out laughing.

Krim turned around and said he had an urgent meeting.

'With who?' Aurélie asked, concerned.

'It's nothing, with my cousin.'

'Stay a bit longer,' she said with as much conviction as he would have wished for. 'You should try the MDMA. I swear, just try it. Come on, you're trying it, right?'

For the first time Krim found her repulsive. She had said *right* one tone above the rest. Posh girls would always be posh girls, no matter what. His hesitation evaporated. He wasn't going to try her drug. He was looking for an honest way to tell her when Tristan said a name that made him jump. He approached him.

'What did you say?'

'What?' Tristan asked defensively, sliding the tray out of range of the row that might break out.

'You said a name, come on, say it again.'

Tristan's blue eyes burned with gratuitous nastiness, that kind of nastiness that a smile of self-derision suffices to justify. 'Fuck, we're having a joke. For Christ's sake, you're not very funny, are you?'

Krim felt like killing him. 'What name?'

'He means Krikri, I think,' one of the other guys offered – the skinny one – to defuse the conflict. His was the girl's voice Krim had heard behind the door.

'Why did you call me Krikri?' he screamed. He shoved Tristan's chest and stepped back over to the fireplace while the other guys tried not to laugh.

Tristan burst into laughter when Aurélie took Krim's scabby hand to comfort him.

'Krim, I'm sorry, don't bother with these morons.'

Touching the smooth skin he'd fantasized over for months no longer did anything for him. He began to observe the love of his life in an attentive, slow-motion stupor: he didn't scrutinize her, didn't stare at her either; it was rather as if his eyes were following the last flames of a torch cast into the abyss. He withdrew his fingers from Aurélie's and took his head in his hands.

He kicked the coffee table and fled just as the guys were getting up to confront him.

Paris, 2 p.m.

He ran out into the street, circled the block, stumbled several times, and ended up calling Nazir. No reply. To calm himself down, Krim went along the Canal Saint-Martin. But there was too much commotion, too much life, too much sunlight. Everyone's good mood hurt him, and the slightest climb took his breath away. His hands were trembling, and his headaches would be back in no time.

The scene was something he'd never seen in the streets of Saint-Etienne – this excitement, this trembling of an order that seemed to him more rich, more noble, more alive than anything he'd experienced up until then. People were better dressed, and with care; the long pedestrian street where the market ended was crowded, but not with old ladies wearing Reeboks and Algerian dresses who heckled him to come and help open their bags. No one here took the slightest notice of him, least of all the Arabs who haggled loudly but went silent when Krim passed by their stall.

A brass band appeared, materializing on a small crowded square at the foot of a fountain. Confident and knowingly dishevelled, the group of happy young students played some jazz tunes. The trombone was one pitch beneath the other instruments, but . . . was it? Krim concentrated, the only one among the passers-by to really listen to their music. But it was a disaster: he could no longer make out where the notes went in the complex scale that his ear was used to creating on its own, like the information screen that separates the external world from the hyperactive little brain inside Arnold Schwarzenegger in *The Terminator.*

'*La Marseillaise! La Marseillaise!*' shouted a woman with long curly hair.

Faced with cheers from the colourful crowd of listeners, the students didn't have to debate for long to play it as an encore. You could hear it sung by several people, of all colours, fathers who carried their babies on their shoulders, groups of teenage girls, activists who pretended to raise their fists while looking at each other out of the corners of their eyes.

When the last notes rang out, Krim remembered his mother's ritual at the beginning of World Cup matches: she always added to the four final notes of the national anthem a booming 'you bunch of pigs' – in response to the line about impure blood watering their furrows – four C notes drummed in with a tone of joyful parody as she frowned and proudly lifted her chin.

A little further on, Krim saw a line that ran the whole street, leading to a school converted into a polling station. He scrutinized each of the faces in the line, especially the white and docile family men, who looked away when Krim passed by. This way they had of not looking at him, as if he had the plague – it was as if a pack of invisible canines had barked upon smelling a dope-smoking little Arab boy. He continued along the pavement, observing the imperfect circle of the sun floating in the gutter. The clouds overtook it as Krim veered off the school's street and away from the overexcited people who talked of the 'great day'.

After half an hour of running, Krim miraculously found the Seine. Thinking he heard gulls' cries, he looked up to the sky and was joined by an old man with blue eyes who also looked up, rubbing his hands behind his back.

'Ah yes, there are the gulls. There's a rubbish dump over there.'

Krim took his leave of the old man and crossed the bridge that looked out on the other side of Notre-Dame. His mobile vibrated.

Received: Today at 2.56 p.m.

From: N

Come on, it's over now. Come to the meeting place or you'll regret it.

Krim called Nazir once, twice, three times. A tear ran down his cheek. He texted him to go to hell.

```
Received: Today at 2.58 p.m.

From: N

With all I've done for you, this is
how you thank me? You drop me like
a piece of shit?
```

Krim stopped at the middle of the bridge and watched a dinghy slipping across the waves, as it had done last summer with Aurélie. He texted Nazir that it was over, that he could no longer trust him, that he was aborting his mission.

```
If you bother me again I'll call
Fouad and explain that you paid me
to shoot at a guy.
```

Nazir replied ten seconds later:

```
Received: Today at 3 p.m.

From: N

We'll see about that.
```

In the two minutes that followed, Krim received three text messages consisting simply of photos, of poor quality, but in which he had no difficulty making out his mother stretched out sideways on her bed, like in a vision of horror, that nightmare vision he'd recounted to Nazir. Except that here she wasn't alone in the darkness, but watched over by Mouloud Benbaraka, Mouloud Benbaraka sitting on the edge of the bed and whose fixed and unhealthy smile left no doubt about his real intentions.

Krim threw his telephone over the guardrail. He heard it land on a pleasure boat where tourists were taking photos of

Notre-Dame's prestigious backside while desperately seeking passers-by to wave at. As a young foreign woman picked up his mobile, Krim collapsed on the pavement, grabbed his knees in his hands and screamed.

Saint-Etienne, neighbourhood of Montreynaud, 3 p.m.

Bouzid took advantage of the red light to remove his suffocating Saint-Etienne Transport Service vest. When his bus started off again, he noticed groups of young people running down the middle of the road, all in the same direction. There were boys, girls, and adults as well. They were coming from all the housing projects on the hill, galloping like zebras in the savannah. Bouzid turned around and saw that his bus was almost empty. Two old men in threadbare jackets strained to hear the news on the radio. Thinking they looked just like Ferhat, he turned the sound up and followed the parade of runners along this winding road he knew by heart.

Sundays were typically difficult for Bouzid: he could listen to neither Ruquier on Europe 1 nor the *Loud Mouths* on RMC, his favourite programme. But the news of this particular day was better than anything. Hordes of people were gathering in towns across the country, on the Canebière in Marseilles, all shouting 'Cha-ouch, Cha-ouch, Cha-ouch'. Near a bend in the road, Bouzid noticed an impressive crowd massed on a small square where a large screen had been erected since his last pass-through an hour earlier; usually it was set up for football away matches.

The street was jammed, and for the first time in his life Bouzid felt it for real – that famous 'electricity in the air'. After

232

a few beeps of the horn he gave up on splitting the dense crowd. Some small boys were climbing the plane trees to see the screen. Instead of calling the central office Bouzid stood up on his seat and saw what everyone was looking at: candidate Chaouch greeting photographers, accompanied by his wife, his daughter and his adviser, the one who had a stump instead of a right hand.

His first reflex was to call Rabia to recount the scene. When something extraordinary happened, Rabia was the best person to call: she was both very impressionable and a very good audience. You never wasted an anecdote by choosing to share it with her.

But Rabia didn't pick up. Not one of his four calls. He left a message on her voicemail, where he described what he saw.

'*Wallah*, all Montreynaud's here, they've all come down to see Chaouch voting! It's just so crazy, Rabia, if you could see this . . . Completely crazy . . .'

He sought the approval and enthusiasm of his two passengers. They had left their seats and were nodding in admiration. Bouzid even thought he could see tears of joy running down the wrinkled olive cheeks of the more smiley of the two mates. He reflected that you could never really be sure with old men: age made them emotional. But he changed his mind when he himself was suddenly submerged by a tide of sobs, sobs that he hadn't known since the end of the seventies, during the epic adventure of the Saint-Etienne football team: collective happiness, the desire to kiss strangers who, in the warm madness of the moment, turned out to be, to have always been, our brothers.

He went up to the old men and their shiny eyes. He took off his cap and passed his finger along the vein on his head. For the first time in years it wasn't anger but joy that made it bulge.

Paris, 3.15 p.m.

When Krim finally knocked on the apartment door through which he'd heard Nazir shouting a few hours earlier, he realized this was a mistake and that it would be best to return to Saint-Etienne to save his mother himself. But the door opened to a red-haired guy with a goatee, who stared at him with his eyebrows raised.

'What, *you*'re Krim?"

'Yes,' he replied in his most assured voice. 'Where's Nazir? What are you going to do to my mother?'

The guy with the goatee didn't reply and led Krim into the living room. He was wearing a dirty t-shirt and seemed to have woken up just ten minutes ago.

'You want some coffee?'

But his mind had already moved on to something else. He took his phone and exiled himself in the kitchen, leaving Krim to devour the nails off his bloody hands.

The guy with the goatee came back into the living room dressed and ready to leave. Krim thought his heart was going to give out.

'Well, you coming? It's okay.'

'What's okay?'

'Come on, let's go.'

'I want to speak to him,' Krim shouted. 'If I can't speak to him—'

'What are you going to do?' the redhead snapped, giving him a hard stare.

They went down to the underground garage and got into the redhead's car. They drove without speaking for ten minutes, until they'd left the ring road. A sign at the motorway exit indicated GROGNY, and on the endless avenue traversing that town, Krim noticed several cars with Algerian, Moroccan and Tunisian flags.

'Where are we?' he asked in a panic.

The guy with the goatee took a big padded envelope from the back seat and handed it to Krim, shaking his head. 'So,' he finally said, 'you know how to use it? You should have been training. You've trained, right? It's a—'

'I know, a nine milimetre calibre with a fourteen bullet magazine. I've got the same at home. But I don't understand, who do I have to shoot? I want to speak to my mother.'

'The nose,' the driver said. 'You aim for the nose. And above all don't look at the roof, okay? There'll be marksmen on the roofs all around. One with binoculars, another with a gun and telemeter. I'm telling you so you won't be tempted to see what it's like. Do you understand what I'm saying?'

Krim nodded, mustering all his strength to stop from shaking. On the wooden butt of the pistol, four letters were engraved: S, R, A, F.

'Fucking hell,' the redhead blurted for no reason.

He seemed on the verge of turning the car round. When the light turned green, Krim watched him bite his nails.

'I'm not getting out of this car if I don't speak to my mother first.'

'Stop it! You're getting out of the car and you're doing what Nazir has paid you to do.'

'Call Nazir,' Krim retorted. 'Tell him I'm not moving if I haven't had my mother on the phone.'

'Go to hell!'

The car started off again gently and passed in front of two

white-gloved policemen blocking access to a street so crowded it looked like the end of a football match in Saint-Etienne. The traffic was stopped in the whole neighbourhood – people were flocking, crossing the boulevard, slowing down buses draped with tricolour flags. A group of old bare-footed Berber women wearing blue make-up sang songs in a little square, accompanying each other with *darbukas*.

The redhead called Nazir and explained the situation. He hung up a few seconds later, waited for an endless minute and dialled another number. 'I'm putting him on,' he suddenly said.

Krim took the phone and recognized Mouloud Benbaraka's voice.

'Your mother's fine. Nothing will happen to her if you do what you have to do.'

'I want to speak to her.'

'She's asleep.'

'I want to speak to her. I want to hear her and I want you to take her to my cousin Fouad. As long as she's not safe I'm not doing anything.'

Krim heard his mother's voice, which was indeed sleepy, a bit stoned, but safe and sound.

'Krim, what's going on? Darling, what's . . .'

'Well, you've heard her,' Benbaraka spat after taking the phone back. 'Now stop fucking around.'

He hung up. The redhead's fist was clenched, and he looked in the rear-view mirror.

'Okay, you reassured? We're going there now.'

'I'm not moving if I don't have a photo of her with Fouad.'

A series of nervous tics took over the redhead's face. One of these tics lifted his chin and the goatee with it. He called Nazir and explained the problem. Krim could hear Nazir's shouting, which made the phone vibrate. He was terrified.

'It's okay,' the redhead declared as he hung up, 'you'll have the photo. But we've got to hurry now. Come on, get out of the car and get ready.'

'For what?' Krim asked.

He obviously knew the answer, knew perfectly well without ever having put it into words.

The dense crowd did it for him.

'Cha-ouch, Cha-ouch, Cha-ouch!'

The sound of chanting surprised Krim as they threaded their way through the crowd. It was like a wedding.

The guy with the goatee brandished a press card to get through more quickly. He was also carrying a big rucksack with a microphone that recorded the sounds of the highly charged street. The security barricade at the entrance to the town hall was made up of about twenty riot police officers and yellow barriers. There must have been tens of thousands of people around the building. Chaouch's bodyguards had mixed with the crowd; they made up the second circle of protection. One of them stared at Krim, who thought he was saved. The work of these men consisted of spotting suspicious faces. Krim knew that his was, but the redhead with the goatee exchanged a look with the bodyguard who'd noticed him and pushed Krim to the front row.

Suddenly murmurs spread through the sea of these elated faces. People turned around to pass on the news:

'He's voted! He's voted!'

And it was then that Krim saw the candidate appear on the steps. He was smaller than on TV, but his entire person was beaming, exuding an air of majesty and vigour.

The crowd shouted, 'Cha-ouch, Cha-ouch, Cha-ouch!'

Valérie Simonetti brought the wrist microphone to her mouth and murmured, 'Walkabout, walkabout.'

Chaouch came over to shake hands. A woman fainted behind the barrier opposite Krim's. Chaouch turned round, and Valérie, who opened the way and moved forward like a crab, gestured to him to continue. Behind Chaouch was another bodyguard, the Kevlar, who scanned faces one by one. On the roofs of the buildings on the square, the marksmen had nothing to report. In truth they were focused on the women in burkas sprinkled throughout the crowd: Chaouch had expressly forbidden that they be refused passage, so as not to 'ostracize them even more'.

The candidate therefore continued to shake hands until he reached Krim, his right hand feverishly held out above the blue-lined shoulder of a policewoman. Blood throbbed in Krim's temples, but his left hand was sure. It was the one with his Swatch, the one by which his life was seven seconds late. Was that a good thing? Was it not better to shoot with the one that was seven seconds fast? And how would he get out of this? Would they shoot him down before he even had the time to lift his weapon?

He remembered the sessions with Fat Momo, the extraordinarily easy handling of the 9mm, its minimal recoil, its comforting weight.

'I want to see the photo!' he cried on the edge of tears.

The redhead didn't reply. He looked at his phone and pushed Krim against the barrier.

'You'll never see your mother again if you don't hurry up! You hear me? You'll never see your mother again! So get on with it!'

'I don't trust you,' Krim implored in a child's voice. He was now crying as though his heart would break.

'You've got no choice!' the redhead screamed.

Krim saw that he was right. He had no choice. He looked for Chaouch's nose. It was astonishing, that nose, it was straight, too straight, the nostrils were thick but lacked the Kabyle bump, the Nerrouche bump.

Suddenly it was too late: the candidate had missed Krim's hand and was already moving towards the next one.

The redhead shoved Krim a little further into the crowd. He gave him a dark look and pushed him to elbow his way through. 'Go on!' he shouted. 'Go on!'

Commander Simonetti pressed on her earpiece and winked to the candidate who, although side on, spotted her and mentally prepared to refuse the hands that followed. A little girl held up by her father was leaning forward to kiss him. Chaouch took the little girl in his arms, over the security barrier. The father took a photo.

Krim found himself right against this chubby man who was taking loads of photos. Suddenly he felt something on his thigh underneath his tracksuit. It felt like warm slugs were crawling in his leg hair.

He had pissed himself.

The sweaty redhead started to jab at his ribs. Krim jostled the photographer father and noticed his little daughter's bare, caramel-coloured legs as she went back over the barrier. The blonde bodyguard was helping the girl regain her father's arms right at the moment Krim's palm brushed Chaouch. He thought of the photos of his mother with Mouloud Benbaraka, he thought of his mother's naked body in the bluish semi-darkness of her bedroom.

He lifted his arm, protected on the right by the redhead's silhouette and on the left by the little girl's body. He closed his eyes for half a second and reopened them on Chaouch's. In the apotheosis of this afternoon, which shimmered with sunlit spangles, Krim realized that fear also inhabited the eyes of the gods.

He fired only one shot, and had the time to appreciate its neatness and perfection. The bullet hit the candidate's left cheek and made him fall flat on his back.

In the chaos that followed, Krim heard nothing more. Blows rained down on him. He suffered from the first one, but those that followed seemed to strike a different body, his own body in truth, but a freed one, finally freed from the tyranny of its nerve endings. From the ground where he had been thrown, he saw a crowd of twisted, hateful faces, of bloody and pitiless eyes.

An immense blonde woman suddenly tore away the security barrier and, with superhuman strength, scooped Krim up from the ground where he'd collapsed. She was soon assisted by three men including the one who'd let him pass. They kept Krim a few centimetres from the ground, his face to the tarmac where the sun crushed the slightest spot of moisture, just like down south that previous summer, just like that, like the sea and the sun gazing at each other during the very rich hours of the afternoon. And while he was being brutally treated, while there was talk of lynching and hospital, Krim could see it once again, the sun's majestic 3.30 p.m. column of silvery reflections, a column he followed because Aurélie had followed it, as far as beyond the buoys, as far as that strange zone where coral suddenly emerged beneath their bare feet, darkening the turquoise water as if the coral were sleeping sea monsters.

Saint-Etienne, 3.30 p.m.

Dounia got up from the side of the bed and switched on the TV perched above them, hoping that Zoulikha was genuinely asleep. But she woke up suddenly and asked her to switch it off again. Dounia obeyed and approached her big sister. She was putting her hand on her forehead to see if she still had a fever when a scream from the neighbouring bedroom eviscerated the peaceful slumber of the floor. It was followed by a second scream, and a third, and a commotion that was so incongruous in these light pink halls that it sounded like a police raid on a nursery. Unsteady on her feet, Dounia inched towards the corridor and saw two nursing assistants running in opposite directions shouting:

'Chaouch's been shot! Chaouch's been shot!'

She followed them like a ghost and had to stop halfway and lean on the handle of a stretcher to catch her breath. Her first reflex was to phone Rabia, but she didn't pick up. She called her landline, she called Luna, she called Nazir, she called Fouad and finally Slim.

When Slim answered, she began to cough in a sickly and phlegmy way, mixed with hiccups, sobs and cries. She could hear Slim's scarcely stifled voice on the phone, the voice of her youngest child who was screaming 'Mum, Mum, Mum', but she couldn't stop coughing, she was now even expectorating some blood.

A nurse paralysed in front of the TV at the end of the corridor finally came to her aid and reassured her son on the phone, in a voice broken by sobs.

At the other end of the city, Fouad hadn't heard his mobile vibrate: for the past fifteen minutes he'd been knocking on the door to Rabia's flat, where he'd been led by a bad premonition. A BMW had sped off just as he'd parked his car at the foot of her block, making him worry even more. He knocked louder and tried the other door on the landing. There was no reply.

He finally went down to the basement, thinking of what he'd heard about Krim getting up to strange things down there. Each cellar unit had a number listed on a dilapidated noticeboard where Fouad managed to make out Rabia's name: Nerrouche-Bounaim. He followed the long neon-lit corridor, went through a few fire-safety doors and heard some noise behind the wooden door of the little room he was looking for. When he knocked, the door opened on its own . . . onto Fat Momo, who was slumped in the shadow, his face lit by a luminous screen.

'What the fuck are you doing here?'

Fat Momo got up and tried to escape. Fouad held him back firmly and looked around the small room, which looked like Ali Baba's cave. There were boxes of shoes piled up in columns, half a dozen game consoles, and two flatscreen TVs.

'Momo, what's all this?'

'Fuck, I'm sorry, we didn't want to—'

'What are you up to here? Answer me, for fuck's sake!'

'Nothing, nothing, just a bit of . . . of business, you see, but nothing serious. It was Krim, with the money he got from his cousin. We bought some things and we sell them, we make a little profit but nothing much, I swear.'

Fat Momo was undeniably sincere, but Fouad noticed that he'd moved in front of another pile of boxes.

'What are you hiding in there?'

He pushed Fat Momo aside and discovered the barrel of a weapon jutting out of an untidily rolled bath towel.

'It's nothing, I swear, we were just training to shoot, you know, in the woods, it was just to pass the time.'

Fouad took his head in his hands. He looked at his mobile, saw the number and variety of missed calls, and realized something had happened. Dizzy, he almost fell flat on his back but was held up by Fat Momo, whose horrified plump face had begun to shine from perspiration. Fouad got his breath back and looked at the screen that Fat Momo hadn't had the time to put on pause. It was a shooting game, from the shooter's viewpoint: the barrel of a machine gun was trained on a patch of silent mangrove trees, which remained deserted for a few more seconds before a camouflaged soldier appeared suddenly and fired in the viewer's direction, gradually covering the screen with blood.

Paris, at the same moment

Nazir had seen one of his mobiles vibrate on top of his harpsichord. He'd paid no attention to it, as he'd been too engrossed in the score of 'The Savages', that piece by Rameau that he'd been working on unsuccessfully for weeks.

He finally closed the lid and ran his hand over his chin. In a week, his hair hadn't grown enough for him to know if it was going to go curly; he felt somewhat sorry about this. He walked over to the window of his bedroom, which was empty except for the golden instrument, a campbed and a stuffed macaque. The Haussmann-era street noise was shut out by the double glazing he'd installed. But a movement attracted his attention to the fourth floor of the opposite building. Through the window, composed of red and green panes, his young neighbour was having a piano lesson with someone hidden from sight by a thick beige curtain. The sun rid itself of cloud, and from a darkness suddenly streaked with oblique bright strips where the dust passed, Nazir enjoyed the sight of the little girl's determined elbow and the velvet of her right sleeve stitched with tiny plastic mirrors that glittered when she rolled towards the high notes.

After one last glance at his faithful stuffed monkey, Nazir went down with his small maroon suitcase and took the metro to meet Fares and the car that would drive him out of Paris. He could have called a taxi, but he wanted to be in the company of others at that fateful moment.

The metro stopped for a long time at Saint-Michel, in front of the lift that went up to place Saint-André-des-Arts. People had begun to run in every direction, to share the news, and to stop each other from fainting.

Nazir lifted up his black jacket collar and took off his headphones to hear properly what was being said around him.

A woman who had just heard the news put her hand on her mouth and staggered. A student held her up and helped her to sit down so that she could fan herself with the supplement of *Le Monde*, which he had been calmly reading a few minutes earlier.

Nazir took out his mobile and saw that he had thirty calls from Farid in his absence, four from his mother and, above all, one from Fouad. His surprise was all the greater as they hadn't spoken on the phone or face to face since their father's funeral three years earlier.

He stretched and bit the flesh of his lips while avoiding his reflection in the window. There was almost no white in his eyes: his pupils, which were permanently dilated by a rare illness, gave the impression that his eyes were made of some thick, unhealthy matter, that if one day he was to cry, his tears would probably be black, a sort of muddy oil flowing down his cheeks. But crying was not on Nazir's agenda.

A girl in a blazer and sailor's t-shirt caught his attention: she'd been staring at him from inside the lift. Her slightly over-arched eyebrows and the fine and arrogant lips of her mouth amused Nazir until he noticed that the electronic noticeboard above her read, 'Out of Order'.

There was a two-minute wait, followed by an inaudible and devastated announcement on the intercom, and then a siren that sounded like an ululation. The metro wasn't going to start up again. The network was paralysed. Nazir got out and hailed a taxi. He reached Porte d'Orleans fifteen minutes later. Some police cars were driving by at full speed; he feared that roadblocks had already been set up around Paris. Fares called him on his mobile, and Nazir was going to answer when he noticed the Maybach's gleaming fuselage, parked on a metered space. He knocked twice on the driver's window, and Fares got out to open the boot for him.

'So weird, all these cops around, something must have happened.'

Fares wanted to shake his hand, greet him properly before speaking to him about what had happened to his brother and what had to be done to help him.

But Nazir stopped him with a wave of the hand. 'The effusions can come later.'

He then took his place in the back seat, where he immediately carried out mysterious transfers of chips with his three mobile phones.

'Are we off?' Fares asked. Despite Nazir's bad mood, he wasn't unhappy to finally have some company.

'Head for the border,' Nazir confirmed, licking his lips.

With that, the Maybach 57S, licence number 4-CD-188, which belonged to an Algerian diplomatic consul, headed towards the east-bound motorway under the dazzling sun of that tumultuous first Sunday in May.

To be continued ...